HEATHEN

SHAUN HUTSON

timewarner
paperbacks

A *Time Warner* Paperback

First published in Great Britain
by Little, Brown and Company in 1992
This edition published by Warner Books in 1993
Reprinted 1994, 1995, 1997, 1998, 1999
Reprinted by Time Warner Paperbacks in 2002
Reprinted 2004

A CIP catalogue record for this book
is available from the British Library

ISBN 0 7515 0136 0

Typeset by Hewer Text Composition Services, Edinburgh
Printed in England by Clays Ltd, St Ives plc

Time Warner Paperbacks
An imprint of
Time Warner Book Group UK
Brettenham House
Lancaster Place
London WC2E 7EN

www.twbg.co.uk

This book is dedicated to my wife,
Belinda, without whom there would be nothing.

'Truth is rarely pure, and never simple'
                                    – Oscar Wilde

Acknowledgements

The following is a list of people who, in some way, shape or form, helped with the book you are about to read. I am indebted to them all and, those whose names are listed should know why.

Many thanks to Gary Farrow, Damian Pulle (and Christina) and Chris. If a Pit Bull could walk it'd be called Gary. Thanks, mate.

To everyone at Little, Brown/Warner especially my ever-ready, ever-battling Sales Team. There are none to match them.

To Mr James Hale whose advice and expertise was, as ever, invaluable.

And, to the following who, as I said before, should know why they are listed here: Brian Pithers, Malcolm Dome, Jerry Ewing, Phil Alexander, Jo Bolsom, Gareth James, John Martin, Chas Balun, John Gullidge, Nick Cairns, Bert and Anita, Maurice, Trevor (and anyone else at Broomhills pistol club I've left out), Krusher, Steve, Bruce, Dave, Nicko and Janick. Rod Smallwood and everyone at Sanctuary Music. Merck Mercuriadis, Howard Johnson. Gordon Hopps, James Whale, Jonathan Ross, everyone at The Holiday Inn, Mayfair and the

Adelphi, Liverpool. Ian Austin, Zena, Julie and Colin (for keeping us fit). The quite marvellous Margaret Daly. Mr Jack Taylor, Mr Stuart Winton, Mr Amin Saleh, Mr Lewis Bloch and Mr Brian Howard. Indirectly I thank Metallica, Queensryche, Judas Priest, Sam Peckinpah, Martin Scorsese and Oliver Stone. As ever, I thank Liverpool F.C.

Special thanks to Mr Wally Grove, valued friend and pursuer of etiquette . . .

Love and thanks to my Mum and Dad for so many things I can't list them.

And to you, my readers, as ever, without whom everything would be a little bit pointless.

Let's go.

Shaun Hutson

One

The handkerchief was covered in blood.

PC John Stigwood cradled it in the palm of his hand and gazed at it through the plastic bag in which it was encased.

As daylight fled from the sky and night began to encroach, the sun was sliding towards the horizon. It left a crimson tint to the heavens. A little like the colour of the blood on the handkerchief, Stigwood thought.

He sighed wearily and glanced at his companion.

PC Andrew Cobb was older by two years. Older. *More experienced?*

'You do it,' Stigwood said, handing the bloodied parcel to his colleague.

'Does it matter which one of us does it?' Cobb said, a hint of irritation in his voice. 'Someone's got to tell her.'

Stigwood shook his head.

'I can't,' he said quietly.

'We don't even know if it's *him*,' snapped Cobb.

He glared at Stigwood then swung himself out of the car, slamming the door hard. He swallowed hard and began the short walk up the path which led to the front door. Jesus, he didn't want to do this. He pushed the handkerchief into the pocket of his tunic and rubbed his hands together as he approached the door. Dark wood. Elegant. Like the rest of the house. Large without being ostentatious, and secluded without being isolated. It was an imposing building, its dark stonework covered with clinging ivy. A moth fluttered around a lamp that was activated by a sensor, Cobb noticed as he reached the doorstep. He heard its wings pattering against the glass.

He had no speech rehearsed, no words ready on his tongue. All he had was the dreadful apprehension he knew his companion shared.

Across the street were lights in windows. He thought he saw shadows, figures moving behind closed net curtains, gazing out, wondering why a police car should be parked in the driveway of the large house.

There were no lights on in this house. Perhaps no one was home. Cobb told himself it would be better that way. He would ring the bell but there would be no answer. End of story. But he also knew that once the information was radioed back to base he and Stigwood would be told to wait until the occupant returned.

He glanced back; Stigwood was watching him impassively. The two policemen locked stares for a moment, then the younger of the two concentrated on the Escort's steering wheel.

Cobb slipped one hand into his tunic pocket

and felt his fingertips brush against the plastic bag that held the handkerchief. He closed his eyes briefly, sucked in a deep breath and held it for a second.

Come on, do your job.

He exhaled, opening his eyes in the process, one index finger aimed at the doorbell.

He noticed that his hand was shaking.

Two

Donna Ward thought she heard the two-tone chime of the doorbell and cocked an ear in the direction of the front door. The music continued to flow from the ghetto-blaster propped on the kitchen unit beside her. Donna wondered for a moment if she'd imagined it. She eased the volume down slightly, then continued with her task. She stepped back from the picture, trying to see if it was straight or not. She smiled to herself. Chris wouldn't even notice when he came in. She'd hung three small pictures in the kitchen, military prints of men in uniform. She'd found them in a box under the stairs a day or two ago. Chris had owned them for years, as long as she could remember. He'd once had a passion for military history. Years ago.

This time, when the ringing of the doorbell came, she *did* hear it. She jabbed the 'off' button and silence dropped like a blanket over the house as she walked across the hall towards the front door.

Donna didn't bother to check the spy-hole but she always left the chain in position and now, as she eased the door open, she only pulled it as far as the restraints of the metal would allow.

Through the gap between door and jamb she saw PC Cobb.

He nodded his head with such exaggeration it looked almost like a bow.

Donna felt a sudden, unexpected coldness run through her, as if someone had suddenly injected her with iced water. She didn't know why; perhaps it was just the sight of the uniform. She'd seen policemen often enough when her father had been alive. They'd arrive at her parents house to tell her mother that the drunken wreck she'd married was either too pissed to get home and was sleeping it off in the cells, or that they had him in the car outside.

But that, as the saying went, had been then. This was now.

What was a policeman doing ringing her doorbell at seven in the evening?

She brushed a hair from her face and looked at him impassively.

'Mrs Ward?' he asked, his tone subdued.

She swallowed hard.

'Mrs Donna Ward?'

'Yes. What is it?'

'Can I come in, please?' Cobb asked, running a

swiftly appraising glance over the young woman. Blonde, pretty. Slim. Late twenties, he guessed. She was dressed casually in jeans, sweatshirt and trainers. She had grey eyes, eyes which flickered back and forth, regarding him now with a combination of bewilderment and concern. He wondered for a moment if she was going to let him in but she pushed the door to and he heard the chain being slipped. The door opened to allow him entry, then was closed behind him.

'I'm sorry,' she said quickly. 'I was going to ask you in.' There was a pleasant smile on her face, but it never touched her eyes.

Do your job.

Cobb stood rigidly in the hallway.

'Mrs Ward,' he began. *Go on, you can do it.* 'I'm afraid to tell you there's been an accident. It's . . .'

She cut him short.

'Chris,' she murmured, her eyes riveted to the uniformed man.

'Your husband has been involved in a car crash. At least, we think it's your husband . . .'

She closed her eyes tightly for a second.

'Is he hurt?' she demanded, her voice cracking.

'We need you to identify him,' Cobb said.

There were tears forming in her eyes.

'How do you know it's him?' she said frantically.

'We're not sure; that's why we need you to come with us and look at him. We have this.' He reached into his pocket and pulled out the small, plastic-wrapped package. With a trembling hand he held it out towards Donna, who snatched it from him.

'Those are your husband's initials, aren't they?' Cobb said, indicating the CW on one corner of the bloodied handkerchief.

'Oh God,' Donna said, her eyes brimming with tears. She put one hand to her mouth. 'Is he dead?'

Cobb had been expecting the question but he still didn't know how to deal with it. No amount of training could prepare you.

'If you come with me, there's a car outside,' he said, trying to sound efficiently detached. 'We'll take you to . . .'

'Is he dead?' she snarled through clenched teeth.

'Yes.'

'Oh God, no, please.' She tried to swallow but couldn't. The tears began to flow.

Cobb felt helpless. So fucking, pathetically, screamingly helpless. Jesus Christ, he wanted to help this woman, but what did he do? What *could* he do, except drive her to the hospital to inspect the body of the man they were convinced was her husband?

There was a coat stand close by. Donna reached for a leather jacket and pulled it on, pushing past Cobb and out of the front door towards the waiting police car. He slammed the front door behind her and followed her to the car, helping her into the back, scurrying around the other side and strapping himself in.

Donna wiped tears from her face.

'We don't know for sure that it *is* your husband, Mrs Ward,' he said, as if that were some kind of comfort.

'Just take me to him, please,' she said.

The car sped away.

The sun slipped away, leaving the last of its colour to fade from the sky. Night closed in.

Now there was only darkness.

Three

She might as well have been blindfolded for the journey. Donna saw little or nothing of the houses and countryside that flashed by. Stigwood guided the police car along the streets with sometimes bewildering speed. She could see her own face reflected in the glass of the windows when other vehicles passed: her eyes looked blank. There was no expression behind them other than that of fearful expectation. Or desperate hope.

They'd said they weren't sure if it was her husband or not.

You're holding his handkerchief, for Christ's sake. Look at it.

It could be someone else.

Someone who looked like him?

It was possible.

Someone who had the same initials?

Please God let them be wrong.

There was so much blood on the handkerchief she could have wrung it out. As she sat in the back of the car she ran her fingers over the plastic. Occasionally she would clasp her hands together.

The silence inside the car was as uncomfortable as it was impenetrable, but what were the uniformed men supposed to say? Stigwood was too busy concentrating on the road to strike up a conversation and Cobb couldn't even bring himself to look round at the distraught woman. The only indication of her presence was the occasional sniffle.

If it wasn't Chris, then how did they know where to find her? From his driver's licence? She gripped the handkerchief more tightly, one part of her mind filled with the unshakeable conviction that the man she was being taken to identify was indeed her husband. The other part of her being fought to believe, prayed that there had been some terrible mistake. She tried to make herself think that there *could* be another Christopher Ward.

The police car slowed down as it approached a set of traffic lights, the glowing red in the gloom. The single scarlet circlet was like an unblinking eye. As red as the blood on the handkerchief.

Donna shifted position, pulling her jacket more tightly around herself, aware of the same

8

bone-numbing chill that had enveloped her from the time Cobb had stepped into her house. But now that chill was deepening, freezing her blood, turning her bones to glacial props encased by bloodless skin. She had never felt cold like it.

Was death as cold as this?

Did Chris already know?

She closed her eyes for a moment but images of him appeared there, images she wanted to see but also ones she feared she might never see again. Images which would become only memories. Never again to be witnessed. She was to be left with nothing *but* memories, now.

In the night air the sound of sirens echoed stridently and amidst a blurr of flashing blue lights an ambulance hurtled from the main gates of the hospital.

Stigwood watched it go, checked that the way in was clear, then guided the car through the main gates.

As the car came to a halt and Cobb opened the door for her, Donna felt as if the very life were being sucked from her.

She brushed a tear from her cheek and followed Cobb inside the hospital.

Four

There were three of them waiting.

Donna had been guided through the labyrinthine corridors of the hospital by Cobb, hardly aware that her feet were touching the ground, seeing the activity around her but not registering it.

The nurse hurrying to casualty with packets of blood for a transfusion.

Two interns running along with a gurney.

Somewhere close she heard crying; always, there was that smell, simultaneously reassuring and nauseating. The disinfectant smell. It mingled with the stench of excrement as a nurse hurried to empty a bed-pan, walking past Donna without even glancing at her. Everything was happening in slow motion; the journey through the hospital took an eternity.

Until they reached the morgue.

That was where the trio waited to greet her, two men – one in a suit – and a WPC who smiled efficiently and took a step towards her, eyeing the bloodstained handkerchief that Donna still clutched.

The man in the suit also stepped forward, introducing himself as Detective Constable Mackenzie. Donna looked at him blankly and followed him through into the morgue.

Please God, don't let it be him.

The WPC took her arm as she moved into the small room beyond. It was grey and white, bare except for a single slab in the centre of the room. On that slab lay a shapeless form covered by a green plastic sheet. The room was barely twelve feet square, but it might as well have been the size of a football pitch. The slab seemed to grow in Donna's mind until it was the only thing she could see. The antiseptic smell was even stronger now.

She felt sick. Felt faint.

Please God.

The other man, dressed in a sweatshirt and trousers, said that he was the coroner, his name was Daniel Jordan. Something like that.

Donna felt a sudden feeling of light-headedness, thought she was going to faint. The WPC shot out an arm to steady her, sliding another arm around her waist, but Donna shrugged it off, pushing the offered support away from her with her cold hands.

Look at him.

No, don't look. Turn and run.

A tear forced its way from her eye and trickled slowly down her cheek.

'It won't take a second, Mrs Ward,' said Jordan, holding out a hand to beckon her closer.

And now every part of her mind centred on that shape in front of her. Moving like an automaton she stood beside Jordan, looking down at the sheet.

She clutched the handkerchief more tightly.

11

'All right,' she whispered.

He pulled back the sheet.

'Oh, no,' she gasped. 'No.'

Jordan looked at her, then at Mackenzie, who merely shook his head slightly.

'Chris,' murmured Donna, her eyes transfixed on the face of the corpse.

The corpse of her husband.

'No,' she said again, tears pouring down her cheeks. She studied his features, the awful gashes in his forehead and cheeks. She saw how the blood had soaked his jacket and shirt.

So much blood.

'Is it your husband, Mrs Ward?' Mackenzie asked.

Donna nodded and reached for her husband, touching one of his lacerated cheeks.

Jesus, he was so cold.

His skin was white, those areas that weren't discoloured by bruises or hideous cuts, as if all the blood had been drained from him. She smoothed one of his eyebrows, then touched his lips with her index finger.

So cold.

She touched her fingertips to her own lips and kissed them, then pressed those fingers to his cold lips once more.

She shook her head again, allowing herself to be eased back by the WPC, allowing herself to be guided towards the door.

She saw Jordan replace the sheet.

It was then that she collapsed.

12

Five

How many tears could the human eye produce?

As Donna sat sobbing she wondered.

How much pain was it possible to feel at the death of a man you loved? Could pain be measured, calibrated and categorised like anything else?

Chris would have known.

She felt a hand clasp hers; it seemed to exude strength and feeling.

The nurse who sat beside her was in her mid-thirties

(*maybe a year or two older than Chris*)

and she had the most piercing blue eyes Donna had ever seen. But in those eyes there was only concern now. The small room had yellow walls, two or three threadbare chairs and posters which bore slogans like

SAVE THE NHS

OVERWORKED DOCTORS ARE A DANGER TO EVERYONE: CUT HOURS

On the small table beside her there were tea cups; one was still steaming.

'Drink it,' said the nurse, holding the cup towards Donna, gripping her other hand firmly.

Donna looked at her, then at the WPC who sat opposite. She took the cup and sipped the tea.

'Good girl,' said the nurse, still holding her hand.

Donna swallowed a couple of mouthfuls then put the cup down. She sucked in a deep breath, as if to replace air that had been knocked from her, then sank back in the chair, one hand over her face, her eyes closed. Her sobs subsided into a series of quivering inhalations and exhalations. She could feel how wet her own cheeks were.

'Oh God,' she whispered, swallowing hard, aware for the first time of the heavy silence in the room and of the ticking of a clock above her.

11.06 p.m.

'What happened?' she asked, looking at the nurse and the WPC in turn.

'You fainted and we brought you in here,' the policewoman told her quietly.

'Oh God,' Donna murmured again. The words were like a litany.

The room was lit by a sixty-watt bulb that cast thick black shadows. Outside, beyond the closed curtains, she could hear the wind. The hospital seemed very quiet. Donna sat for interminable minutes just staring ahead, wondering why her mind was so blank. It was like a blackboard wiped clean of chalk, all feelings wiped away. She just felt a terrible emptiness, so intense it was almost physical, as if a hole had been gouged in her soul. Could so much emotion be expended that a person was left without feeling? When Donna looked down at her own

14

body she saw only a shell, with nothing left inside. Just a husk, devoid and emptied of feeling.

She put down the teacup, touched the nurse gently on the back of the hand and released her grip, resting both arms on the worn arms of the chair. Tilting her head back she closed her eyes and took another deep, racking breath.

'How did it happen?' she asked finally, her voice low.

The policewoman looked at her and then at the nurse, as if for permission to speak.

'How was Chris killed?' Donna had no recollection of Cobb telling her about the accident.

'A car crash,' the WPC said quietly.

'When did it happen?'

'I'm not really sure, Mrs Ward,' the police-woman told her apologetically. 'I wasn't on duty when it happened.'

'Is there anyone here who could tell me?' Donna asked, smiling thinly. 'Please.'

The policewoman got to her feet, excused herself and slipped out of the door, closing it behind her.

The clock continued to tick loudly above Donna's head.

'You must have done this so many times,' she said to the nurse, 'comforted the grieving relatives.' Her voice cracked and a tear rolled down her cheek. She wiped it away hurriedly. 'I'm sorry.'

'Don't be,' the nurse told her, clutching her arm warmly. 'Don't apologise for the way you feel. I was the same when my father died; I was saying sorry to everyone. Sorry for being a nuisance, sorry for crying all the time. Then I realized that it didn't matter. You have a right to your grief. Don't be ashamed of it.'

Donna smiled, despite her tears. She touched the nurse's hand.

'Thank you,' she whispered.

The door of the room opened and the WPC re-entered. Mackenzie was with her. He nodded awkwardly to Donna before sitting down opposite her.

'You wanted some information about your husband's death, Mrs Ward?' he said.

She nodded.

'The crash happened some time this afternoon,' the DC said. 'We think at about four o'clock. His body was brought here for identification. It was easier to reach *you*.'

'*How* did it happen?'

'His brakes failed, as far as we can tell. He hit a wall.'

Donna felt that feeling of despair rising once more like an unstoppable tide.

'Was anyone else hurt in the crash?' she wanted to know.

Mackenzie hesitated, licking his lips self-consciously.

'I'm afraid there was another death. We . . . er . . . we found another body in the car with

16

your husband. A young woman. Her name was Suzanne Regan.'

Donna sat forward in her chair, a frown creasing her brow.

'Oh my God,' she murmured. 'And she was killed, too?'

'Unfortunately, yes. Did you know her?'

'She worked for my husband's publishers. I don't know why she would have been with him, though.'

'She obviously knew your husband quite well?'

'They worked together,' Donna said, her confusion growing. 'Well, not really worked together. Like I said, she worked for his publishers. She was only a secretary, as far as I know. What makes you think she knew him?'

'Well, she *was* in the car with him, for one thing, Mrs Ward. I suppose he could have been giving her a lift home, something like that.'

'What are you trying to say?' Donna snapped, sucking in a deep breath.

Mackenzie clasped his hands together and looked evenly at the distraught woman.

'One of the reasons we couldn't identify your husband after the crash was because he had no ID on his person. No driver's licence, no credit cards, no cheque book. Nothing.'

'He always got *me* to carry his credit cards for him,' she protested.

'That's what I'm trying to tell you, Mrs Ward. He *did* have credit cards *and* his cheque book but *he* wasn't carrying them. After we'd taken the bodies from the wreckage we found your husband's cheque book *and* credit cards in Suzanne Regan's handbag.'

Six

'What are you trying to say?' Donna demanded angrily.

'I'm not trying to *say* anything, Mrs Ward. You merely asked me for some information and I gave it to you,' Mackenzie told her.

'I want to see her,' Donna said flatly.

'That's impossible, Mrs Ward.'

'You could be wrong about her. It might not *be* Suzanne Regan. I've seen her; I could identify her.'

'That's already been done. Her brother confirmed it earlier.'

There was an awkward silence, which was finally broken by Donna.

'Why was she carrying his credit cards?'

'We don't know that, Mrs Ward,' Mackenzie said, almost apologetically.

'What else did you find in her bag? Anything that belonged to my husband?' There was a trace of anger in her voice now.

'I can't disclose information like that, Mrs Ward.'

'Was there anything else?'

'There was a photo of your husband in Miss Regan's purse, and we found two letters from your husband to Miss Regan in her bag as well.'

'Where are they?' Donna demanded.

'Her brother took them. He took all her belongings with him.'

'And my husband? Did he have anything of *hers*?'

'Not as far as we can tell. There was a card – it looks like a business card – in his wallet, but it was blank apart from a phone number and the initial S written on it.'

'Suzanne,' she hissed, her jaws clenched.

The silence descended again and Donna sat back in the chair. Her mind was spinning. First dread, then shock, now confusion. What was next? What other revelations were to be revealed to her?

Why had Suzanne Regan been in the car with him?

Why had she had his photo in her bag? Why was she carrying his credit cards?

Why?

Letters. From Ward to *her*.

She raised a hand to her face once more, covering her eyes.

'I *will* need to speak to you again, Mrs Ward,' Mackenzie said. 'Once everything has been taken care of.'

'You mean after the funeral,' she said, quietly.

'I'll be in touch.' He moved towards the door,

19

pausing before he left. 'I'm very sorry.' And he was gone.

'I want to go home,' Donna said, her voice quivering. She sounded like a child, a lost child. And lost she most certainly was. She felt more alone than she could ever remember.

Seven

She'd been alone in the house often, but until now Donna had never felt truly lonely.

The silence and the desolation crowded in on her almost palpably. The clock on the wall opposite showed 1.32 a.m. She cradled the mug of tea in her hands and sat at the breakfast bar, head lowered. The central heating was turned up to full and Donna was seated close to a radiator, but she still felt that ever-present chill. She wondered if it would ever leave her.

The policewoman had offered to stay with her for the night, to call a relative. A doctor at the hospital had recommended sleeping pills. She had declined all the offers, accepting only the one to drive her home around midnight.

Home.

Even the word had an empty ring. How could it be home without Chris there? She sniffed back a tear then thought about what the nurse had said: '*You have a right to your grief*'. It was one of the few things from that interminable evening she *did* remember.

That, and Mackenzie's revelations that her husband had been in the car with another woman when he'd been killed.

Donna thought how her mind was trying to dismiss this particular piece of knowledge now in the same way as she had tried to shut herself off from the possibility that her husband was dead.

Another woman?

There was an answer, there had to be. There had to be a reason why Suzanne Regan had been in the car with her husband when he died. Had to be a reason why she was carrying his credit cards and cheque book in her handbag. Had to be a reason why she had two letters from him, and a photo.

There had to be a reason other than the most obvious one, that they were involved somehow.

Involved.

What a pleasing euphemism. It sounded so much more civilized to say that Christopher Ward, her dead husband, had been *involved* with another woman. So much more civilized than saying he was having an affair.

Was that what she was trying to deny now?

First his death, now his infidelity.

For now she had only nagging doubts, doubts which became more tangible the more she considered the matter. She got to her feet and wandered out of the kitchen, holding her mug of tea, snapping off the lights as she went. She

21

walked into the hall, her footfalls soft on the carpet as she headed for the sitting room. She pushed open the door, flicked on the lights and the room was illuminated.

It seemed no more hospitable than the kitchen had done.

Over the fireplace hung the framed covers of three of Ward's books.

He'd written fifteen novels in the last twelve years, each one a massive bestseller. Two had been turned into badly-made and unsuccessful films, but he'd been well paid for the rights; Ward had washed his hands of the adaptations and continued writing.

How long ago had he met Suzanne Regan?

Donna sat in the chair where he always used to sit and where he would never sit again.

Never.

She gazed across the room at the television and saw herself reflected in the blank screen. There were videos beneath the set, her husband's chief form of relaxation.

When he was alive.

Donna felt a tear roll down her cheek.

Had he described the house to Suzanne Regan?

Donna got to her feet and walked out of the sitting-room, leaving it in darkness. Back across the hall she walked, to the dining-room with its large dark wood table and its bookcases where Ward's own books were displayed. She took one from a shelf and turned it over, studying the photo on the back, running one index finger over it. He

22

had been an attractive man. It was hard to believe that this was the same man whose face she had seen earlier, gashed and bloodied by the crash. She studied his features carefully, the steely blue eyes, the shoulder-length brown hair.

Was that what had attracted Suzanne Regan?

Donna replaced the book, still crying softly, aware that she would never see that face again in life, never feel the touch of his hands. The unbearable chill seemed to close tightly round her, like a freezing glove.

It followed her into every room.

In the bathroom she touched his razor and ran her thumb across the blade, scarcely aware that she cut the pad. She watched blood well up from the small gash, forming a globule before running down past the first knuckle.

Every room she walked into and looked around, she picked out the objects which were Ward's, objects which made her think of him even more strongly. And the more she thought about him, the stronger the pain became. The chasm in her soul expanded with every recollection.

She paused at the door to his office.

Her hand quivered over the door handle.

She couldn't enter it.

The memories were piled high in there, as high as the copies of his manuscripts. As high as the filing trays, filled with their letters and notepads.

She closed her eyes and pushed the door open.

In the dull light from the desk lamp she gazed around. One half of the room was occupied by two huge bookcases, the other by his desk. On part of the desk sat a typewriter, an old portable manual model. Ward had never invested in a WP; he'd never found the need to fill his room with technological gadgetry. He wrote long-hand, then typed. It was as simple as that.

Beside the typewriter were loose sheets of notepaper with hastily scribbled notes. She saw a dictionary, a thesaurus, the pocket tape-recorder she had bought for him one Christmas. The filing cabinets and drawers remained shut, their secrets hidden from her.

Donna noticed that the small clock on the desk had stopped, its hands frozen and still.

Like Chris.

She flicked off the light and closed the door behind her, walking into their bedroom. The effort of getting undressed seemed too great; she sat down on the edge of the bed, her head bowed as if under some enormous weight. Tears were rolling down her cheeks, her quiet sobs loud in the stillness of the bedroom. Grief she thought she had expended at the hospital now seemed to crowd in on her. She fell back on the bed, her legs drawn up to her chest, and lay in that foetal position, her body quivering as she cried.

The darkness outside was impenetrable but it was radiant compared to the gloom in her soul.

And she knew this was only the beginning.

Eight

A dream.

It had to be a dream.

She heard the sound but thought it was part of her subconscious. The persistent two-tone bell.

She sat up quickly, her eyes wide and staring, red-rimmed. It was no dream. Daylight poured in through the open curtains of the bedroom. The ringing of the doorbell was virtually unabated now, occasionally interspersed with the banging of the brass knocker.

Donna put both hands to her face and felt the stiffness in her neck and shoulders, the beginning of a headache.

The ringing continued. And the banging.

Donna finally swung herself off the bed and moved mechanically across the landing and down the stairs. She paused beside the front door, she put one eye to the spy-hole and recognised the figure outside. She pulled open the door.

'I thought there was something wrong . . .' Jackie Quinn began. Then, as she looked at Donna, she realized that there was. Something terribly wrong.

Donna stepped away from the door, allowing Jackie into the hallway.

'Donna, what's wrong? What is it? You look

terrible,' Jackie said quickly, shocked by her friend's appearance.

'What time is it?' Donna mumbled quietly.

'Sod the time,' Jackie rasped. 'What's happened?'

'It's Chris,' Donna said, tears already forming in her eyes. 'Jackie, he's dead.'

The two women embraced, Donna clasping her friend to her with a strength born of desperation. Jackie could feel tears soaking into the shoulder of her blouse, could feel Donna trembling helplessly in her grasp. And she too felt that awful sense that someone had punched her in the stomach, knocked the wind from her. Shock struck like a clenched fist.

Jackie guided her weeping friend towards the kitchen and sat her down, keeping her hands on Donna's shoulders, stroking her hair repeatedly. She found herself looking into eyes that bulged in the sockets, eyes criss-crossed by veins.

Eyes without any semblance of hope.

At twenty-eight Donna was a year older than Jackie, but her face might have belonged to a person of forty. Beneath her puffy eyes the skin looked bruised, the lids themselves swollen. Her nose was red, her cheeks untouched by make-up. Her hair was unkempt, tangled like intertwined lizard-tails. Two nails were broken on her right hand and another chewed down as far as the tip of the finger. Her face was tear-stained and Jackie could see patches on Donna's sweatshirt and jeans. She thought the dark stain on her thigh was blood.

Jackie found tears coursing down her own cheeks, so touched was she by the plight of her friend.

Gradually Donna stopped sobbing. Jackie held her close again, rocking her as she would rock a child. She kissed the top of Donna's head, pressing her face against the other woman's hair. Donna pulled back slightly and looked at her.

'It happened yesterday,' she said quietly. 'A car crash. I had to identify his body.'

'Donna, I'm so sorry,' Jackie murmured, wiping tears from her own face before pulling a tissue from her handbag and wiping Donna's face. The older woman sat still and allowed her friend to minister to her.

'Have you been here on your own all night?' she asked.

Donna nodded.

'Why the hell didn't you call me? You need someone with you.'

'I need Chris.'

Jackie nodded slowly and swallowed.

'Have you slept?' she wanted to know.

'A few hours. I must have dropped off on the bed last night. You woke me up, ringing the doorbell.' She smiled thinly.

'Come on,' Jackie said, holding out a hand and beckoning her. 'You're going back to bed.'

'I can't sleep. I couldn't sleep. Not now.'

'You're out on your feet. If I hadn't woken you up you'd still be asleep now. Come on.'

'I'll never be able to sleep, Jackie.'

'I've got some sleeping pills in my handbag; you can take those if you have to. Please, Donna. You need some sleep now.'

Donna got to her feet and allowed herself to be led upstairs to the bedroom. There, Jackie drew the curtains and turned down the bed while Donna slipped off her clothes and threw them to the floor. Naked, she slipped between the sheets. Jackie sat on the edge of the bed stroking her hair until she saw her friend's eyes begin to close. It took a matter of minutes before she was asleep. Jackie took one more look at her then hurried downstairs.

In her sleep Donna rolled over, her lips parted slightly, her breathing even.

One hand slid across the bed to rest where her husband would normally have slept.

Nine

She awoke with a start for the second time that day, sitting bolt upright, her head spinning.

Donna looked round to see Jackie standing by her bedside, a tray in her hand. On the tray was a bowl of soup, some bread and two mugs of tea. Donna smiled thinly and sank back onto her pillows, pulling the sheet round her breasts. She glanced across at the clock on the bedside table and saw that it was almost two-thirty. A watery afternoon sun was trying to fight its way out from behind a bank of thin, high cloud.

'You should have woken me earlier,' she said, rubbing her eyes.

'You needed the sleep,' Jackie told her, setting the tray down on the bed. 'You need food, too.'

'Jackie, I can't,' Donna murmured wearily.

'I don't care whether you can or can't, you *need* to eat. Take it.' She pushed the tray towards her friend and perched on the edge of the bed. Donna looked so tired, so drained. Normally, the two women were not dissimilar in appearance. Both were blonde and about the same height, Jackie perhaps a little bigger around the hips and bust, but they shared the same well-defined features; on more than one occasion they had been mistaken for sisters. At the moment, Jackie thought, Donna could have passed for her mother.

Reluctantly Donna reached for the soup and began sipping it.

'The doctor will be here at about four,' Jackie announced, raising a hand to silence the protest she saw forming on Donna's lips. 'I don't care how much you complain, it's better he looks at you. He might give you some tranquillisers or something.'

'I don't need bloody tranquillisers,' Donna said irritably.

'You need something to help you through this,

Donna. They'll do you good. Our doctor prescribed them for my mum when my dad died.'

'What are you trying to do, turn me into a junkie?'

'He'll probably give you valium, not cocaine.'

Donna managed a smile. She reached out and squeezed Jackie's hand.

'Thanks for what you've done, Jackie. I appreciate it. I'm sorry if I've put you to any trouble . . .'

'Don't be so stupid. What was I supposed to do this morning, just turn around and walk away? What would you have done if you'd found me the same way?'

'Exactly what you've done. But I'm still grateful.'

She sipped more of the soup, then some of her tea.

'Do you want to talk about it?' Jackie asked quietly.

'No, not really, but I suppose I'm going to have to eventually. People will have to be told.' She sighed and rubbed a hand across her face.

'Chris didn't have any family, did he?'

Donna shook her head.

'Neither of us did, but there's my sister. I'll have to let Julie know.'

'It's all taken care of. I phoned her before I phoned the doctor. She said she'll be here tomorrow morning. She's taking time off work.'

Donna looked blankly at Jackie.

'She's your sister, Donna; she *should* be with you. You shouldn't be alone. Not now.'

'Thank you,' Donna said softly.

'So, do you want to talk?'

Donna nodded.

'It was a car crash, somewhere in Central London as far as I know. He was working there for a couple of days, researching a new book. He'd been using the British Museum Library a lot. So he said.' She repeated the sequence of events which led up to the identification of her husband's body the previous night.

'It must have been terrible for you. I'm sorry, Donna.'

'Jackie . . .'

I think he was having an affair.

The words were there but Donna could not bring herself to say them.

'What?' Jackie wanted to know.

Donna shook her head.

'It's all right,' she lied. Then, trying to change the subject: 'Did anyone ring while I was asleep?'

'Two or three people rang. They wanted to speak to Chris. I just told them he wasn't available.' Jackie shrugged. 'I didn't think it was my place to tell them the truth. You're not mad, are you? I suppose if I had done it would have saved you the trouble. Perhaps I should . . .'

'You were right,' Donna said. 'As usual.'

It was Jackie's turn to smile.

'The police rang,' she said after a moment or two, the smile fading. 'They said that you could

31

pick up Chris's belongings whenever you wanted to. Some bloke called Mackenzie. He said he wanted to speak to you when you felt better.'

'He was there last night,' Donna said. Then she frowned. 'I wonder why they need to speak to me again? I identified Chris.' She swallowed hard. 'What more could they want to know?'

Some details about Suzanne Regan, perhaps?

Could you tell us how long your husband had been having an affair, Mrs Ward?

She wiped a tear from her eye and sniffed, pushing the tray away.

'I can't eat any more,' she announced apologetically.

'There's some stuff in your fridge, I checked. I'll warm it up for you later. Chops, that kind of thing.'

'I can't eat anything, Jackie, I told you. Anyway, you can't stay here all the time. Dave gets home at about six, doesn't he?'

'Dave is on a training course for a couple of nights in Southampton. I've got nothing to rush back for, anyway.'

Are you sure that's where he is, Jackie? Are you certain he's not driving around with another woman? Positive he isn't involved?

That word again.

'If you want me to stay the night with you I will,' Jackie said.

'I appreciate it, really, but I've got to face things sooner or later.'

'It's only the day after, Donna; be fair to yourself. Don't try to be *too* strong.'

'I'll be okay.'

'I'll stay until the doctor's been, how's that?'

Donna smiled and nodded, watching Jackie pick up the tray and head for the door. She heard her footfalls on the stairs and lay down, eyes closed for long moments.

A car crash in Central London. He was working there.

Was he? Was he really working?

On a book or on Suzanne Regan?

Donna opened her eyes, felt the moisture there.

Had it been an affair?

Somehow she had to find out.

Ten

It was about seven-thirty when Jackie finally left. She had tried to encourage Donna to eat something, using a combination of threats and cajolements. The two women had ended up smiling at each other across the kitchen table. Both of them knew that there was no relief in that smile, however; no hint of a respite from the suffering Donna felt.

The doctor had prescribed a mild dosage of Valium, just 2mg, the minimum dose, but Donna was wary of the drug and said she'd only take it if she found she had no option.

Alone in the house now, seated at the kitchen table dressed in tracksuit bottoms and a T-shirt several sizes too big, she stared at the bottle reproachfully and ran a hand through her hair. She had showered and washed her hair after Jackie had left, standing beneath the spray for more than twenty minutes, as if the powerful jets of water could wash away some of her grief.

She'd sat in the sitting-room and tried to watch television but the images on the screen did not register in her mind. She had flicked aimlessly from channel to channel before switching the set off and turning on the stereo instead. It didn't seem to matter what she did as long as she didn't have to put up with the silence. In the kitchen she had switched on the ghetto-blaster, but every tape she selected seemed to bring different memories. If she played one of Chris's tapes it made her think of him. If she played one of her own then the words she normally sang along to quite happily had added poignancy. He always used to joke with her about her choice of music, telling her the sad love songs she was so fond of would make her depressed. They never had. Until now.

She sat alone and silent in the kitchen, tapping the lid of the valium bottle, wondering if she should take just one.

It *might* help.

She shook her head. Tranquillizers helped to

alleviate symptoms of stress and suffering; they didn't remove the cause.

She got to her feet and padded barefoot from the kitchen back towards the stairs, climbing them slowly.

The phone rang again but she ignored it, allowing the message to be taken by the answering machine. The green light was already flashing three times but Donna had no inclination to learn the identity of the callers just yet. As she reached the top of the stairs she heard the click as the machine recorded the latest call and stored it.

The house was silent again as she wandered down the corridor that led off the landing to her husband's office.

It was cold inside there, colder than the rest of the house, she thought, but realized that this was merely fanciful supposition. She touched the radiator and found it was hot. She switched on the desk lamp and sat down behind the typewriter, running her fingers over the black keys as if it were a musical instrument.

There was a framed picture of her husband on the wall to the left of the desk, from a photo shoot he'd done in Madame Tussaud's Chamber of Horrors for the launch of his last book. It showed him standing beside the guillotine, pointing up at the blade and smiling.

Donna stared at the photo, her eyes filling with tears. She fought them back and glanced around at the other things on his desk. It was organised chaos. File trays were marked with white sticky labels, each one supposedly home, according to the legend on the sticker, to various documents.

CONTRACTS

RESEARCH AND NOTES

FAN MAIL

She picked a letter from the top of the tray and glanced at it. It was the usual thing. *'I enjoyed your books very much. I look forward to the next one. Please can I have a signed photo etc. etc.'*

Ward received a lot of fan mail and was always grateful for it. The readers, he used to tell her, paid their mortgage.

Did they pay for his mistress, too?

Donna slid open one of the drawers and peered in. More notepads, more envelopes. Elastic bands, paper clips, Tipp-Ex.

A letter.

She pulled it out and spread it out on the desk, scanning it through tired eyes.

Dear Suzanne.

Donna stiffened, sucked in a shallow breath.

Suzanne.

One part of her wanted to read the letter; the other part told her not to continue.

'Dear Suzanne,' she read aloud. 'Just a quick note to tell you that everything is taken care of.' She swallowed hard. 'I hope you are well and I will see you next Thursday. Love, Chris.'

Love.

Donna closed her eyes for a moment, her body shaking. Then she looked at the letter again. There was no date on it.

See you next Thursday.

She snatched at the letter and balled it up, crushing it between her hands, finally hurling it across the room with a despairing grunt. Tears were coursing down her cheeks. She glared across at the photo of her husband on the wall.

He smiled back at her.

'You fucking bastard,' she roared at the photo.

She didn't know whether her tears were of pain or anger.

And it didn't really seem to matter any more.

Eleven

Donna hadn't expected so much coverage in the papers.

She'd thought there would be a mention of her husband's death in the trade magazines, and perhaps a line or two in one of the nationals, but she was unprepared for what actually appeared.

Three of the tabloids ran two-column stories (one with a photograph) while even *The Times* mentioned Chris's death. A little ironic, Donna thought, considering how they had lambasted his books when he'd been alive. The coverage provoked a flood of phone calls to the house.

She moved around irritably, not picking up the phone, leaving the answering machine to cope with the deluge. Occasionally she would stand beside the machine and listen to see who was on the other end of the line, but by the afternoon she had unplugged all the phones except the one connected to the answerphone in an effort to get some peace.

She hadn't slept much the previous night and what rest she'd managed had been fitful. She'd woken twice from a nightmare but had been unable to remember the images that had shocked her into consciousness.

Car crashes, perhaps?

Funerals?

Mistresses?

She didn't go near Ward's office that day; she feared what she might find in there. The letter she had discovered had only reinforced her conviction that her husband had been having an affair with Suzanne Regan. What Donna *was* aware of was how little she had cried since finding the letter. More and more of the emotion she felt was tinged with anger now.

She ate a bowl of soup and some bread at about two o'clock and sat staring at the Valium bottle. She thought about taking one of the tablets but decided against it.

The phone was silent now. As she dropped her bowl into the sink, Donna decided to check the messages before a new batch came in.

The house seemed very quiet as she walked

through the hallway and flicked the switch marked 'Incoming Message'. She heard a high-pitched squeal, a cacophony of indecipherable noise as the tape rewound quickly then began with its catalogue of calls.

A reporter from the local paper.

Diana Wellsby, Ward's editor, offering her condolences.

Nick Crosby, Managing Director of his publishers, also offering his sympathies.

No message.

Chris's accountant; could he ring him? (Obviously not everyone read the papers, Donna thought.)

Her mother, who said she refused to speak to a machine but would ring back.

Donna smiled thinly when she heard her mother's voice.

Jackie. Ring her, just to let her know how things were going.

'Mrs Ward, this is Detective Constable Mackenzie. I'd appreciate it if you could call me as soon as possible. Thank you.'

Donna chewed her bottom lip thoughtfully. The policeman had called yesterday, too. What was so important? She reached for the pad and pen beside the phone, rewound the tape and took down the number he'd left.

'Donna, it's Martin Connelly,' the next voice announced. She smiled at the warmth in the tone. It was Chris's agent. 'I realize what you must be feeling and I'm very sorry about what's happened. I'll call you back later. Take care, gorgeous.'

One more call.

She waited for a voice but there wasn't one.

A wrong number, perhaps?

She could hear breathing on the tape, slow, rhythmic breathing. No background noise. Nothing but breathing.

Then the message was brought to an abrupt end as the phone was put down.

Donna flicked her hair from her face and was about to walk away from the phone when it rang again.

Her hand hovered over the receiver. She thought about picking it up but finally allowed the machine to click on.

Breathing.

The same breathing as on the message she'd just listened to.

Pick it up.

Donna stared at the phone, listening to the breathing. Then finally she heard, 'Shit.' The phone was put down, *slammed down* hard at the other end.

Donna backed away from the machine as if it were some kind of venomous serpent. If it was a crank call, it was either bad timing or a particularly sick bastard getting his rocks off at the other end of the line. She suddenly felt very lonely and vulnerable.

It was then that the doorbell rang.

Twelve

For long moments she hesitated, standing rigid in the hallway.

The chain was off.

Donna swallowed hard and took a step towards the door as the two-tone chime sounded again. She gently eased the chain into position and finally peered through the spy-hole.

She saw her younger sister immediately.

Donna hurried to open the door, throwing it wide and holding out her arms.

When Julie Craig embraced her the two women clutched each other tightly, unwilling to be parted. Finally Donna pulled back slightly, with tears in her eyes.

'Thanks for coming,' she whispered.

'Nothing would have stopped me,' Julie told her. They embraced again. 'Donna, I'm so sorry.'

Both of them were crying now, weeping softly against each other's shoulders. At last Donna guided her sister inside the house and pushed the front door closed.

'I'll get my stuff out of the car in a minute,' Julie told her, wiping a tear away. She touched her cheek and shook her head gently. 'You look *so* tired.'

'I haven't been sleeping too well,' Donna said, smiling humourlessly. 'You can guess why.' She wiped her eyes. 'I'm glad you're here, Julie.'

When she'd finished telling her story Donna didn't even raise her head. She merely shifted slightly in her seat, running the tip of her index finger around the rim of her teacup.

Julie watched her sister seated at the other end of the sofa, legs drawn up beneath her. She reached out a hand and touched Donna's arm, gripping it.

'Why didn't you call me as soon as it happened?' she wanted to know.

'There was no point. Besides, I could hardly remember my own name, let alone call anyone,' Donna explained, running a hand through her blonde hair. She looked at Julie and smiled. 'Little sister helping *big* sister out this time.'

'You've helped me enough times in the past,' Julie said.

There was only two years' age difference between the women. Julie, at twenty-six, was also a little taller, her hair darker, chestnut brown compared to her sister's lighter, natural colour. They were dressed similarly too, both in black leggings and baggy tops, Julie wearing white socks, Donna barefoot. They had always dressed similarly. They had similar views on life, men and the world in general, too. Best friends as well as sisters, they had shared a closeness throughout their lives most siblings only discover with advancing years. There had been no teenage rivalry between them, only a bond of love that had grown deeper as they'd developed. It had intensified when Julie left home first to attend photographic college and Donna had moved into her own flat after securing a job with a record company. The very fact that the women saw less of each other made their closeness more palpable when they met.

Julie had married when she was twenty-two. It was a doomed relationship with a man ten years older, whose affections seemed divided between her and the contents of whisky bottles. Their short marriage had ended acrimoniously less than a year after they'd promised each other, 'Til Death us do Part'. Alcohol, it seemed, was as effective a destroyer of marriages as death.

Julie had set up her own photographic business with her share of the settlement money, a business she now owned and operated with the aid of a partner, employing three people. It was thriving.

Donna had married two years later. Both had known love; both had known grief. The latter tended to predominate where men were concerned.

'How far have you got with the arrangements?' Julie asked. 'Sorting out the undertaker, things like that?'

'I haven't even picked up Chris's things from the hospital yet,' Donna said guiltily. She looked at her sister, opened her mouth to say something, then paused a moment longer before finally breaking the silence.

'Julie, I think Chris was having an affair.'

Julie shot her an anxious glance.

'What makes you think that?' she demanded.

'There was another woman in the car with him when he died,' Donna began, then went on to explain what had come to light.

'She could have been a friend,' Julie offered.

Donna raised an eyebrow quizzically.

'A friend? Yes, I suppose she could have been.' She shook her head.

'I'm not saying you're wrong, I'm just saying you've got more important things to think about right now.'

'More important things?' Donna snapped. 'My husband was having an affair, Julie. He died with the woman he was fucking behind my back. I think *that's* important.'

'You loved him, didn't you?'

'Of course I loved him. I loved him more than I thought it was possible to love anyone. That's why it hurts so much.' Tears were beginning to form in her eyes. 'I miss him so much but I'll never know the truth.' The tears were flowing freely now. 'And I have to know.' Julie embraced her, stroking her hair. 'I *have* to know.'

Thirteen

Donna was crossing the hall when she heard the car pull up outside.

She paused as she heard the car door shut and footsteps approach. She moved towards the front door, peering through the spy-hole. She smiled as she recognised her visitor and opened the door before he could ring the bell.

Martin Connelly looked surprised to find himself gazing into her face.

'I heard your car,' she said, beckoning him inside.

Connelly accepted the invitation and stepped in, turning to hug Donna briefly.

'When you didn't call me back I thought I'd come round and see how you were. I hope you don't mind,' he said.

'It's very thoughtful of you,' she told him as they walked into the sitting-room.

Julie was glancing at a magazine when Connelly entered. She looked up and saw him, smiled tightly and nodded a greeting.

'Martin, this is my sister Julie,' Donna announced. 'Martin Connelly. He was Chris's agent.' The two of them shook hands a little stiffly and Connelly looked at Donna.

'If I'm interrupting,' he apologised. 'I just

wanted to see if you were okay. I won't stay.' He smiled at Julie again.

'Stay and have a drink.'

'If I do it had better be coffee. I'm driving,' Connelly explained.

'I'll make it,' said Julie. 'You two talk.' And she was gone, closing the sitting-room door behind her, leaving them alone.

Connelly wandered over to the fireplace and glanced at the framed book covers that hung there. Donna studied him.

He was in his mid-thirties, smartly dressed (he was always smartly dressed, she remembered), his light brown hair impeccably groomed. He had been Ward's agent for the last five years. The relationship between them had never been business-orientated, though; it was something stronger than that. Although it was not powerful enough to be true friendship, there was nevertheless a mutual respect of each other's abilities coupled by a ruthless streak they also both possessed. It had been a formidable combination.

'You're okay for money, aren't you?' Connelly asked her.

'I won't starve, Martin.'

'I always made sure Chris had enough insurance policies and stuff like that.' He turned and looked at her. 'But if you need anything, anything at all, you call me. Right?'

She smiled.

'I mean it, Donna,' he insisted. 'Promise me you will.'

46

'I promise.'

He reached into the pocket of his jacket and took out a packet of cigarettes, lighting one with his silver lighter. He regarded her coolly through the haze of bluish smoke. Despite the dark rings beneath her eyes and the fact that her hair needed brushing she still looked extremely attractive. Prior to Ward's death he'd seen her dressed up, her make-up done to perfection. On some of those occasions the only word he could find to describe her was breathtaking. Now he ran appraising eyes slowly over her, a little embarrassed when she looked up and caught him in the middle of his furtive inspection.

'How long's your sister here for?' he asked, feeling the need to break the silence.

'For as long as she wants to be. Certainly until after the funeral.'

'Do you know when it is yet?'

She shook her head.

'I've got to sort all that out tomorrow,' Donna told him.

'Do you need any help?'

'I'll be all right. Thanks, anyway. It's probably better in some ways. The more I've got to do, the less time I've got to sit around and think about what's happened.'

'I know what you mean. No good brooding about it, is it?' He realized the clumsiness of his statement and apologised.

'It's okay, Martin. Say what you think. People can't tip-toe around the subject for the rest of their lives. Chris is dead, and there's nothing I can do about that. Ignoring it isn't going to make it any more bearable.'

'You know that he had it written into all his contracts that, if anything happened to him, you were to become beneficiary of all his money from royalties and advances?' Connelly said.

She nodded.

'I remember when we first met, before Chris was earning decent money from his books. People used to tell me I was crazy to stay with him, that he'd never earn a good living. Then, when he *did* start earning good money, those same people told me that was the only reason I'd stayed with him.' She shook her head.

'Jealousy. You'll always get it. The wives of successful men always get that thrown at them, that they're only with the bloke because of his money. It happens the other way round, too. Behind every successful woman is a spongeing bastard; behind every successful man is a gold-digger.' He smiled and took another drag on his cigarette. 'Of course sometimes it's true.'

Now it was Donna's turn to smile. The atmosphere seemed to lighten a little.

Connelly moved away from the fireplace and sat down opposite her, chancing another swift glance at her as she ran a hand over her face.

'How much did you know about Chris?' she asked.

Connelly frowned.

'What do you mean?' the agent asked, looking a little puzzled.

'I mean about his work, his character. What he did in his spare time. How much did you know about what he thought?'

Connelly looked bemused.

'Would you say you *knew* him, Martin? Knew him as a person, not just as a client?'

'That's a strange question, Donna. I don't see what you're driving at.'

Their conversation was momentarily interrupted as Julie arrived with a tray of coffee cups, milk and sugar. She set it down and poured cups for Donna and Connelly, saying she had some things to unpack. 'I'll leave you to talk.' She smiled at Connelly. 'It was good to meet you.' Again she disappeared and Donna heard her footsteps on the stairs.

Connelly dropped sugar cubes into his cup and stirred gently.

'What do you mean, did I *know* Chris?' he asked.

'You were pretty close, weren't you? I mean, he must have told you things. About himself, about his work, about me.'

'Donna, I was his agent, not his bloody confessor. If my clients want to tell me their problems, that's up to them. I care about them, and I like to think it's not just on a professional level.'

'Did Chris tell you his problems?'

'What kind of problems?' Connelly said, taken aback by her questions. 'What made you think he had any? If he had, you'd know more about them than me. You *were* his wife.'

'I hadn't forgotten, Martin,' she said acidly. 'But there might have been things he told you that he *couldn't* tell me.'

Connelly shook his head.

'Did he tell you he was having an affair?' she demanded.

The agent looked at her evenly.

'What makes you think he was?' he wanted to know. 'And even if he *was*, which I doubt, what makes you so sure he'd tell *me*?'

'You said you were close to your clients. He couldn't very well tell me, could he?'

'What gives you the idea he was having an affair, for Christ's sake? He loved you. Why would he want to screw around with other women?'

'Does your professionalism run to protecting him when he's dead, Martin?'

'Donna, I know you're going through a bad time, I understand that. But this is shit.' There was a hint of anger in Connelly's voice. 'Chris wasn't having an affair and if he was, he didn't say anything to me about it. You're on about that crap in the paper about him being found in the car with a woman, aren't you?'

'He *was* found in the car with a woman.'

'That doesn't mean she was his mistress. Jesus Christ, Donna. Think about it logically.'

'I don't know what to think any more, Martin,' she hissed. 'But I'll tell you this, if you're keeping quiet just because you think it's saving me hurt then you may as well tell me what you know. I couldn't suffer any more than I'm suffering now.'

'Just listen to what you're saying, Donna,' Connelly told her, trying to keep his voice even. 'Your husband is dead and all you can think about is whether or not he was having a fucking affair.'

An uneasy silence descended.

Donna rested her head on her hand, her eyes averted. Connelly kept his gaze on her. When he sipped at his coffee again it was cold. He put the cup back on the tray and got to his feet, taking a step towards her.

'He never said anything to me, Donna, believe me. I know as much as you.' He wanted to reach out and touch her shoulder but resisted the temptation. 'If I knew anything I'd tell you.'

'Would you, Martin?' she said, eyeing him challengingly.

'I'd better go,' he said quietly. 'I'll let you get on.'

She got to her feet and they walked to the front door where she paused on the step and pecked him on the cheek.

'Don't forget,' he said. 'If you need *anything*, just let me know.'

She nodded and watched as he walked to the waiting Porsche and slid behind the steering wheel. He started the engine and waved, watching her disappear back inside the house. Connelly pulled away, the house falling away behind him.

On the landing, hidden by the curtains, Julie Craig also watched the agent leave.

Fourteen

They had done all they could that day. The two women had risen early and begun the tasks which needed completion. Now, as night began to creep across the sky, they sat in the dining-room eating, occasionally glancing at each other and smiling.

Donna, wearing make-up for the first time in two days, looked pale and tired still but she also looked a little stronger.

There had been tears when they'd called at the hospital that morning to pick up Chris's belongings but Julie had expected that.

His clothes were now upstairs in one of the spare bedrooms, the blood-spattered garments laid out on one of the beds until they could be washed. It was as if Donna needed to keep looking at them; despite Julie's entreaties, she had returned regularly to the room that day to view the torn clothing.

Next to his clothes lay his wallet and his cheque book, similarly splashed with blood.

After the hospital they had travelled to the undertaker. He'd been helpful and sympathetic in his practised way, a fat, middle-aged man with too much hair that looked as if it had been dropped onto his head from a great height. He asked the relevant questions:

'*Open coffin?*'

'*Cremation or burial?*'

'*How much did she want to spend?*'

The enquiries had begun to blur into one another; Donna had left feeling that she was no longer in control of events. The undertaker would arrange everything, he assured her. She need have no worries. As she and Julie had left another group of people had entered, doubtless to be asked the same questions. Death had become like a conveyor belt, it seemed.

From the undertaker's they travelled to a florist's and ordered the flowers.

There were catalogues full of suitable wreaths and arrangements. Wreaths for all occasions. Donna noticed, with acute poignancy, that one page was devoted to 'The Death of a Child'. How terrible, she thought, for parents to be confronted by that particular ordeal.

Everything appeared ready now; there was just the funeral to come. The time Donna dreaded most. The awful finality of it all. At the moment, she knew the body of her dead husband lay in the Chapel of Rest. Once it was laid in the earth then it was as if he was to be wiped from her consciousness, not just her mind. All she had to look forward to now were memories.

Memories and pain.

And anger.

Donna pushed her plate away from her and sat back in her chair, exhaling deeply.

'You okay?' Julie asked.

'I feel so tired,' Donna told her. She smiled wanly at her sister. 'I'm sorry, Julie.'

'Go and have a nap, I'll take care of this,' Julie said, waving a hand over the dirty plates and glasses. 'Go on. I'll bring you a cup of tea up in a while.'

Donna thanked her and walked away from the table, touching Julie's shoulder as she went.

The younger woman smiled and kept on smiling as she heard her sister's footfalls on the stairs. The steps groaned protestingly as she made her way to the bedroom. Julie continued eating, looking first at her watch then at her plate. Eventually she, too, pushed it away, got to her feet and began gathering the utensils, ready to take them through to the kitchen.

As she reached the dining-room door she glanced across at a darkwood cabinet inside the room. There were a number of photos on it, each of them in a silver frame.

Photos of Donna and Ward together.

Julie stood close to them, gazing at the pictures for long moments. Then she reached out one slender finger and gently drew it around the outline of Ward's face, a slight smile creasing her lips.

Then she did the same around the image of Donna's face.

By then, though, the smile had faded.

Fifteen

He used to call it The Cell.

The room where he imprisoned himself for six hours a day, five days a week. The room where Christopher Ward sat, with only his thoughts for company, pounding away at a typewriter until a new book was completed.

The silence in the room was something Donna had always found unsettling. Only the sound of the water in the radiators broke the oppressive stillness. One day, jokingly, she had said to him that he had an easy job, just sitting behind a desk alone all day. He had locked Donna in there behind the typewriter. After just ten minutes she had called to him to let her out. Laughing, he had agreed.

Laughing.

She had almost forgotten what the sound was like. At times she wondered if she would ever hear such joyous noise again. Certainly not now, seated in The Cell, peering round her at the notes scattered over the desk, at the books and the files.

He had always kept his work private. What went on inside his head was his concern, he'd once told her. And what went on inside his office was his concern, too. He hadn't excluded her through any act of antagonism; he preferred to keep his work and his life with her separate. She had asked him about his methods of working, about how each of his books was progressing; she'd even been allowed to read portions of them before they were published. But as a rule Ward kept his work to himself. What little else she discovered was by reading interviews with him in newspapers or by hearing him on radio, watching him on television.

And now, as she sat amongst the remnants of his work, she felt a heavy sadness at this exclusion. Now it was too late for him to tell her, she felt she wanted to know every single stage of the processes involved in turning an idea into a finished book. But she knew it could never be.

She began by searching his attaché case, going through the papers. She needed the insurance policies, for instance.

She wondered why she felt as if she were intruding in the small room. It was as if she had no right to be in here, with the night closed tightly around the house like a tenebrous glove. Only the dull glow from the desk light illuminated the blackness.

Donna felt that chill she had come to know only too well over the last few days.

She found what she sought and pulled it clear of the case.

The photos came loose with it.

They fluttered into the air and then fell to the floor. Half a dozen of them.

Donna picked them up.

There was a publicity shot of Chris, unsmiling. His sinister face, he called it. She smiled thinly as she gathered the other photos, turning the next one over.

Chris again.

With other men.

She searched their faces but didn't recognise any of them. They were sitting at a large table, two younger men, no older than Chris, then her husband, then an older man. Very much older. She squinted at the picture but could not make out his features. It was as if that particular part of the photo were blurred.

It was the same with the next man.

Very old again and, once more, the image was blurred.

Not so with the last of the group, a young man in his early thirties, handsome but with cruel eyes and short dark hair. She could feel those eyes boring into her as she studied the picture.

The next one was the same, except that Chris was in the centre this time.

And again she saw those two blurred images. As she looked from one to the other she realized that it was just the faces that were blurred; the rest of the image was as sharp as a knife.

No one in the photo was smiling. Chris and the other five looked impassively into the camera. She assumed that was what the two older men were doing, too, just looking at the camera. She knew they were old from the wrinkles on their hands;

there were deep folds of skin around the knuckles and the base of the thumb. Their clothes looked old, too. Almost archaic, in fact.

What did stand out with sharp clarity was something on their hands.

Both the blurred figures wore rings on their left index fingers, large heavy gold signet rings.

She peered closer at them, aware that there was a symbol of some kind at their centre, but no matter how closely she looked she could not make it out.

Donna sat back on her haunches, breathing heavily.

Then she picked up his diary, flicking through it.

JANUARY 11th: Phone Martin.

JANUARY 15th: Confirm interview for next week.

JANUARY 17th: Shooting – 7.00–9.00.

The entries were mostly uninspiring, some scribbled in pencil, others in pen.

FEBRUARY 5th: Check train times.
She read on.

FEBRUARY 9th: Ring S.

Donna gritted her teeth and flicked back and forth through the diary. There were numerous entries of a similar nature. Sometimes just the initial. Others just bore the initial D.

Well, it didn't refer to Donna, that's for sure.
Another mistress?

Donna flicked to the back of the diary, to the addresses, and ran her index finger down the list.

Through the hotels and restaurants, the business addresses, the private addresses, the . . .

SUZANNE REGAN.

Donna read the address, then reached for a pen and scribbled it down on a piece of paper.

SUZANNE REGAN,
23 LOCKWOOD DRIVE,
NOTTING HILL GATE,
LONDON W2

She got to her feet, the piece of paper gripped in her fist.

Sixteen

'Where the hell are you going?'

Julie looked up in surprise as her sister entered the sitting-room, her long leather coat flying open as she headed across the room.

'Out,' snapped Donna, brandishing the piece of paper.

Julie got to her feet. She noticed that Donna had pulled on a pair of suede boots and tucked her jeans into the top of them.

'You were tired; you were going to have a nap. Donna, tell me what's happening.' She could see the tearstains on the older woman's face.

'I know where she lives,' Donna said angrily. 'I found her address in his diary. I know where she lives.'

'*Lived*,' Julie reminded her. 'And so what if you do?'

'I want to see where she lived.'

'Donna, this is crazy. She's dead. It's over. *She's* dead. Chris is dead. That's all there is to it. Stop this now, before it drives you mad. You're becoming obsessive about it.'

'And wouldn't you?' Donna rasped. 'You lost *your* husband to the bottle, but it didn't matter to you. I *care*.'

Julie took a step back, her face losing its colour.

'I wish I could argue with you,' she said resignedly. 'Yes, I did lose my husband to the bottle, not another woman. But the difference between us is I didn't blame myself for his drinking. It's as if you're blaming yourself for what Chris did before he was killed. It isn't your fault, Donna.'

'Then why did he need to have an affair?' she rasped. 'What the fuck was so special about this bloody Suzanne Regan? I want to know what she had that I don't. I want to know what she wore, what she smelled like. I want to know what kind of music she listened to. I even want to know what she bloody well ate.' There was a vehemence in Donna's words Julie had never seen before, a hatred that burned as brightly as a beacon. It danced in her eyes like fire.

'It's becoming an obsession with you,' Julie continued. 'I'm beginning to wonder which has upset you the most, the fact that Chris is dead or that he was unfaithful.'

'Well, perhaps even *I* don't know any more,' Donna told her. 'He's not here for me to ask, is he? I can't find out from him why he wanted her. So I have to find out myself. It might just keep me sane.'

'Why do you have to know?' Julie asked imploringly. 'Why do you have to torture yourself?'

'I told you, I need to know whether she was better than me.' There were tears forming in Donna's eyes now. 'I lost my husband, Julie, that's the worse thing I could ever have imagined. I don't want to lose my self-respect, too.'

For long seconds the two women stood staring at each other, neither speaking. Then Julie took a step forward.

'What are you going to do?' she asked quietly.

'Go to her house.'

'And do what?'

'Look around, see what I can find.'

'You're just going to break in? As easy as that?'

'I don't know what I'm going to do. All I know is, I have to see where she lived.' She handed the piece of paper with the address on to Julie. 'You're my sister and I love you. If you love *me*, then help me.'

'Help you do what? Go crazy? Because that's what you're doing. Please think about this, Donna. Think about what you're doing to yourself. Isn't Chris's death enough to cope with?'

Donna's stare was unflinching.

'Are you going to help me?' she asked, holding out her hand for the piece of paper.

Julie exhaled deeply and wearily.

'Yes, I'll help you,' she said finally.

'I want to go there now.'

Julie knew that it was futile to argue. She nodded.

'Let me get my coat,' she said. 'I'll drive.'

Seventeen

Number Twenty-Three Lockwood Drive was a converted house off Moscow Road, part of the maze of Notting Hill.

It was white, or had been at one time. Now the painted brickwork was grey with the accumulated grime of the years. Even the flowers in the window box on the ground floor looked as though they'd been sprayed with dust. It was difficult to tell which were alive and which weren't. A row of iron railings, rusted in places, protected the front of the house and a gate with one hinge missing guarded the short path to the front door. The neighbouring houses were in a similar state; many had FOR SALE signs displayed.

Lights burned in windows and shadowy figures could be seen moving behind curtains. There were few people on the streets and those that were hardly glanced at the two women sitting in the Fiesta parked opposite Number Twenty-Three.

Donna Ward gazed at the house, studying every

aspect of it: the colour of the front door, the curtains that hung at the windows. She saw a dark stain at the meeting of the roof and front wall and realized that water had obviously been dripping from a hole in the guttering. Somewhere close by she heard a dog bark.

Street lamps burned with a dull yellow light, casting deep shadows. Inside the car it was silent.

The drive into the heart of London had taken less than an hour. Traffic had been unexpectedly light and Julie had guided them skilfully to their destination. Now she sat in the driver's seat, one hand pressed to her forehead, her impatience growing.

'How long are we going to sit here?' she wanted to know.

Donna ignored the question, her eyes still fixed on the dirty white house across the road.

'It's expensive around here,' she said. 'A bit grand for a secretary's wages. Perhaps he was paying her rent, too.'

'Let's go. You've seen the place, that's what you wanted.'

Donna reached for the door-handle and pushed it open.

'What are you doing?' Julie asked, bewildered.

'Wait for me,' Donna instructed her, swinging herself out of the car. She walked briskly across the street and headed for the house, lifting the gate on its hinge as she made her way up the short path and four steps.

Julie, watching from the car, shook her head.

Donna studied the panel beside the front door and saw a number of names attached to the intercom buttons. She ran her index finger down the list:

Weston.

Lawrence.

Regan.

She gritted her teeth when she saw the name, then pressed the main door buzzer and waited.

She heard movement behind the door. A moment later, it was opened and she found herself looking into the face of a man in his sixties, short, balding and with tufts of white hair sprouting from each nostril. It looked as if two snow-white caterpillars were trying to escape from his nose. He was wearing impeccably-pressed trousers, a blue shirt that looked freshly ironed and a spotted bow-tie. On his feet he wore scuffed carpet slippers.

He smiled warmly when he saw Donna.

'Can I help you?' he asked.

'It's about my sister,' she lied, her tone sombre. 'Suzanne Regan.'

The old man nodded, his smile fading.

'I was very sorry to hear what happened. She was a lovely girl,' he offered. 'There's a family resemblance.'

Donna controlled herself with difficulty.

'My brother said he was going to call round for some of her things,' she said, sounding remarkably convincing. 'But I thought I'd better check whether he had or not.'

'No one's been round, Miss Regan,' he said, glancing down at her left hand, catching sight of the wedding ring. 'Or is it *Mrs*?' He smiled again.

She shook her head.

'My name is

(*careful now*)

Blake. Catherine Blake.'

'Mercuriadis,' he announced, holding out a hand. She shook it lightly; his hand felt soft and warm. 'I know it's a bit of a mouthful. Would you like to come in?'

Bingo.

Donna accepted the invitation and closed the door behind her, looking briefly around the hall. There was a small antique chest to her left with flowers propped in a vase on its scratched top. A pay-phone on the wall. To the right was the half-open door to the landlord's own flat, presumably. At least she assumed he was the landlord. Ahead of her was a flight of stairs.

'I'd just like to check my sister's flat if that's all right?' Donna said, trying to hold the old man's gaze.

'I'll get the key,' he said, and disappeared into the room on the right. Donna could hear the sound of television coming from inside.

Jesus, this was too easy.

See how easy it is to lie.

He returned a moment later clutching the key and ushered her towards the stairs.

'Did you see much of my sister?' she wanted to

know as they climbed the stairs slowly, the old man wheezing every few steps.

'No, she kept herself to herself. Very quiet. A lovely girl.'

'Did she have many visitors? I was always joking with her about getting a boyfriend.' Donna laughed as convincingly as she could.

'There was a young man,' Mercuriadis said. 'I saw him with her two or three times.' He lowered his voice into a conspiratorial whisper. 'I think he spent the night more than once.' He smiled.

Donna tried to smile but it came out as a grimace.

'What did he look like?' she asked.

'I can't really remember. Age plays tricks with memory, you know. My wife always used to say that, God rest her soul.'

Had Chris been here? Had he slept here with her?

They reached the first landing and Donna hesitated.

'It's up another flight, I'm afraid,' he told her. 'It's a good job my tenants are younger than I am. It never used to bother me, all this climbing. My wife and I bought this house forty years ago. After she died I decided to let the rooms. I don't like being in a house this size on my own. There aren't so many tenants now, though. I've had to put the rents up and some moved out. The recession, you know.' He nodded as if to reinforce his statement.

'Look, I can check out the room myself,' Donna

told him. 'There's no need for you to struggle up the stairs. I'll return the key to you on my way out.'

'All right, then. That's very thoughtful of you,' he said, looking at her.

Was it her imagination or did she see a look of suspicion in his eyes?

Come on, don't get paranoid.

'I'm surprised I don't remember seeing you before,' he said, still holding onto the key. 'I don't usually forget a pretty face.'

Donna smiled with impressive sincerity.

'Thank you. I live on the South Coast. I didn't get to see Suzanne as often as I'd like.'

Lying was easier than she'd thought.

He nodded again and handed her the key.

'I'll leave you to it, then,' he said. 'But I would just like to offer my condolences once again. I know what you must be going through.'

Do you? Do you really?

She smiled thinly, took the key from him and set off up the second flight of stairs, emerging on the next landing. She looked down to see the landlord making his way back down the stairs. She waited until she heard the door to his room close before turning around.

Only then, faced by four locked doors and with the key in her hand, did she realize that she hadn't got a clue which of the doors would lead her into Suzanne Regan's flat.

Eighteen

What the hell was she going to do?

Donna looked at the key, then at each of the doors in turn. They all looked the same.

Only one way to find out.

She crossed to the first door and edged the key into the lock, listening for any sounds from the other side. She didn't relish the prospect of having to explain herself to both an irate tenant *and* Mr Mercuriadis. She heard nothing and pushed the key as far as it would go into the Yale lock, turning it as gently as possible.

It wouldn't turn.

She withdrew it with equal care, looking behind her at the other doors just in case someone emerged and caught her at her furtive business.

She moved to the next door and pressed her ear close to the white-painted wood.

From inside she heard classical music. Someone was obviously in there.

Donna turned and moved towards the third of the four doors. Once more she pushed the key slowly into the lock and tried to turn it.

Again it wouldn't move.

She allowed herself a thin smile as she realized, by process of elimination, that the door she wanted was the last one. Donna pulled the key.

It wouldn't budge; remained stuck fast in the lock.

She swallowed hard and gripped it more firmly but still the recalcitrant object stayed where it was, held by the grooves and threads of the lock.

She had to free it.

There was movement on the other side of the door.

Oh Jesus, what if the tenant was coming out?

Donna pulled at the key again frantically but still it remained firmly wedged.

The movement behind the door ceased and she stood still for a moment, listening.

Across the landing she could still hear the classical music.

She waited a second longer then tried again, working the key back and forth this time, feeling it give a little.

And a little more.

She pulled hard and the key came free with a metallic rasping sound.

Immediately she heard footsteps coming towards the door from the other side.

She had to get inside Suzanne Regan's flat as quickly as possible. Donna took the three paces across to the other door, slid the key in and turned it.

The door of the flat next to her was beginning to open.

Hurry.

She pushed the door open, slipped inside and closed it. She leaned her back against it, trying to control her breathing as she heard footsteps on the landing. In the darkness of the flat she listened to them move towards the top of the stairs, the top step creaking protestingly.

For interminable seconds she stood in the blackness, awaiting the knock and the confrontation. Her mind was racing, her thoughts tumbling in different directions. She closed her fists tightly.

Closed one around the key.

The key.

As she stood in the darkness she realized that it was still stuck in the door, protruding from the lock.

Nineteen

On the landing the footsteps thudded back and forth, were still for a second then receded.

Donna listened to the silence. Like a spring uncoiling she slowly turned the handle, shot her hand out and plucked the key from the lock, pushing the door shut again.

She let out a breath explosively in relief.

She stood there in the gloom, waiting until she had stopped shaking. Then she slipped the key into the pocket of her coat, ran a hand through her hair and turned, feeling for the light switch. Her hand brushed against it and she flicked it on.

70

A sixty watt bulb flickered into life, illuminating the flat.

She was standing in the entry-way. Coat hooks had been attached to the wall to her right. Two short jackets and a longer wool coat hung there. There was a phone on a table close by.

Donna moved into the sitting-room proper and noticed how small it was. There was a sofa and one easy chair, a table and four chairs in one corner. These stood on a beige coloured carpet. On the other side of the room was an oven and hob and several fitted cupboards. A small fridge stood alongside.

There was a stereo, a small TV set, dozens of records, tapes and compact discs on a DIY unit with one screw missing at the top. A video recorder, surrounded by a number of tapes, lay at the bottom of the unit. The automatic clock on the machine was flashing constantly. Four green zeros flickering in the dull light.

The cooker was clean. There were no dirty dishes in the sink, no pots and pans on the hob. Everything seemed to be in its place.

A framed picture of a muscular man dressed only in a baseball cap and a thong stared down at her from one wall. Donna glanced at it for a moment, then wandered back towards the main door. There had been two others.

She opened the first and found herself in a tiny bathroom. Pulling the cord, she looked around at the contents. A bath which seemed to fill most of the room, a toilet and a sink. There was a cabinet on the wall and for a second Donna caught her own reflection in the mirrored doors. Clean washing was piled up at one end of the bath: blouses, T-shirts, skirts. A predominance of blues, she noted.

Donna opened the cabinet and peered at the contents. Some anti-perspirant, a Mudd Mask Facial Cleanser, nail varnish remover, some Lil-lets and two packets of contraceptive pills.

She moved to the next door and opened it, stepping into the bedroom.

This, too, was small; there was barely room to manoeuvre around the bed. Wardrobes and bookshelves covered three walls. On one of the bookshelves there was also make-up, perfume. Donna sniffed it, inspecting the bottle. It was Calvin Klein. Good perfume, expensive.

Had he bought it for her?

She opened the wardrobe closest to her and regarded the hanging clothes in there impassively. There was a lot of silk and suede.

How much of that had Chris paid for?

Shoes, boots, trainers.

She pulled open drawers and found underwear, more blouses.

The envelope was in the bottom drawer.

A brown manilla A4 envelope.

Donna sat on the edge of the bed and upended it, the contents spilling out onto the duvet. She rummaged through the pieces of paper, inspecting each one. There was a motley assortment. Bills, some paid, some unpaid. Bank statements, business cards, a couple of old birthday cards. She opened them to check the sender's name. Neither had been sent by her dead husband. A party invitation, a free pass to a London nightclub.

She found the first of the photos sandwiched between a Medical card and a bank statement.

It showed Chris and Suzanne together.

Pale. Unsmiling.

Donna swallowed hard and looked at another.

It was of Chris dressed in a leather jacket and jeans. He was smiling, leaning against a tree. The land behind him looked barren: only fields and hills.

Where the hell was that?

There was another of Chris, alone again, hands tucked in the pockets of his jacket.

Donna felt that all too familiar feeling building inside her, that combination of rage and sadness.

Then she found the last two pictures.

'Jesus,' she murmured, her breathing deepening as she studied them. For long moments she sat looking at the pictures then, as quickly as she could, she gathered the spilled contents of the envelope together and replaced them, shoving the manilla container itself back into the drawer.

The photos she tucked into her jacket.

She moved quickly through the flat, switching off lights as she went, heading for the main door, concerned to make sure she had left everything as she'd found it.

She paused at the door, listening for any sounds of activity from the landing or other rooms. Hearing none, she slipped out and closed the door behind her. She scuttled downstairs, the photos still tucked in her coat, returned the key to Mercuriadis, thanked him for his help and hurried from the house, resisting the temptation to run back to the waiting Fiesta.

As Julie saw her approaching she leant across and unlocked the passenger side door, watching as her sister slid in and buckled up.

'Did you find what you were looking for?' she asked, starting the engine.

Donna was staring straight ahead, but even in the dull glow of the streetlamps Julie could see how pale her sister was.

'Are you all right?' she asked.

Donna continued staring out of the windscreen.

'Get us home,' she said quietly, 'as quick as you can.'

Twenty

Julie was the first to see the police car, parked close to the front door of the house. Even in the darkness she could make out two figures inside.

As the headlights of the Fiesta illuminated the short driveway the car was picked out and held in the beams as if by some magnetic force.

'Donna . . .' Julie began but she was cut short.

'I can see them,' her sister said curtly. She gripped the photos inside her coat, tucking them into the waistband of her jeans.

One of the figures inside the car clambered out and watched as the Fiesta parked. Donna could not make out his features in the gloom.

Had someone reported her?

What were the police doing here at this time? She glanced at the Fiesta's dashboard clock and saw that the time was 11.23 p.m.

Had the occupant of the flat next to Suzanne Regan's reported mysterious movements in the dead girl's place?

How would they know to look for *her*?

Had Mercuriadis become suspicious?

Why should he?

Donna knew that the police could not possibly be at her house in connection with the visit to Suzanne Regan's, yet she felt uneasy, the way teenagers feel who have stolen penny chews from a sweetshop.

She swung herself out of the car and walked across to the police car and its occupants.

The plain-clothes man approached her, clearing his throat.

Donna Ward, you are under arrest.

'Mrs Ward, I'm very sorry to trouble you this late,' he said apologetically. 'My name is Mackenzie. I was at the hospital the other night.'

Donna felt a sudden, joyous feeling of relief sweep over her.

I realize this is a difficult time for you,' Mackenzie went on, 'but I would like to talk to you if I may.'

'Come in,' Donna said and the policeman followed her. When Julie entered she introduced them briefly. Then, as Julie went through into the kitchen to make tea, Donna ushered Mackenzie into the sitting-room.

'I hope you're feeling better,' the policeman said, standing self-consciously in the centre of the sitting-room.

'Sit down, please,' Donna said, slipping a hand inside her coat with her back to him, dropping the photos onto a coffee table. She pushed the newspaper over them, then turned back to face him and pulled off her coat.

Mackenzie perched on the edge of one chair, his hands clasped together as if he were cold.

'The other night, when you arrived at the hospital, I know you probably weren't thinking straight. It probably didn't occur to you it was unusual that a plain-clothes man should be present at an identification. I didn't think it was a good time to explain.'

'Explain what?' Donna asked.

'There were questions I needed to ask you about your husband; only trivial things. Well, trivial to you, probably.' He attempted a comforting smile but failed miserably. 'I need to know how often he had his car serviced.'

Donna looked puzzled, then she too smiled thinly.

'I know it sounds like a stupid question but it is important, believe me,' Mackenzie told her.

'He had it serviced once a year,' she said.

'And he never complained about it? About things going wrong with it?'

'Like what? Everyone complains about their cars, don't they?'

'Did he ever complain about the brakes?'

Donna met the policeman's gaze and held it, the colour draining from her face.

'It's a routine question, Mrs Ward,' the DS said quietly. 'When your husband's car was examined following the crash, his brakes were faulty. It could have been that which caused him to crash.'

'Are you saying the brakes were tampered with?' Donna said, her voice low.

'No, definitely not,' the policeman qualified. 'We have no proof that anyone interfered with the brakes on your husband's car. I'm sure it was an unfortunate accident and nothing more.' He shuffled his fingers together like fleshy playing cards, then looked at her again. 'And your husband was hardly the kind of man to make enemies, was he?' Donna shook her head.

'No, Chris didn't have any enemies,' she said quietly.

'None.'

'Well then, that's it. It was the brakes, I'm afraid.'

Julie arrived with the tea but Mackenzie declined and insisted he must go. It was the younger of the two women who saw him out.

Donna sat alone in the sitting-room, listening to the police car pull away. She moved the paper from on top of the photos, her mind spinning.

Enemies.

She looked at the photos lying on the table.

Enemies?

Twenty-One

'Why would anyone want to murder Chris?'

Donna looked at her sister in bewilderment.

'You said they were convinced that he *wasn't* murdered, that it was a mechanical fault with the car,' Julie insisted. 'It's just routine, Donna. They have to be sure of everything.'

The older woman nodded slowly and shifted her position slightly in the seat, looking down at the photos.

In particular of Chris and the five men.

One pile were those she'd taken from his office; the others those she'd taken from Suzanne's flat that very evening.

Identical.

The same young faces, the same blurred images of two of the figures.

Those same gold rings on the left index fingers.

78

Who the hell were these people?

'How could that happen?' Donna said, prodding the photos of the group, outlining the fuzzed shapes of the older men's faces.

'A fault in the emulsion,' Julie told her, inspecting the photos. 'But it's unusual. The negative could have been tampered with. The point is, why? Obviously, whoever these two men are, they didn't want to be recognised.'

'Then why have their photos taken in the first place?' Donna asked challengingly.

'Do you recognise the other three, the younger ones?'

Donna shook her head.

There were so many questions. She sifted through the pictures again, checking through both sets, looking for even the minutest difference, but there was none. The shots of Ward and the five men were identical in every way.

'Perhaps they were the ones that killed him,' Donna said finally.

Julie shook her head.

'For Christ's sake, Donna,' she snapped. 'The police said it *wasn't* murder.'

'I know what they said,' she responded angrily.

Julie studied her sister's features for long moments then broke the silence again.

'*Did* he have any enemies that you knew of?'

'He'd been threatened before while he was working on other books. Not threatened with murder but, well, warned off, I suppose you could say.' She glanced down at the pictures. 'He wrote a novel to do with loan sharks a couple of years ago, how some of the big Security Companies were in business with them. The security men would act as strong-arm men for the loan sharks. Chris was told he'd be beaten up if he published the book.' She smiled thinly. 'Nothing ever came of it, thank God.' Donna swallowed hard. 'When he wrote about the porn industry he lived in digs in Soho for a week; he worked in a peep show to get information. He used a false name, of course. When the owner of the club found out he was getting information, he thought he was an undercover policeman. Chris said they wrecked his room one day while he was out. They left a dead dog in the bed with a note stuck to it saying he'd be next.'

'There must be easier ways of earning a living,' Julie said.

'He used to call it the Method school of writing,' Donna said, smiling at the recollection. 'You know how actors like Robert De Niro research their parts, live them? Chris was the same with the characters he wrote about. He never knew when to stop pushing.' She looked at the photos again. 'Perhaps this time he pushed the wrong people.'

'If you think there could have been a link between Chris's death and the men in these photos, you should tell the police,' Julie urged.

Donna shook her head.

'What difference would it make? They've already decided it wasn't murder.'

'And what if they're wrong?'

'You're the one who keeps telling me they're sure.'

'That was until I found out about Chris's research,' Julie said. 'These pictures could be evidence, Donna.'

'No. The police said the crash was an accident. They have no reason to think otherwise, Mackenzie told me that.'

'And what do *you* think?'

'I don't know *what* to think. I just want to know who these men are and why Chris and *she* had photos of them.'

'Then tell the police, let *them* find out.'

'What am I going to tell them, Julie? "My husband and his mistress had identical pictures of five unidentified men. Could you track them down for me, please?" Something like that?'

'So what's the answer? How do you find out who they are?'

'I have to find out what he was working on. Find out if these five men,' she tapped the picture, 'were anything to do with his new book. I have to find out who they were, but I'm going to need some help.'

'You know I'll help you,' Julie said.

Donna smiled.

'I know. But there's someone I have to speak to first.'

Twenty-Two

The banging on the door woke him up.

At first he thought he was dreaming, next that the racket was coming from the television, but then Mercuriadis realized that the incessant thumping was on his own door.

As he hauled himself to his feet he glanced across at the clock on top of the TV set and groaned when he saw it was well past two in the morning. He had, he reasoned, fallen asleep in front of the screen – something he'd been doing quite regularly lately. It irritated him, and when he got to bed he always had trouble sleeping properly. Better to doze in the chair, he told himself.

When his wife had been alive she had always woken him if he'd dropped off. Woken him with a cup of warm milk and reminded him that it was time for bed. He thought fondly of her as he moved towards the door. The loud banging continued. It seemed like only yesterday that she'd shared his life and he sometimes found it difficult to accept she'd been dead nearly twelve years.

'All right, all right,' he called as he approached the door, anxious to stop the pounding. He slipped the chain and pulled the door open.

'What the fuck is going on?' snapped the tall, dark-haired man who confronted him.

Mercuriadis eyed the man inquisitively, irritated by his abrasiveness. It was too early in the morning for profanity, the older man thought, although he was only too aware of this particular tenant's penchant for it.

Brian Monroe stood before him in just a pair of jeans, fists clenched and jammed against his hips.

'I'm trying to fucking sleep and someone's creating merry hell in the room next door. In number six,' Monroe persisted angrily, rubbing his eyes. He looked as tired as his landlord.

'What's going on, Mr Monroe?' asked Mercuriadis.

'That's what *I'd* like to know,' the younger man told him, running a hand through his short hair. 'I'm trying to sleep and there's banging and crashing coming from the room next to me. I've got to be up early in the morning; I can do without this shit.'

'Noise coming from number six?' Mercuriadis said, his brow furrowing. 'But that's, that *was* Miss Regan's room. It's empty.'

'Well, there's some fucking noisy mice in there then, that's all I've got to say. Are you going to check it out?'

'I'll get the key,' the landlord said, taking a bunch from a drawer in the bureau behind him. 'Is the noise still going on?'

'It finished about five minutes ago,' Monroe

told him. 'I've been banging on *your* door for two minutes at least.'

Mercuriadis selected a key from the ring and followed his irate tenant along the hall towards the stairs to the first floor landing.

'Perhaps one of her bloody relatives had a spare key,' Monroe said, stalking up the stairs two at a time.

'Keep your voice down, please, Mr Monroe,' the landlord asked, climbing the steps after him. 'Think of the other tenants.'

'Fuck the other tenants. I should think they're all awake by now, anyway, if they heard that bloody banging,' Monroe snapped, reaching the first landing.

Mercuriadis shook his head reproachfully and glanced at Monroe's broad back. Such profanity. It was difficult to believe the man was an employee of one of the City's top accountants. The landlord wondered if he spoke to his clients in the same way.

They began ascending the second flight of steps, the older man wheezing slightly as he struggled to keep up.

As they drew closer to the top of the stairs the landlord cocked an ear for any sound but he heard nothing.

Monroe was standing outside the door of number six.

'I'm going back to bed,' he snapped. 'I might get four hours' sleep if I'm lucky.' The door to number five slammed shut behind him and Mercuriadis found himself alone on the landing, the key to number six in his fingers. He inserted it gently into the lock, alert for any sounds or movement beyond.

Banging and crashing, Monroe had said. Could it be burglars? He paused, wondering if it wouldn't be easier just to go back downstairs and call the police. His heart was already pounding from the climb but it seemed to speed up as he thought of the possibility of a break-in. If the noises had stopped five minutes ago, it should be safe to investigate. He pushed the door a fraction, still listening.

The silence was total.

All he could hear was his own breathing and the sound of the blood rushing in his ears.

He pushed the door open, reaching for the light switch.

'Oh my God,' he murmured.

The room had been ransacked.

Everything it was possible to smash had been smashed. Damage of some description, it seemed, had been done to every single object in sight. The sofa was torn apart, the stuffing spilling from it like entrails from an eviscerated corpse. Chairs had been overturned. The television lay in the centre of the room, its screen shattered and holed, as if a heavy object had been thrust into it. Cupboard doors had been torn off their hinges, their contents scattered across the floor. Shattered. Destroyed.

Records had been pulled from their sleeves,

the black vinyl broken and scattered amongst the other debris. The video lay ruined against the opposite wall, as if thrown there with great force. The plug it had been attached to was still in the socket. The stereo too had been smashed, the turntable itself prized out and hurled to one side. CD cases, tape cases, videos and even books had been torn open. Mercuriadis could scarcely move without treading on some broken object.

His heart pounded harder, his head spun. As he looked around it became obvious that nothing had been taken.

The object had been destruction pure and simple, not robbery.

He felt a cold breeze against his hot cheek and realized that the bedroom door was open a fraction.

With infinite slowness he moved towards it, prodding it open slightly, just enough for him to slip inside. He fumbled for the light switch but when he flicked it nothing happened. Looking up, he saw that even the lightbulb had been smashed.

The duvet had been ripped to shreds; the pillows, too. Wardrobe doors, those that hadn't been simply torn from their hinges, hung open revealing the devastation inside: clothes torn and ripped, pulled from their hangers and tossed into the centre of the bed. A framed photo of Mel Gibson had been pulled from the wall and smashed, the picture snatched out, the frame smashed. Drawers had been upended, their contents dumped on the floor.

Mercuriadis felt a growing tightness in his chest, a sickly clamminess closing around him. He tried to control his breathing, aware of a growing pain around his sternum.

Sucking in deep breaths, he realized where the cold breeze was coming from.

The room's single sash window had been prized open, paint scratched and gouged from the frame where entry had been forced.

He swayed slightly and moved towards the window, wincing as the pain in his chest became more acute.

The bedroom door swung gently shut behind him, the sound causing him to turn quickly.

The figure loomed out of the darkness at him, stepping so close until Mercuriadis could feel the intruder's breath on his cheek.

His eyes bulged madly in their sockets as he stared at the intruder.

A heart already strained swelled and burst; the shock was too great, too intolerable.

His vision was clouded red as several blood vessels in his eyes simply erupted.

As he fell backwards onto the bed the intruder stood over him for a second, looking down. In his final minutes of consciousness Mercuriadis was conscious of its presence, and what he had seen – a sight he could not have imagined in even the most depraved nightmare. A sight which questioned his sanity as surely as it took his life.

The figure headed towards the window and

clambered over the sill, disappearing into the welcoming darkness.

Mercuriadis felt one massive surge of pain envelope him, spreading with staggering rapidity from his chest, along his left arm and up into his neck and jaw.

He felt the darkness descending upon him and he feared it but, after what he'd seen, the oblivion which awaited him was to be welcomed.

The flat was silent once more.

Twenty-Three

Martin Connelly sipped at the glass of white wine and peered out of the window of Silk's restaurant. He was seated at his usual table, to the right of the main door. The menu lay close by his elbow and a waiter came over to ask if he was ready to order. Connelly said he was waiting for a guest. The waiter nodded and passed on to another table.

Connelly glanced at his watch; it was almost 1.15 p.m. He wondered where his guest was.

The phone call had been completely unexpected. He'd arrived at his office in Kensington at around ten that morning, the drive in from Beckenham having taken him a little longer than usual. After listening to the messages on the answerphone, he'd returned those calls he thought important and decided that those not so important could call him back. Then he'd settled down to read an unsolicited manuscript he'd begun the day before. Unlike most unpublished material, it showed promise; Connelly was already beginning to wonder whether to invite the author into the office for a chat.

The phone call from Donna Ward had come about 10.30.

Could she meet him for lunch that day?

Connelly had agreed immediately, and told her he'd book the table at Silk's for one. He'd spent the rest of the morning wondering what she could want; she'd mentioned nothing over the phone. The fact that it was to be over lunch pleased the agent. It was less formal than her coming into his office. He smiled to himself, taking another sip of his wine.

He saw the taxi pull up outside and watched her clamber out. As she paid the driver, he took in as much detail as possible of her appearance.

She was wearing a black silk jacket over a white blouse. A short black skirt and black suede high heels showed off her shapely legs. The wind ruffled her blonde hair as she walked and Connelly felt his heart beating faster when she entered the restaurant. She was met by a waiter and then noticed the agent sitting close by. She smiled and joined him, kissing him on the cheek before she sat down.

'I'm sorry I'm late,' she said, running a hand through her hair and dropping her handbag beside her. 'The traffic was terrible. I had to leave the car parked in Golden Square and get a cab.'

Connelly waved away the apology. Unlike the previous day when he'd seen her, she looked tired but she was made up and her clothes were immaculate. She looked wonderful, considering the circumstances.

He told her so.

'Thanks,' she said. She smiled briefly at him and ordered a mineral water from the hovering waiter.

'I hope you like it here,' he said.

Donna glanced around the restaurant. The walls were covered in jockey's silks, riding caps, whips and pictures of racehorses. Paintings or photographs of famous jockeys vied for space on the walls. Rotary fans turned slowly like the blades of a helicopter.

'I usually bring clients here,' he said. 'This isn't business, is it, Donna?'

She raised her eyebrows.

'Sort of.'

'And I thought you just wanted the pleasure of my company.' He smiled and studied her across the table, gazing into her eyes a little too intently.

'How are you managing?' he wanted to know.

'Everything's organised, thanks to Julie. I don't know what I'd have done without her.' She sighed. 'I'm terrified, Martin. I'm dreading the funeral. Part of me wants it over; the other part hopes tomorrow never comes.'

'I understand that. Like I told you before, if there's anything I can do, call me.'

'That's one of the reasons I'm here now,' she told him.

The waiter returned and they ordered. Donna shifted position in her seat and looked at Connelly.

'How much did Chris tell you about the books he was working on, Martin? How much did you know about them?'

'Very little, until I saw the finished manuscript. You know how Chris liked to work, keeping everything to himself until the book was finished. Even *after* the book was finished it was sometimes a job to get him to talk about it. The publishers always wanted him to do promotional tours, interviews and that sort of stuff, but you know, he wouldn't do that for two of the books.'

'So he never talked to you about his projects?' she said. 'You never even had a *clue* what he was writing about, or what he planned to write about next?'

'He mentioned things here and there, rarely anything specific, though. Just plot outlines, ideas sometimes. That was it.'

'And his research? How much did you know about that?'

'Only what he told me.'

Donna shook her head gently.

'You were his agent, Martin, and you're trying to tell me you never knew what he was writing about, what research he did? Nothing?' She looked at him challengingly.

'Only what he *told* me,' Connelly insisted. 'It seems we've had this conversation before, Donna. I can't tell you anything different.'

The starters arrived. Donna prodded her avocado with the fork.

'What did he tell you about this new book?' she wanted to know.

'For Christ's sake,' Connelly said irritably, 'he didn't tell me anything. How many more times?'

'You arranged some of the interviews he did, didn't you? Or can't you remember that either, Martin?' she said cryptically.

'What is your problem, Donna?' he hissed, keeping his voice under control but not his anger. 'What do you want me to tell you?'

'The truth.'

'I don't know the truth. You asked me what Chris was working on. I don't know, but that's not good enough for you. Why did you mention his interviews?' he asked.

Donna reached down beside her and fumbled in her handbag. She produced Ward's diary and flicked it open, turning it around on the table so that Connelly could see it.

'October 25th,' she read aloud. 'Interview in Oxford.' She turned a few more pages. 'November 16th. Interview in Edinburgh.' She looked at Connelly. 'He was gone three days that time. And here, London, December 2nd. He was gone two days then.' She turned more pages. 'January 6th. Dublin.'

Connelly shook his head.

'Did you arrange those interviews, Martin?' she wanted to know. 'Or weren't they interviews? Was he with *her*, then? Did you know about it? Who usually went with him on promotional trips? Someone from the publishers, wasn't it? Someone from the publicity department? Or was it *her*?'

'Donna, I don't know what you're talking about,' Connelly said wearily. '*What* you're talking about or *who* you're talking about.'

'I'm talking about Suzanne Regan. My husband's mistress. Did she go with him on any of these trips?'

'I don't know. Really. Trust me.'

'What about these?' she said, pointing at other entries in the diary. Beside every single interview in London, Oxford, Dublin or Edinburgh was the initial D.

'Who was "D"?' she asked. 'Was that his pet name for her?'

Connelly could only shake his head.

'I really don't know what any of it means,' he said. 'I didn't arrange those interviews, if that's what they were.'

'Did you know he was going to be in those places?' she persisted. 'I thought you and Chris usually let each other know if you were going away, in case one had to contact the other urgently.'

'Donna, I wish I could help you. I can't

93

remember if Chris mentioned those trips or not.'

Donna reached into her handbag again, this time pulling out the photos she'd found of Ward and the five other men.

'Who are they, Martin?' she asked.

Connelly didn't speak.

'Recognise any of them?' she persisted.

He ran his eyes over the pictures.

'Where did you get them?' he asked finally.

'I found them in Chris's office,' she said, realizing it prudent not to mention she'd found identical ones in Suzanne Regan's flat. 'I want to know who they are and I'm going to find out.'

'How?' he enquired.

She flipped through the diary to another entry.

DUBLIN NATIONAL GALLERY

and beneath that

JAMES WORSDALE

The date was about a week later.

'I'm going to Dublin,' she announced defiantly.

'What the hell for?'

'To find out exactly what Chris was working on. To find out who these men were.' She tapped the photo. 'I think they're linked in some way. And I think they're linked to his death. I want to know how and I'm going to find out, no matter what I have to do.'

The rest of the meal was eaten in virtual silence and Donna finally left without having a coffee, having carefully gathered up the photos and the diary. She said goodbye to the agent and hurried out, flagging down a cab that was dropping off nearby.

Connelly paid the bill quickly and ran out after her, calling to her across the street.

Donna hesitated as he approached.

'When are you leaving for Dublin?' he asked.

'In five days,' she told him. 'Why?'

Connelly shrugged and smiled awkwardly.

'I thought you might like some company,' he said. 'I've been there a few times. Perhaps I could help you.'

Donna eyed him with something close to contempt.

'I'll manage,' she said and climbed into the cab. Connelly watched as it pulled away.

Twenty-Four

Julie Craig received the news of Donna's intended trip to Dublin with not so much surprise as weary resignation.

The two women were lying in bed, with only the ticking of the bedside clock an accompaniment to their subdued conversation. Julie lay on her back gazing up at the ceiling, listening to Donna recount her meeting with Connelly that afternoon. It was all she could do to stop herself telling Donna she was sick of hearing about the whole subject. Still she seemed obsessed with Suzanne Regan.

'Do you think it's a good idea you going so soon after the funeral?' she asked.

'The quicker I get this business sorted out the better,' Donna told her.

'And what if you don't get it sorted out? What if you don't find the answers you want?'

Donna had no answer.

'Are you going to let it haunt you for the rest of your life? Are you going to think about it for the rest of your life?'

'It's easy for you to dismiss it, Julie,' Donna said, irritably.

'I'm not dismissing it,' the younger woman said. 'But this has become an obsession with you.'

'Maybe it has. I'll just have to learn to live with it. The same way I've got to learn to live *without* Chris.' She wiped a tear from her eye. 'I have to do things my way, Julie. It's my way of coming to terms with it.'

They lay there in silence for what seemed like an eternity, then Julie broke the stillness.

'If you need me to help you, to come with you to Ireland, or anywhere else, you know I will,' she said softly.

Donna nodded in the darkness.

The light filtering through the window illuminated her face and Julie could see the tears glistening in the dull light. She reached across and wiped them from her sister's cheek, stroking her face.

Donna held her hand and kissed it.

Julie began stroking her sister's hair, smoothing the soft blonde tresses back.

'Everything's arranged for tomorrow,' she said quietly. 'The cars, the flowers, everything.' She continued stroking. 'The caterers will be here before we leave; they'll have the food ready when the service is over. I told them nothing too elaborate.'

'Sausages on sticks?' Donna murmured, managing a thin smile.

Julie smiled too, her initial annoyance giving way to a feeling of helplessness. She could see the suffering in her sister's eyes, feel it in her words, but knew she could do nothing to ease it. All she could do was stand by helplessly and watch. She carried on stroking, seeing Donna's eyes closing.

'Go to sleep,' she whispered. 'You need to rest.'

'Remember when you used to do this when we were kids?' Donna murmured, her voice low, her words delivered slowly. 'It always used to make me drop off then.'

'I remember,' Julie told her. 'You did it for me, too.'

'Little sister looking after big sister,' Donna said, her eyes closed.

She said one more thing before sleep finally overcame her, words spoken so softly Julie barely heard them.

'I miss him, Julie,' she said.

Then all she heard was her sister's low breathing.

She slept.

Julie stopped stroking her hair and rolled over onto her back again, glancing across at the photo on the bedside table of Chris and Donna, peering at it through the gloom.

It was a long time before she fell asleep.

Twenty-Five

Martin Connelly took the suit from the wardrobe and hung it on one of the handles.

He brushed fluff from a sleeve and inspected the garment carefully. He hadn't worn it for over two years, not since the last funeral. The agent noticed a couple of creases in one arm of the jacket and wished now that he'd left it out for his housekeeper to press. He shook his head. The creases would drop out once he had it on. What the hell. He selected a white shirt and then rummaged through his wardrobe for his black tie, hanging it neatly over the shoulder of the jacket. Satisfied that everything was ready for the following day, he wandered back into the sitting-room of the flat and poured himself a drink.

He sat down in front of the television and

reached for the remote control, flicking through channels, unable to find anything suitable. He wondered about watching a video but decided against it.

There were cassette cases underneath the television, both tapes leant to him by Christopher Ward. He made a note to return them. It would give him an excuse to return to the house.

He wouldn't phone first, he'd just turn up, surprise Donna one day. He doubted whether she'd be too happy to see him after their lunch that day. He regretted his suggestion to travel with her to Dublin.

You should have waited.

And yet what better time to speak to her than now? She was emotionally vulnerable, looking for kindness, wanting to be needed. As time went on and her emotional strength returned, his task would be more difficult.

Connelly finished his drink and poured himself another, rolling the glass between his palms.

It was one of a set Kathy had bought.

The thought of her brought the memories flooding back into his mind.

They had lived together for ten months and, whilst it had scarcely been idyllic, both had been happy. She was beginning to make a go of her career in modelling; she'd been signed up by an agency and the work had begun to flood in. At first he'd been overjoyed, proud of her and more than a little smug to think that his girlfriend was a fashion model.

When the nude work started to take over he began to change his mind. Kathy had never been ashamed of her body and when she was approached by a top men's magazine to do a spread she jumped at the chance. The pay was good and it opened up even more opportunities. Modelling assignments took her abroad. It got to the stage where they hardly saw each other and, all the time, Connelly was plagued by doubts. By thoughts of his girlfriend and a photographer he'd never met cavorting about on some sun-kissed beach in the Caribbean. He'd challenged her several times about it. Had she ever slept with a photographer while she was away? The usual thing. Blind to the fact that the only thing that interested her was furthering her career, Connelly had finally made life unbearable for both of them with his jealousy. As she reminded him, during rows over her assignments, he was always having lunch or dinner with female clients, editors or journalists. Connelly insisted it was different. Besides, the women *he* dealt with didn't sit in restaurants naked.

It took less than a year before she left him. He simply returned home one night to find that she was gone, all her clothes and belongings gone with her.

That had been almost two years ago. He hadn't heard from her since. He'd seen photos of her in some of the tabloids, looking decorative on the arms of rock stars or others of that ilk. Apart from that, he hadn't seen her or heard from her since the split. He'd lived alone ever since.

A housekeeper came in twice a week to clean the place and do his laundry, but apart from that he lived a more or less solitary existence outside working hours.

Connelly finished his drink, set the glass down and headed for the bedroom, glancing at the black suit hanging on the wardrobe door.

He wondered what Donna was doing now.

It was 12.36 a.m. She was probably in bed.

Bed.

Connelly tried to picture her lying between the sheets. It was a pleasing image.

He smiled crookedly.

He had failed that lunchtime, a trifle impetuous perhaps.

There would be other opportunities.

He had time.

Twenty-Six

There was a bird singing in the tree close to the grave. It chirped happily throughout the service, bouncing from branch to branch, rejoicing in the blue skies and the warmth of the day.

Donna heard its shrill song but the priest's words were lost to her. The words of the service were meaningless; it was as if he'd been speaking

101

a foreign language. All she was aware of was that solitary bird in the tree. And the sound of a woman crying.

The crying woman was her.

Supported by Julie, she stood at the graveside surrounded by crowds of other mourners. Dressed in black, those paying their final respects to Christopher Ward looked like a menacing horde against the green of the cemetery grass. Splashes of brilliant colour afforded by the flowers at the graveside made the dark mass of mourners look incongruous in the peaceful setting.

A light breeze stirred the cellophane wrappers on some of the flowers, causing them to rattle.

Donna, looking down into the grave and seeing the coffin, was aware even more now of the appalling finality of the occasion. When they shovelled six feet of earth on top of that casket her husband would be well and truly gone. Nothing remaining except a marble marker which bore his name and an inscription:

CHRISTOPHER WARD, BELOVED
  HUSBAND
SLEEP UNTIL WE ARE TOGETHER
  ONCE MORE

Not much to signify the sum total of thirty-five years, Donna thought.

All around the grave others were standing in orderly lines, some with heads bowed, others gazing around as the priest spoke.

Beyond them stood the line of cars that had ferried the mourners from the church.

Again, Donna found it difficult to remember what had happened in the church or, indeed, since she had got up that morning. She had seemed to be moving like an automaton, not really aware of anything she did or said, or of anything which was said to her.

Julie had tried her best to coax her along but she too had found the solemnity of the occasion sometimes too much to bear. As she stood beside Donna now there were tears rolling down her cheeks. Inside the church she had stared at the coffin, raised up on a plinth and surrounded by flowers, her own mind struggling with the thought that inside that box lay her brother-in-law.

She had ridden in the leading car with Donna, neither of them speaking as the driver guided the vehicle towards the cemetery, never more than a few yards behind the hearse.

And then to the grave itself, yawning open to swallow the box that contained Christopher Ward.

Connelly had acted as one of the pall-bearers. He now stood on the other side of the grave, his hands clasped across his groin, his head bowed. Beside him were people from Chris's publishers, friends and relatives. There were even some fans there, readers of his books who had come to pay their last respects.

More than once Donna felt her legs weaken; she was sure she was going to fall.

Fall into the grave, perhaps?

But she held onto what little strength she had left and felt Julie's arm around her waist, supporting her but also needing that closeness herself. And Donna had felt this terrible feeling before, the night they had first told her that her husband had been involved in a crash. As she looked down into the grave she felt the same crushing desolation she'd felt as the coroner had pulled back that green sheet in the hospital morgue. How long ago was it now? Four days? More? Time seemed to have lost its meaning since his death. She wondered if *life* would lose its meaning, too.

As the priest came to the end of his service he stepped back a pace, beckoning Donna towards the graveside.

It was a monumental effort for her to walk those few steps; again she felt as if her knees were going to give way. Sobbing gently she made that short journey, Julie close by her. They both looked into the grave then Donna stepped back, her head lowered.

The breeze brought the smell of flowers to her, an aroma so strong, so thickly scented she felt sick. The cellophane rattled again and a petal from a red rose came free and fluttered across the grass towards the graveside, where it was blown in, floating gently downwards until it settled on the coffin lid.

Julie, trying to control her own emotion, led Donna away. The other mourners filed past.

From the tree close by the bird took flight, soaring high into the blue sky.

Like a soul en route to heaven.

Twenty-Seven

Donna stood by the car, a handkerchief clutched in her hand. The priest spoke softly to her but she heard little of what he said. She smiled every now and then, grateful for his concern but anxious only to be away from this place.

Julie stood beside her, reaching over once to pull a blonde hair from her sister's jacket. She lovingly touched the back of her hair as she did so.

The priest finished what he had to say and retreated, to be replaced by various mourners. Words of condolence were offered. Donna was confronted by a parade of people, many of whom she found it difficult to place. What she felt now was more akin to shock than grief; it was as if she was numb. Every part of her body and her soul, burned out. She looked at people with blank eyes, red-rimmed and glazed; she might have been on drugs.

Cars were beginning to leave the cemetery, mourners driving away back towards her house for the wake. Donna was suddenly aware how archaic the word sounded. Wake. The thought of having her house filled with people seemed abhorrent. She wanted to tell each and every one of them to leave her alone with her grief and her pain. Let her enjoy it unhindered. Their presence would only seek to prevent her complete immersion in despair.

Friends and relatives spoke words of comfort to her before climbing into their cars. She nodded gratefully at each word, unable and unwilling to answer.

Julie finally urged her to get into the car, wiping tears from her own eyes as she pulled gently at Donna's arm.

Martin Connelly walked over, arms outstretched, and Donna found herself embracing him. Embracing him and holding him tightly. His touch was reassuring and he allowed her to bury her head in his chest as he held her.

Only Julie saw the slight flicker of a smile on his lips as he spoke to her softly.

'It'll be okay,' he said. 'Just let it out.'

She sobbed uncontrollably in his arms.

Aware of Julie's probing gaze Connelly looked at the younger woman, their eyes meeting for uncomfortable seconds before he finally stroked Donna's cheek with one hand and she stepped away from him slightly.

'I'll see you back at the house,' he said and walked off to find his car.

Julie watched him go, then held out her hand for Donna to join her in the car.

'Come on, Donna,' she said gently, but then

noticed that her sister was gazing in the direction of the grave. Julie followed her gaze.

'I don't know who they are,' Donna said quietly, wiping her nose with her handkerchief.

There were three men standing by the graveside, the one in the centre tall and powerfully built. All three of them wore dark suits.

At such a distance Donna couldn't make out their features.

'Friends of Chris's, I suppose,' Julie said. 'You didn't know *all* his friends, did you?'

'Most of them,' Donna told her, eyes still fixed on the trio of mourners.

She noticed one of them kneel beside the grave, squatting down on his haunches and leaning over the edge, as if he were looking for something in the deep hole.

'Who are they?' Donna murmured, finally allowing herself to be coaxed into the car by Julie.

The driver asked them if they were ready, then pulled slowly away.

Donna turned in her seat and looked out of the back window.

The three men were still beside the grave, all of them standing again now, still looking down intently at the coffin.

The car rounded a corner and they were lost from sight.

Donna sank back in her seat, her eyes closed, the vision of the three men fading from her mind.

Had she been able to, she would have seen the tallest of the three kick a clod of earth into the hole.

It landed with a thud on the coffin lid.

Twenty-Eight

She didn't count the cars parked outside the house but there seemed to be at least a dozen, parked on the driveway and in the road.

As Donna moved through the sitting-room she glanced out of the window at the horde of vehicles. Inside, a low babble of chatter rose from the mourners who had returned to the house.

The caterers Julie had hired to provide food and drinks had set up a large table in the sitting-room, where they served guests with sandwiches and other snacks. In the kitchen they were using a tea urn and countless coffee pots to keep thirsts quenched.

The talk was subdued but interrupted by the odd laugh here and there. Laughs of relief, perhaps, now that the worst of the solemnity was over. A number of the men present loosened their ties.

Donna sat down by the window with a cup of tea in her hand, her eyes sore from crying, her head aching. She received the kind words and the advice with humility, concealing her desire that they should all simply leave her house as quickly as possible. They had paid their respects; now they had no reason to remain. But she pushed that thought to one side, grateful also for the concern.

Jackie Quinn glided across to her, kissed her on the cheek and squeezed her hand tightly, perching on the arm of the chair.

'Today seems to be lasting forever,' Donna said, smiling wanly. She squeezed Jackie's hand more tightly. 'Thanks for coming, Jackie.'

'I wish there was more I could have done to help,' she said, 'but your caterers seem to be coping.' She smiled.

'Where's Dave?' Donna asked.

'Getting himself a drink. I told him to get *you* one, too.'

'Jackie, I couldn't drink. Not now,' Donna protested.

'Yes, you can,' Jackie said quietly. 'A brandy will help you relax.' She turned and saw Dave Turner entering the room, a glass in each hand. He smiled at Donna and made his way past a group of guests standing by the door talking.

As he stepped clear of them another man almost walked into him.

Donna frowned as she saw him.

It was one of the men who had been standing at Chris's grave when the car had brought her away, she was sure of it.

The man apologized to Dave and made his way out of the room, followed by a companion.

Another of the trio of mourners she'd seen as she'd left the cemetery. Donna was certain of it. She still didn't recognize them.

Turner handed her the brandy and watched as she sipped, wincing as it burned its way down to her stomach.

'Thanks, Dave,' she said. He smiled down at her. 'That guy you just bumped into. Did you recognize him?'

'Should I?' Turner wanted to know.

'I can't place him. I saw him at the cemetery, him and two other men. I knew all of Chris's friends, or so I thought, but I can't seem to put a name to those three.'

'I wouldn't worry about it,' Jackie told her, squeezing her hand again. 'Drink your brandy.' She smiled.

Donna took another sip, wincing again, then she got to her feet, looking around the room.

From one corner, hidden from her view, Martin Connelly watched intently.

'Have you seen Julie anywhere?' Donna wanted to know.

Jackie shook her head.

'I'll be back in a while,' Donna said, excusing herself.

She made her way across the room, pausing to speak to Chris's publisher, then to a couple of magazine editors he'd been friendly with. More condolences were offered.

How many different ways were there to say, 'I'm sorry?'

She found more people in the hallway. They smiled politely at her as she passed, making her way upstairs, anxious to be away from everyone, wondering how long it would be before the guests started to leave. She paused on the landing for a moment and exhaled deeply. The top storey of the house seemed quieter, the atmosphere heavier. Donna crossed to her bedroom and entered.

Julie looked up in surprise as her sister entered. Tears had stained her cheeks and her mascara had run, causing ugly black marks around her eyes. She wiped self-consciously at them as Donna entered, a worried expression on her face.

'I'm sorry, Donna,' Julie said, wiping her face. 'I didn't want this to happen. I didn't want you to see me like this.'

Donna crossed to her and the two women embraced.

'I wanted to be strong for *you*, to *help* you,' Julie said, angry with herself. 'That's why I came up here.' She sniffed and smiled. 'I'm okay.'

'Stay here for a while if you want to,' Donna said.

'It's me who should be saying that to you,' Julie told her, waving away the suggestion. 'I told you, I'm okay now.'

'You don't have to feel sorry for missing him, too, Julie. A lot of people will,' Donna told her.

The younger woman nodded slowly and stood up. She glanced at her reflection in the mirror and shrugged.

'Perhaps I'd better just touch up the worst bits first,' she said, smiling thinly.

Donna smiled too and walked out of the room.

She stepped back in only seconds later.

'Julie,' she said, her voice low, her expression troubled, 'did anyone else come up here with you? Follow you up here?'

'Like who?' Julie wanted to know.

'You haven't heard anyone come up here since *you* did?' Donna persisted.

'No,' Julie replied, looking puzzled. 'Why do you ask?'

Donna stepped back onto the landing, followed by her sister. The older woman was looking down the short corridor towards the door which was normally kept shut.

'I think there's someone in Chris's office.'

Twenty-Nine

As the two women approached the door, Donna noticed it was indeed ajar. From inside there was very little sound; just the soft rustling of paper on paper. Occasionally there came the furtive squeaking of a drawer or filing cabinet. Then there was silence.

Donna pushed the door open and stepped inside.

The man turned slowly and looked directly at her.

He was tall, his hair short and dark, cropped close at the nape of his neck. He had a thin face which rested on a very thick neck. Instead of looking surprised by the discovery, he met Donna's gaze with one of such intensity as to make *her* appear the intruder.

'What the hell are you doing in here?' she snapped, looking first at the man and then at the office.

He still had a piece of paper in his hand, taken from one of the open drawers in Chris's desk.

'Who gave you permission to break in here?' Donna hissed angrily.

The man smiled.

'I'd scarcely call it breaking in, Mrs Ward,' he said, his lip curling contemptuously. 'I realize that perhaps I should have asked your permission first, but you seemed otherwise engaged.' He made a theatrical show of dropping the piece of paper back onto the desk.

'Get out of here now,' she said, her angry stare never leaving the man.

'If you'd just let me explain,' he began.

'There's nothing *to* explain,' she told him. 'Now get out of here before I call the police. How *dare* you do this?'

The man looked at Julie, then back at Donna.

'I was looking for something which belonged to me,' he said evenly. 'Your husband and I had been

113

working together. He'd borrowed some reference books from me.'

'Working together?' Donna said incredulously. 'Chris always worked alone. He never mentioned you or anyone else that he was working with. What's your name?'

'Peter Farrell. Your husband must have mentioned me at some time,' the man said, smoothing his short hair down with a large hand.

Donna shook her head.

'Why were you going through his papers?' she demanded.

'I told you,' Farrell insisted. 'I was looking for the books I lent him. I didn't want to trouble you. You seem to have enough to worry about.'

'Thanks for the concern,' Donna said, sarcastically. 'So, instead of worrying me you thought you'd just come up here and break into my husband's office?'

Farrell laughed and shook his head.

'Don't laugh at me, you bastard,' Donna snapped. 'If you're not out of this room, if you're not out of this *house* in one minute, I'm calling the police.'

Farrell shrugged and immediately headed for the door, holding Donna in that steely gaze for a second before passing by.

'I'd like the books back, Mrs Ward,' he said. 'I'll leave you my phone number. If you find them, I'd appreciate a call.' He reached into the inside pocket of his jacket and took out what looked like a business card. On the back he wrote a number and his name and then passed it to Donna.

'What are the books called?' she wanted to know.

'They're books about paintings. Catalogues. As I said, if you find them I'd appreciate a call.' He walked briskly towards the staircase and descended. Donna watched him from the landing.

'Do you know him?' Julie asked.

Donna shook her head. She glanced down at the name and number written on the card.

PETER FARRELL

Books about paintings?

'Jesus Christ,' Donna murmured.

'What is it?' Julie asked, looking concerned.

Books about paintings.

What was the entry in Ward's diary? JAMES WORSDALE: DUBLIN NATIONAL GALLERY.

Coincidence?

She looked over the bannister again and saw Farrell leaving, followed by two other men. The ones that had been at the funeral.

Donna walked across to the window on the landing and peered out, watching the three men as they clambered into a blue Sierra. Farrell sat in the passenger seat, glancing round once as the car pulled away.

A look of realization crossed Donna's face and she spun round, hurrying to the bedroom where she pulled open the bedside cabinet.

The photos she'd taken from Chris's office and Suzanne Regan's flat were there; she spread them out on the bed.

'I knew it,' Donna said softly, her voice barely audible.

'Look.'

She pointed to the photos of Chris and the five other men.

'I *knew* it,' she said again, more forcefully this time.

She recognised the dark cropped hair, the thin face and bull neck.

The image of Peter Farrell glared back at her from the photos.

Thirty

The last of the mourners left at just after six that evening and it was with something akin to relief that Donna graciously accepted the last words of comfort and bade the final farewells of the day. Those who had been friends of her husband told her to keep in touch, that they would ring her. The usual things people feel they have to say to widows. She wondered how many of them would keep their promises.

Martin Connelly was sitting in the kitchen when Donna walked in. He stopped chewing on a sandwich and smiled at her. She returned the gesture, wondering why the agent was still there.

Julie was pushing plates into the dishwasher.

Donna wondered briefly whether or not she should mention the incident with Farrell, then decided against it.

'He had a lot of friends, Donna,' said Connelly.

'Did he, Martin?' she said wearily.

Connelly looked puzzled.

'There were lots of people at the funeral, but I'm not sure how many of them Chris would have counted as friends.' She sighed. 'He was popular but I don't think he had any *real* friends. He couldn't give a fuck about anyone.'

'Come on, Donna,' Connelly began.

'I'm not being nasty,' she explained. 'I'm just telling you. People liked Chris but *he* rarely let anyone get close to *him*. People would ring him, write to him, but he hardly ever rang them back. You and a couple of others, that was it. He used to say, "If people want me bad enough *they'll* call *me*".' She smiled at the recollection. 'He was a solitary man. He liked his own company.'

And the company of Suzanne Regan.

'I think that's why a lot of women found him attractive,' she continued rather sadly. 'He genuinely *didn't* give a shit.'

Connelly dropped the remains of his sandwich onto the plate, wiped crumbs from his mouth and got to his feet.

'I think you're being too hard on him, Donna,' he said.

She smiled.

'That was one of the things *I* loved about him,' she said.

Connelly kissed her gently on both cheeks.

'I'd better go, unless there's anything I can do.'

'We'll be fine now, Martin. Thanks, anyway.'

He headed for the door.

'See you, Julie,' he said, looking at the younger woman.

She didn't turn to face him.

'See you,' she said and continued loading the dishwasher.

Donna walked with Connelly out to his waiting Porsche, watching as he fumbled in his jacket pocket for the keys.

'You're determined to go on this trip to Dublin still?' he asked.

She nodded.

Should she mention Farrell?

'Humour me, Martin,' she said as he slid behind the wheel and placed the key in the ignition.

'Is Julie going with you?'

'She's going to stay and look after the house.'

Connelly tapped the wheel gently and looked up at Donna.

'If you want company . . .'

He allowed the sentence to trail off.

'I'll speak to you when I get back, Martin,' she said sharply.

The agent nodded, started the engine and pressed down hard on the accelerator. The back wheels spun noisily for a second before the car pulled away.

Donna stood in the driveway, watching as the tail lights disappeared around the corner.

As she headed back to the house a cool breeze ruffled her hair and she shivered.

That involuntary movement might have been more extreme had she realized she was being watched.

It took the two women less than thirty minutes to check through the books in Chris's office.

There were atlases, dictionaries and at least a dozen books on weapons but not one about paintings.

'Paintings,' muttered Donna irritably.

'Donna, try his number,' Julie suddenly said.

The older of the two women hurried back into the bedroom for the card the tall man had given her, then picked up the phone and jabbed out the digits. Julie wandered into the room, watching intently.

Donna heard the hiss and buzz as the number was connected, then all she heard was the single unbroken tone of a dead line.

'Nothing,' she said. 'We should have known.' She tried once more, got the same monotonous sound and dropped the receiver back onto the cradle.

'His name's probably fake, too,' Julie offered.

'Maybe, but *he's* real enough and whoever he is he wanted *something* in Chris's room.' She looked at Julie, her brow furrowed. 'But what was it?'

Thirty-One

The roar of the Porsche's engine filled the garage as Martin Connelly left his foot on the accelerator a second before easing off. Through the open window he could smell the acrid stench of carbon monoxide fumes. He took his foot off the pedal and sat back, switching off the engine. It gradually died away.

Connelly rubbed both hands over his face and sighed wearily.

'I'll call you when I get back,' he said, raising the pitch of his voice slightly, imitating Donna's words. He swung himself out of the car and slammed the door hard.

Connelly walked to the garage door and pulled it down behind him, locking it from the inside. There was a connecting door through to his house; he didn't switch on the fluorescents inside the garage as he locked up. The only light coming into the garage was from a tiny skylight window above him. Glancing up, he saw that night was now in command of the sky. The blackness outside was almost as total as that surrounding him in the garage.

He could smell the drink on his breath. He'd

stopped off at a pub on the way home for a couple of vodkas. Neat. No fucking about. He promised himself a couple more when he got in. The agent selected a key on the bunch in his hand and slipped it into the lock of the door which joined the house and the garage. He stepped through into the hall.

The arm which snaked round his throat took him by surprise, both by its speed and its strength.

Connelly was practically lifted off his feet by his assailant.

He tried to cry out but a powerful forearm was wedged hard across his windpipe.

The tip of a knife was pressed against his neck just below his left earlobe.

The touch of it made him squirm; he felt his bowels loosen slightly.

'Keep still,' the voice behind him rasped.

In front, the shadows in the hallway seemed to be moving independently, dark shapes detaching themselves from the umbra and gliding towards him.

Two more figures stood close to him; because of the darkness he couldn't see their faces. They stood like sadistic spectators at some violent exhibition.

'Where's the book?' said one of them.

'What book?' Connelly managed to rasp as the arm loosed its grip slightly.

The respite was only temporary, however. The grip was re-applied with even greater ferocity.

The leading figure stepped forward a pace and drove a fist into Connelly's stomach with incredible force. The blow tore the wind from him and left him wheezing, wanting to drop to his knees but still supported by that choking grip.

The knife was pressed slightly harder into the soft flesh beneath his ear.

'You stupid bastard,' said the first man contemptuously. He leaned forward so that his face was only inches from Connelly's. The weak light coming through the hall window illuminated parts of the visages, but otherwise Peter Farrell remained bathed in shadow. 'Do you want to play games?' He snapped his fingers and the knife was handed to him.

He pressed the point to the tip of Connelly's nose and pressed gently, hard enough to make an indentation but not with sufficient force to draw blood.

'I don't know where the book is, I swear to Christ,' Connelly gasped, still held by that vice-like grip.

'Liar,' said Farrell. He began tracing the tip of the blade around the agent's cheek, pausing at the corner of his eye. 'I could have your eye out with one turn of this knife. You know that?'

'I don't know where the fucking book is, I swear to you,' Connelly gasped, his eyes bulging madly in their sockets.

'You were his agent. You knew what he was working on.'

Farrell trickled the knife point down to Connelly's bottom lip and pressed. Gently at first.

'No,' Connelly said, fearing that to move his mouth would cause the blade to cut it.

Farrell withdrew it slightly.

'Did he tell you what he was working on?'

'Some of it. He was very secretive about his work.'

'And you never asked?'

Farrell pressed the point against the underside of the agent's chin.

'Tell me what you *did* know,' the big man demanded. 'Tell me what you knew about the book.'

'I told you, he never spoke about what he was writing.'

Connelly's words were interrupted as Farrell pushed the blade up harder beneath his chin, hard enough to break the skin. Blood welled up from the puncture and ran down Connelly's throat, staining his shirt collar.

'Find the book,' Farrell said quietly, drawing the blade across the agent's cheek, stroking his earlobe gently with it. 'Find it. Someone will be watching you, not all the time, but you'll never know when. If you go to the police I'll personally come back here and cut your fucking head off. Understand?'

Connelly closed his eyes, aware that blood was still running from the cut beneath his chin.

'Understand?' snapped Farrell angrily.

'Yes,' Connelly croaked.

Farrell whipped the blade to the right swiftly and powerfully. The cut sliced open the lobe of Connelly's left ear. The fleshy bud seemed to burst, blood spurting from the gash. As the pressure on his neck was eased the agent fell forward, one hand clutching at the bleeding lobe. Crimson liquid streamed through his fingers.

Farrell looked down at the injured man as he opened the door, allowing his companions out first. He saw the blood puddling on the hall carpet as Connelly tried to staunch the flow.

'We'll be in touch,' Farrell said.

Then he was gone.

Thirty-Two

At first she thought she was dreaming, that the sound was the residue of a sleep-induced image. But as Julie sat up she realized that it wasn't.

She listened intently for a moment, the silence of the house closing in around her, then she heard it again.

Below her.

Movement.

Soft and furtive, but nevertheless movement.

She shot out a hand and pushed Donna hard, shaking her when she got no response. The other woman rolled over slowly and looked up, her eyes heavy with sleep.

'What's wrong?' she murmured, rubbing her face lazily with one hand.

'I heard something,' Julie told her, keeping her voice low. 'I think there's someone in the house.'

Donna blinked hard, her head suddenly clearing. She swung herself onto the side of the bed and sat there, her feet just touching the carpet, ears alert for the slightest disturbance.

'There,' said Julie as she heard another sound beneath them.

Donna nodded and got to her feet, moving swiftly and quietly across the room towards one of the wardrobes.

'Call the police,' she whispered to Julie, who needed no prompting and had already reached for the phone beside the bed. She frowned and flicked at the cradle. The line was dead.

'Nothing,' she said, a note of panic in her voice. 'They must have cut the lines.' She replaced the useless receiver, her attention now divided equally between listening to the sounds from below and watching her sister.

Donna slid the wardrobe door open, pulling the light cord inside. In the dull glow she was hunkered over what looked like a safe, a metal cabinet encased in oak. She took a key from the top of the cabinet and inserted it into the small lock, pulling the door open.

'My God,' Julie murmured as she stared at the contents.

There were four pistols inside the gun cabinet. The light reflected dully off their metal lines.

A .38 Smith and Wesson. A 9mm Beretta 92S Automatic. A chrome-plated .357 Magnum and a Charter Arms .22 Pathfinder revolver. Stacked at the bottom of the cabinet were boxes of ammunition.

Donna took the .38, pushed open a box of shells and flipped out the cylinder, thumbing the high-velocity ammunition into the chambers.

Julie looked on in disbelief, jumping involuntarily as Donna snapped the cylinder into position. She got to her feet and Julie found the image before her disorientating: her older sister, hair still ruffled, dressed only in a thin, short nightdress, gripping a gleaming revolver in her hand. It would have seemed absurd but for the seriousness of the situation.

'What are you going to do?' Julie asked, moving across the room, pulling her dressing gown on, glancing warily at the pistol Donna gripped expertly in both hands. 'You can't shoot whoever it is, Donna. This isn't a film, for Christ's sake.'

'I know. And whoever is down there isn't going to back off when someone shouts cut, are they?'

The two women locked stares, Julie blenching as she saw the determination in her sister's eyes.

'Come on,' said Donna, moving slowly towards the bedroom door.

Julie hesitated a moment.

'Do you want to wait until they're up *here*?' Donna asked challengingly.

Julie shook her head. Both of them paused by the door, listening.

The sounds were still coming from downstairs.

Donna heard a creak, a sound she recognized well.

One of the hinges on the sitting-room door squeaked.

The intruder was moving into the hall.

It wouldn't be long before he made his way up the stairs.

Thirty-Three

'Open it,' Donna said, nodding towards the handle of the bedroom door.

Julie reached for it, hesitated, then closed her shaking hand around the cold brass. The chill seemed to fill her entire body. Goose pimples rose on the flesh of her forearms. She wondered if she would find the strength to force the door open.

What lay beyond in the gloom?

'Let me out first,' whispered Donna. 'When I tell you, put all the lights on.'

Julie nodded, remembering that there was a panel of four switches close to the door which controlled the lights on the landing, the stairway and the hall.

Donna gripped the gun more tightly, her own

body quivering slightly in anticipation as much as fear.

What if the *intruder* was armed?

What if she *had* to fire?

She remembered the hours she and Chris had spent standing on a firing range, the shooting designed as a hobby to begin with. As they'd attended more regularly they'd become proficient shots, then accomplished marksmen. When firing at a target, anyway, Donna thought.

Targets didn't shoot back.

Was he still in the hallway?

If so, what would be her best strategy?

Confront him? Hold him in the sights of the .38 until the police arrived? And how were they to arrive when the lines had been cut?

Thoughts tumbled through her mind madly.

What if he was already outside the door, waiting for her to emerge?

She closed her eyes momentarily, trying to push the thoughts aside, trying to clear her mind.

Come on, come on.

She could feel her heart thudding hard against her ribs, the blood rushing in her ears.

You can't wait all night.

Donna held the gun out in front of her.

Do it.

'Now,' she said, and Julie pushed the door open, allowing Donna to slip out onto the landing.

She scrambled across the carpet, the gun held

out moving awkwardly as she attempted to keep the .38 raised.

It was pitch black on the landing; the only light came from a small window about half-way up the stairs.

In the light from that window Donna saw a figure.

The figure was moving up the stairs.

'The lights,' she shouted frantically and Julie joined her on the landing, slapping at the switches.

The landing, the stairs and the hall were all bathed in light. In the explosion of radiance the intruder could be seen clearly.

Julie screamed.

The sound echoed off the walls and drummed in Donna's ears as she too recoiled from the figure's features.

She could scarcely find the strength to stand up as she saw him freeze, startled by the sudden appearance of the two women and, she thought, even more so by the sight of the gun.

Julie put a hand to her mouth to stifle another yell of terror as she looked at the man's face.

It was pale, almost yellow, the eyes only sunken pits. There didn't seem to be any whites. The flesh itself was rutted with a dozen or more deep gashes, some of which looked as though they'd partially healed only for the scabs to picked away again, revealing purple welts beneath. On the forehead and cheeks were large protuberances, nubs of flesh that looked like boils on the verge of bursting, brimming with corpulent pus. The man's head was covered by fine white hair that swirled around his ravaged face as he moved. The mouth was nothing more than a gash between the chin and nose filled with moulding teeth.

Julie took a step back, her eyes riveted to the horrendous sight.

Donna dragged herself upright, the gun still pointing at the hideous intruder.

As he began to move towards her she realized that the repellent features were not those of a man at all.

The intruder was wearing a mask.

The sudden realization fortified her and she took a step towards *him*.

'Stand still,' she shouted.

The venom in her command seemed to take the man by surprise. He looked at her, then down into the hall at something she couldn't see.

Donna heard the sound of the front door bolts being drawn, the chain being pulled free.

The figure on the stairs turned to run.

'I'll shoot,' Donna bellowed.

As she ran towards him the figure vaulted the bannister.

He either misjudged his jump or failed to calculate the distance from the landing to the hall.

From fifteen feet he crashed to the hard floor, landing with sickening force on his left foot.

The snap of breaking bone was devastatingly loud inside the house.

The man screamed in agony as he felt uncontrollable pain shoot up his left leg.

The cuboid and navicular bones in his foot had simply disintegrated under the impact and, so huge was the force with which he fell, the left fibula had snapped, part of it impacting into the talus at the top of the foot, the other part tearing through both the flesh of his shin and also the material of his trousers. A jagged point of bone projected from the leg like an accusing finger. The man screamed again as he toppled to one side.

And now, from over the banister, Donna saw that there were two intruders, one urging the injured one to follow him out of the front door.

Donna swung the pistol round and drew a bead on the injured man who was being lifted by his companion.

Kill the fucker.

The second man looked up and saw the wild-haired woman with the gun.

He too wore a mask.

Kill them both.

He hooked one arm around the waist of his crippled companion and the two of them hurried through the front door.

Oblivious to any danger she might be in Donna raced down the stairs after them, stumbling at the bottom.

'Stop,' she roared, her breath coming in gasps. But she could already hear a powerful motor start up. As she reached the front door she saw

131

a car hurtling away from the house, its tail-lights disappearing into the night.

Donna banged the floor with her free hand and crouched by the door, the cold breeze rushing past her. She sucked in a deep breath and hauled herself upright. As she turned she noticed blood on the hall floor.

Julie descended the stairs slowly, using the banister to support herself.

'We'd better get the police,' said Donna. 'I'll go over to Jackie's and call them. One of them was hurt badly.' She smiled thinly as she said it. She tried to slow her breathing but it was an effort.

The blood on the floor glistened beneath the bright lights.

Thirty-Four

'It doesn't make sense,' said Detective Constable David Mackenzie. 'They disable the alarm, use a glass-cutter to get in, don't leave any prints behind and wear masks in case they're spotted. They cover every eventuality but they don't take anything.' He shook his head.

Standing in the sitting-room he looked around in bewilderment.

'Nothing's even been *broken*, let alone taken. Burglars usually ransack the place. These two look as if they were being careful not to disturb things too much. As if they didn't even want anyone to know they'd been inside.' Again he shook his head. 'I've never seen anything like it before.' He looked at Donna, who was sitting on the edge of the sofa stroking her neck slowly. 'You're sure nothing was taken, Mrs Ward? I know you say you've checked . . .'

'Nothing was taken,' she interrupted him.

The clock on the mantlepiece said 2.36 a.m. The police had arrived more than thirty minutes ago. Already they'd dusted for fingerprints but found none that shouldn't have been there. Donna had called them from Jackie Quinn's house, telling Jackie there was nothing to worry about.

Did she really believe that herself?

She'd told Mackenzie that one of the men had been injured, badly, as far as she could tell. Word had been put out to surrounding hospitals that all casualty admittances with leg injuries were to be reported.

The two women had not been able to help much by way of descriptions apart from recounting details of the horrific masks the burglars wore and that one appeared to be rather thin (the one with the broken leg).

Mackenzine had no doubt that the masks and the clothes they wore would have been discarded by now.

'You say no shots were fired by you *or* the burglars, Mrs Ward?' the policeman enquired again, checking his notepad.

'No. You only have to check the gun for that,' Donna said wearily.

'And you can verify that the guns are licenced?'

'My husband and I both held Firearms Certificates. We were members of a gun club; we shot there regularly. I'll give you the number if you want to check it out.'

'Just routine,' he said, smiling. 'Why did you have guns in the house, Mrs Ward?'

'My husband was away from home a fair bit. He said I should have more adequate protection than a burglar alarm. It was my husband who insisted I learn to shoot.'

Mackenzie nodded.

'Am I the one on trial, Detective Constable?' she said irritably.

'I have to ask these questions, Mrs Ward,' he said apologetically. 'I mean, this isn't New York. It's not every day a young woman pulls a gun on a burglar. This is new to me.'

'I didn't pull a gun on him,' Donna corrected. 'I was protecting myself and my sister. God knows what would have happened if he'd got upstairs.'

'Would you have shot him?' Mackenzie asked flatly.

'My house has been broken into, my sister and I could have been in danger and all you're concerned about is whether or not I would have shot the bastard who did it.' She glared at him for a moment. 'To tell you the truth, I don't know, but I'd like to think that I could have pulled the trigger if I'd had to. But if I had, it'd be me you'd be arresting, wouldn't it? To hell with saving my own life and my own property.' She ran a hand through her hair.

Mackenzie lowered his gaze a moment, his voice softening.

'Mrs Ward, do you think this break-in could have anything to do with your husband's death?' he asked.

'You're the policeman; you tell *me*.'

Mackenzie could only shrug.

'It was just a thought,' he added belatedly.

Donna was already certain there *was* a link.

Mackenzie looked around him. 'I don't think there's anything more we can do here now. We'll leave you in peace.'

Donna got to her feet, ready to show him out, but the DC motioned her to remain seated.

'There is one thing, Mrs Ward. The fact that they broke in but didn't *take* anything, and also that they were obviously professionals, makes me think they were looking for something specific. Something particularly valuable, perhaps. Can you think what it might be?'

Donna shook her head gently.

'Do you think they'll come back?' Julie wanted to know.

'Normally I'd say no, especially after having had a gun pointed at them. But if they *were* looking for something, and it's *that* important

135

to them, then it's possible.' He looked at both women. 'Be careful.'

Thirty-Five

The pain was excruciating.

Howard James had felt pain before, but nothing to compare to the agony he felt from his shattered leg.

'Get me to a fucking hospital,' he said, frantically shaking the arm of the man who sat next to him.

Robert Crossley looked down at his companion huddled in the passenger seat of the Orion, his broken leg stretched out before him. The splintered bone was clearly visible poking through the rent in his trousers. Blood had congealed thickly on the end of the smashed fibula. There was dark matter oozing slowly from the centre of the bone which, Crossley concluded with revulsion, was marrow. The stench inside the car was almost overpowering.

'How much longer do we have to sit here, waiting? I need help,' wailed James, his cheeks tear-stained, his skin milk-white.

Crossley wiped perspiration from his face and looked at his watch.

3.27 a.m.

It was almost thirty minutes since he'd made the phone call, stopping off quickly at a pay-phone before swinging the car off the main road and into Paddington Recreation Ground. The vehicle and its two occupants now stood silently in a children's playground. The wind, blowing across the open ground, turned the roundabout and Crossley looked up nervously every time he heard it creak. Swings also moved gently back and forth in the breeze, as if rocked by some unseen hand. Beside him, James continued to moan loudly as the pain seemed to intensify.

'I can't take this much longer,' he hissed through gritted teeth. 'Please.'

Crossley nodded and looked round again, as if seeking inspiration from the children's slides and climbing-frames.

He heard the soft purring of a car engine and saw the Montego rolling slowly towards them, its driver flashing his lights once as he approached.

'Who is it?' gasped James.

Crossley didn't answer. He pushed open the driver's side door and clambered out, unsure whether to approach the Montego or wait. He decided to wait, watching as the driver switched off the engine and slid from behind the wheel. He walked with brisk steps.

A strong breeze ruffled Crossley's hair and made him shiver. Inside the car James was huddled in the seat like a whimpering child.

'What went wrong?' Peter Farrell snapped, looking at Crossley then down at the injured James.

'She had a fucking gun,' Crossley told him. 'I wasn't going to argue with a gun.'

'So you found nothing?' Farrell persisted.

Crossley shook his head.

'Did you check his office. Upstairs?'

'We didn't get that far,' Crossley said. Then, turning towards his injured companion, 'We've got to get him to a hospital, he's hurt bad.'

'The police will have put out checks on every hospital for miles. How bad is it?' Farrell demanded.

'Look for yourself,' Crossley told him and pulled open the passenger door.

Farrell saw the smashed bone sticking through skin and material.

'You were careless,' he said irritably.

'We were unlucky,' Crossley protested.

'Same thing.'

'And what the fuck would you have done if she'd pulled a gun on *you*?'

'Pulled one on *her*,' Farrell rasped, taking a step closer so that his face was inches from Crossley's. 'You could have jeopardized everything. We won't be able to get near the house for a while; they'll be expecting it. You fucking idiots.' He turned his back on them for a moment, hands planted on his hips.

'So what do we do about James?' Crossley asked. 'He needs help, for Christ's sake.'

Farrell turned slowly. His hand went to the inside of his jacket.

Crossley's mouth dropped open as he saw the taller man pull a gun into view.

The silencer jammed into the muzzle of the .45 made the weapon look enormous.

Farrell fired two shots into James's head.

The first hit him on the bridge of the nose, almost severing the appendage and taking out an eye as it exited. The second blasted away most of the back of his head, spraying it across the driver's seat and the side windows.

The body toppled sideways, the eyes still staring wide in shocked surprise, the mouth still open.

'Get rid of the body *and* the car,' Farrell said flatly. 'Call me when you've done it.' He turned and headed back to the Montego, pausing as he opened the door. 'Crossley, you fuck up this time and I'll kill you, too.' He climbed into the car, started the engine and drove off, his lights still out, disappearing into the darkness.

Crossley looked down at the corpse, the breeze bringing the stench of blood and excrement to his nostrils. He shivered and he knew it wasn't just the wind.

The roundabout creaked again. The swings moved gently back and forth.

Thirty-Six

The porter accepted his tip gratefully, nodded and glanced at Donna as he left, smiling approvingly when her back was turned.

She waited until the door was closed and then crossed to the window of her suite, pulling the curtains aside. The Shelbourne Hotel in Dublin overlooked St Stephen's Green and Donna gazed out onto the park for a moment, glad to be safely at the hotel. 'The most distinguished address in Ireland,' boasted the legend on the desk notepad. Donna stood at the window a moment longer, gazing out at the people in the street below. Finally she lifted her small suitcase onto the bed, flipped it open and began taking clothes out, sliding them into drawers.

The flight had been smooth but Donna didn't enjoy flying. It didn't frighten her; she merely disliked the physical act of getting on a plane and sitting there for the duration of the journey. Fortunately the Aer Lingus 737 had delivered her from Heathrow in less than an hour, so she'd barely had time to become bored.

She'd promised to phone Julie that night to let her know she'd arrived safely and to check on her sister. The break-in of the previous night had shaken them both, but Julie more so.

Donna finished unpacking and crossed to the desk where her handbag was. She sat down, reached inside and took out an envelope, removing the contents.

There were a dozen American Express receipts inside, each bearing the name of a hotel. One of them bore the name of The Shelbourne.

She flipped open Chris's diary and ran her finger down the entries.

She checked the date on the Amex slip against the entry for Dublin in the diary.

It matched.

So did the one for Dromoland Castle, County Clare.

And The Holiday Inn, Edinburgh.

The Mayfair, London.

Every entry in the diary was matched to a receipt. Only some of them had the initial D beside them; it was these which Donna was interested in.

It had been simple to find out which hotels Chris had stayed in. He always paid by credit card and he always kept the receipts for his accountant. She had merely unearthed them from his office.

How many of these places had he stayed with Suzanne Regan?

Donna swivelled in her seat and looked across towards the bed.

Had he stayed here?

She tried to drive the thought from her mind, feeling an all-too familiar surge of anger and sorrow. If only she'd been able to ask him why,

141

perhaps it would have been more bearable. For a moment, Donna felt tears welling up in her eyes but she fought back the pain, forced the thoughts away. There would be plenty of time for them in years to come, she thought wearily. For now she replaced the receipts in the envelope and pushed it into a drawer beneath some clothes.

She put the photo of Chris and the five men in there too.

The diary she dropped back into her handbag.

Donna got to her feet and padded across to the bathroom where she showered quickly, rinsing away the dirt of the journey. Travelling always made her feel grubby, no matter how luxurious it was. She pulled on one of the towelling robes and wandered back into the bedroom, selecting clean clothes. A white blouse, jeans and some flat suede boots. She dried herself, dressed, brushed her hair and re-applied her make-up, then inspected her reflection in the mirror.

Satisfied, she slipped on her jacket and picked up her handbag, pausing to look at the diary once more and its mysterious entry:

JAMES WORSDALE: DUBLIN NATIONAL GALLERY.

As she made her way to the lift and jabbed the button marked 'G' she found her heart thumping a little faster than normal.

Outside the hotel she asked the doorman to get her a cab.

She was at the gallery in less than five minutes.

Thirty-Seven

It was as imposing an edifice as she'd ever seen. A massive grey building, its frontage decorated with stone pillars, its grounds were dotted with statues. The gallery itself looked as if it had been carved by some giant sculptor, minute details in the stonework wrought by caring as well as skilful hands.

Donna had only seconds to appreciate its beauty; she had other things on her mind. She paid the taxi-driver and walked briskly towards the main entrance of the building, slowing her pace as she reached the flight of broad stone steps that led up to the doors.

This was going to cause more problems than she'd thought, but it was the first place to try.

For one thing, there was no time in the diary for meeting Worsdale. Coupled with that, she had no idea what the man looked like.

As Donna climbed the stairs slowly she looked around at the dozens of people entering and leaving the building, wondering how the hell she was supposed to find someone she'd never seen before. Perhaps her husband and Worsdale had agreed a certain meeting place inside or even outside the gallery.

She entered the building, wondering how she was to find this elusive man, wondering again what she was going to tell him even if she *did* succeed in locating him.

She gazed around at the paintings which hung on the walls, looking but not really seeing.

It was quiet inside the gallery, an atmosphere akin to a library. That same hushed reverence pervaded the place. Donna glanced at the other visitors, noticing how diverse an audience were drawn to such a building.

There were people of all ages, wandering back and forth, some studying the paintings for long moments others just glancing, some checking their guides, some making notes.

As she looked up she saw what looked like a loud speaker in one corner of the room.

A public address system.

The idea hit her like a thunderbolt and she spun round, heading back towards the main entrance, remembering that there was an enquiries desk there. She could get them to broadcast an announcement for her, spread the word around the gallery that Mr James Worsdale was to come to the main entrance.

She smiled at her own ingenuity, the smile fading as she realized the ploy would only work if Worsdale was actually in the gallery. But, she thought again, her mind accelerating now, there was another way. She could leave a message at the desk. Get them to put a sign up telling Mr

Worsdale to contact the Shelbourne Hotel and ask for Mr Ward.

Pleased at her plan, she smiled as she approached the desk.

She'd find him yet.

There was a man seated behind the desk reading a book. He looked up as Donna approached and smiled at her.

She returned the gesture, struck by his good looks. He was in his late twenties, thick-set, dressed in jeans, with his long hair pulled back in a pony-tail.

'Can I help you?' the attendant said happily.

'Yes, I think you can,' Donna told him. 'I'm looking for someone. I'm supposed to meet them here but I've forgotten where,' she lied. 'I was wondering if you could put out a message over the public address system to tell him I'm here. If that's okay?'

'It's not supposed to be used for that, really,' he said apologetically. 'It's newly installed. We've had a couple of bomb threats lately and it's been installed to warn staff to clear the building. I'm sorry.'

'This is *very* important,' Donna insisted. 'Please.' She could feel her heart sink. If this failed she was lost.

'I shouldn't,' the attendant said, but then smiled broadly.

'But what the hell. What's the name of the person you're looking for?'

Donna smiled broadly.

'Thank you, I appreciate it,' she said, relieved. 'His name is James Worsdale.'

The attendant's smile faded rapidly and he looked at Donna with narrowed eyes.

'Are you sure?' he asked.

'Yes, I'm sure. Is there a problem?' Her own smile was replaced by a frown.

'I can put out the announcement but I don't think James Worsdale will show up.'

'Why not? How do you know?'

'Because he's been dead for over two hundred years.'

Thirty-Eight

The smile on the face of the attendant was a marked contrast to Donna's expression of shocked surprise.

As he saw her concern, again his smile faded.

'Well, let's say the James Worsdale *I* know has been dead that long,' he said apologetically. 'But if there's another . . .' He shrugged. 'It's an unusual name.'

Donna's mind was still reeling but she reached for her handbag, pulling out the diary.

'Look,' she said, thrusting the book at him and pointing at the entry. 'James Worsdale, Dublin National Gallery.'

'You're in the right place, then. His work is exhibited here. *He's* not.'

Donna shook her head, now totally puzzled by what she'd heard. She felt a little foolish, too.

'I'm sorry,' she said, and turned to leave.

'Wait,' the attendant said. 'Have you got five minutes to spare? You came here to see Worsdale's work; the least I can do is show it to you.'

She hesitated, then smiled thinly.

'Five minutes?' she repeated. 'I feel such an idiot,' she said.

'No need to. You wouldn't be the first one through these doors,' he nodded towards the main entrance and smiled broadly.

The gesture was infectious and Donna at last found herself grinning, too. The attendant clambered out from behind the counter, one of his colleagues taking his place. He walked around to where Donna stood and motioned for her to follow him. Again she was struck by his good looks and his relaxed, easy manner. He introduced himself.

'My name's Gordon Mahoney,' he told her.

'Donna Ward. How long have you worked here?'

'Six years. It pays to know whose paintings are exhibited here. People are always asking questions.'

'But not always looking for the artist,' she said. Mahoney grinned.

'What makes Worsdale's work so interesting to

you?' he wanted to know as they walked through the gallery, passing among the tourists and the students and the other visitors.

'It was my husband who was interested in him,' she said a little sadly.

'Is he with you today?'

'He's dead.' She swallowed hard.

'I'm sorry,' Mahoney said quickly. 'Was he interested in obscure Irish painters, then?'

'Was Worsdale like that?'

'He wasn't one of our most famous painters. Maybe obscure is being a little unkind to him, though.'

They climbed a flight of stone steps and reached another floor. Mahoney moved briskly along, glancing at Donna every now and then. He finally came to a halt and made a sweeping gesture with his arm designed to encompass the array of canvases on the wall.

'This is some of James Worsdale's work,' Mahoney explained.

Donna stood looking at them, listening as the attendant pointed out each canvas in turn and told her a little about it. They were unremarkable works: landscapes, portraits and still-lifes. She could see nothing amongst them to explain why Chris should have been so interested in the artist's work. She knew very little about art and couldn't tell if the paintings were brilliant or not. To her, they looked accomplished but ordinary. What the hell made Worsdale so interesting to her late husband?

'What was your husband looking for?' Mahoney wanted to know.

Donna merely shook her head gently, looking from canvas to canvas.

'I honestly don't know,' she said quietly. 'Is this it? All of his paintings?'

'All *we* have. Well, nearly all. There's one in storage.' He smiled. 'In fact, it's permanantly in storage and it's probably the most interesting thing he ever painted, but the subject matter makes it a little, how shall I put it, undesirable for public display.'

'Why, is it obscene or something?' she asked.

Mahoney laughed.

'Anything but.'

'So why is it never put on show?'

'You could say it's something of an embarrassment.' He looked at her and held her gaze.

'Could I see it, please?' she asked.

Mahoney hesitated, his infectious smile fading.

'I don't know. Perhaps I shouldn't have mentioned it.' He looked around, as if afraid that someone might be listening to their conversation.

'It could be important,' she persisted.

He nodded finally.

'Okay. Come with me.'

Thirty-Nine

Nothing about the gallery had been how Donna had imagined it. It was not filled with crusty old men and women poring over the paintings; the whole building had a bright and open atmosphere, instead of the sullen brooding one she'd expected. Most of all, Mahoney didn't look like the sort of man who would work in an art gallery. He seemed too young and vibrant for work she had previously thought to be the province of uniformed men with starched collars and even stiffer demeanours. Every cliché she had held had been exploded by her visit.

The room where paintings were kept in storage was no exception. She had been expecting a small, dusty room filled with paintings draped in cloths that were thick with dust, where air would have a musty scent of old canvas and decay. Instead the room was light and airy, lit by fluorescent lights and smelling pleasantly of air freshener. There was a thermometer on the wall displaying the temperature, ensuring that it was constant so that the paintings were preserved correctly. There was an expel-air machine on a bank of filing cabinets which rattled in the stillness of the room.

The paintings were carefully stored in crates dependent on their size. Others were propped against the walls. These, she noticed, *were* covered by white dust sheets. Some appeared to be covered by what looked like cling film.

'How do you decide which paintings go on display and which are kept here?' she asked, following Mahoney through the room.

'We display them on a kind of rotation system,' he told her. 'Each artist is allocated a certain amount of space in the gallery. The paintings are usually left on display for three months, then one or two are replaced. Those not on show are kept in here.' He reached a canvas covered by a dust cover and paused. 'You wanted to see all of James Worsdale's work?'

She nodded.

'Like I said, this one is hardly ever displayed.' He pulled the sheet clear, exposing the canvas.

Donna took a step closer, her gaze travelling back and forth over the gilt-framed painting.

'Hardly what you'd call shocking, is it?' Mahoney said, smiling.

'Who are they?' Donna moved closer to the painting.

It showed five men in eighteenth-century garb, four seated, one standing, bewigged and splendid in their clothes and obviously, for their time, wealthy men.

'Five of the founder members of the Dublin Hell Fire Club,' Mahoney announced with a sweeping gesture. He pointed each one of the figures out individually, moving from left to right across the canvas. 'Henry Barry, fourth Lord

151

Santry. Colonel Clements. Colonel Ponsonby. Colonel St George and Simon Lutterell. Rakes and profligates, the lot of them.' He chuckled. 'And proud of it.'

'The Hell Fire Club,' said Donna quietly. 'I've heard of them.'

'Most people have, and know something about the legend attached to them. They were rich young men, out for thrills, out to shock the establishment. They used to pass the time being cruel to the poor, gambling, whoring and indulging in most other perversions you could care to name.' He smiled. 'A little like an eighteenth-century branch of the Young Conservatives.'

'Why isn't the painting displayed?' Donna wanted to know.

'The Hell Fire Club were something of a social embarrassment at the time. Lots of them were the sons of well-off men, politicians and the like. Not the sort of offspring you'd be proud of if you were in politics, or some other branch of the upper social orders. Their motto was "*Fay ce Que Voudras*", "Do as you will". And they *did*, most of the time.'

'Was Worsdale a member?' Donna asked, intrigued.

'No one knows for sure. That's the curious thing about this painting, though,' Mahoney said, tapping the frame. 'The two men responsible for actually starting the Dublin Hell Fire Club aren't in it.'

'Who were they?'

'Richard Parsons, the first Earl of Rosse, and Colonel Jack St Leger. You know the horse race, the St Leger? It was named after Colonel Jack's ancestor Sir Anthony. Jack lived near Athy in County Kildare, a great drinker and gambler.'

'What about the other one, Parsons?'

'He was the most vicious of the bunch, from what I've read. He had a fondness for setting fire to cats, apparently.'

Donna frowned.

'A lovely crowd they were. We've got a painting of Parsons here somewhere, a miniature done by another member of the club called Peter Lens. I'll see if I can find it.' Mahoney wandered off to another part of the room, leaving Donna to study the canvas more closely. She reached out to touch the surface, aware of a chill that seemed to have settled around her. As Mahoney returned she shook it free but her eyes remained on the painting.

What had Chris wanted here?

'Richard Parsons,' Mahoney announced, presenting the miniature.

Donna looked closely and frowned. She could feel her heart thumping that little bit faster against her ribs.

'I've seen this face,' she whispered.

Mahoney didn't answer.

Donna traced the features with one index finger but it was not the face that caused her hand to shake.

153

'Are you all right?' Mahoney asked, seeing the colour drain from her cheeks.

She nodded.

'I need to know about these men,' she said, suddenly looking straight into his eyes. 'About The Hell Fire Club. How much do you know?'

'I've read a fair bit about them. What's so important?'

'Will you meet me tonight, for dinner? I'm staying at the Shelbourne. Will you meet me there? Eight o'clock?'

It was Mahoney's turn to look puzzled.

He nodded gently.

'There's something I have to show you. Something I have to know. I think you might be able to tell me,' Donna said. Then she turned her attention back to the painting. Again she found that she was quivering slightly as she studied the picture of Richard Parsons.

On the index finger of his left hand he wore a gold signet ring.

It was identical to the one worn by the man in the photo she had back at the hotel.

Forty

Julie Craig rolled over on the large double bed.

She sat up, her breathing heavy in the stillness. She swung herself off the bed and padded, naked, across to the wardrobe, hesitating there for a second.

Apart from her own breathing, the ticking of the bedside clock was the only sound.

She opened the wardrobe and pulled the cord inside. The small bulb inside exploded into life, displaying his clothes.

His jackets. Shirts. A couple of suits.

Julie ran her hand across them, feeling the different materials, her fingers lingering over the silk of the shirts, stroking gently.

She pulled one from its hanger and rubbed it against her cheek, her eyes closed.

Enjoying the softness she allowed the material to brush against her breasts. The nipples stiffened and she squeezed her breasts through the silk, her breathing growing heavier as she kneaded the sensitive buds with her fingers, her excitement growing rapidly. As she stepped away from the wardrobe she felt the moisture between her legs. She drew one index finger through her dewy pubic hair, lifting the glistening digit, touching it very gently to her lips. She shuddered, then slipped the shirt around her bare shoulders before heading towards the landing.

She paused at the head of the stairs, as if expecting someone to ascend; the house remained silent save for the creaking of settling timbers.

Julie turned and headed back across the landing, down the short corridor towards the office.

Outside she hesitated again, feeling the silk shirt around her shoulders. She pulled it more tightly, rubbing her shoulders, allowing one hand to slide across her breasts and down her belly. Then she pushed open the door and stepped inside the office, flicking on the table lamp.

The dull light cast thick shadows in the small room where her brother-in-law had worked.

The atmosphere was slightly chilly but she scarcely seemed to notice it as she sat herself at Ward's desk. She ran one finger across the keys of his typewriter and looked across the room to the photo of him which hung on the wall, smiling.

She smiled back at it, licking her lips, her breathing now deep, almost laboured.

Julie stood up and faced the photograph, slipping the shirt from her shoulders so that once more she was completely naked.

She moved closer to the picture, her eyes never leaving Ward's face, her feet brushing against the soft silk as she walked over it.

She knelt before the picture as if in prayer, then slowly opened her legs, stroking the insides of her thighs with both hands. Julie had her eyes closed now and her head tilted back, so that her long hair dangled down and brushed against her arched back. Her mouth dropped open slightly, her breathing deep as she allowed her hands to slide up her body, cupping both breasts, rubbing both nipples with her thumbs. She opened her eyes, kept her gaze fixed on Ward's face and allowed her hands to glide over her smooth skin back down towards her pubic mound.

Her fingers stirred the tightly curled hair there,

one index finger probing more deeply, grazing the hardened nub of her clitoris, stroking gently before plunging further to stir the warm wetness of her vagina.

She began to make slow circular movements on her clitoris, gradually increasing the speed, sliding another finger into her slippery cleft. She felt a sensation of heat building up between her legs as she rubbed harder and faster and held her gaze on Ward's picture as the pleasure grew more intense.

'Oh, Chris,' she whispered as the beginnings of an orgasm made her shudder. 'Chris.'

Forty-One

'I owe you an apology,' Donna said, pushing her plate away and dabbing at the corners of her mouth with a napkin.

Mahoney looked puzzled but continued sipping at his soup.

'I never even asked if you had other plans for tonight,' she said.

'I can live with it,' Mahoney told her, smiling.

'I'm not in the habit of picking up men I've just met,' she told him.

Especially when my own husband has only been dead for just over a week.

'I'm not complaining.'

Donna smiled thinly and watched him as he finished his soup.

He was dressed in a black jacket and black shirt, immaculately pressed, as were his trousers. His shoes were shined to perfection. The long hair she'd admired was still drawn back in a pony-tail. They'd drawn the odd inquisitive glance as they'd entered the dining-room of the Shelbourne, but Mahoney had been convinced that was because of the way Donna looked. She would have turned heads anywhere in a navy blue backless dress which rose just above her knee. Moving elegantly on a pair of high heels, she looked stunning. Her long blonde hair, freshly washed, seemed to glow in the dull light from the chandeliers.

Donna looked at him again, wondering why she felt so guilty to be sitting at the table with this man. Perhaps it was because there had been such a short gap between this meeting and the burial of her husband.

Do you think Chris ever felt guilty when he was with Suzanne Regan?

She tried to push the thought from her mind but found that it persisted.

'I used to work here, you know,' Mahoney said, pushing his bowl away and glancing around him. 'I was a trainee chef for six months.' He raised his eyebrows.

'What happened?'

'I managed to tip half a pint of *crème brûlée* over the manager one evening when he came in to see how I was getting on. They sort of decided for me

158

that it wasn't my perfect vocation. I was sacked.'
He raised his wine glass in salute. 'Cheers.'

She echoed the toast and drank.

'From there to the National Gallery,' she said.

'Via half a dozen other jobs. I've been a barman three times. There's always plenty of vacancies for bar work here. We like our drink, the Irish. More drinkers call for more barmen. It's a simple equation.'

She found him looking at her a little too intently and lowered her gaze.

'What made you come here?' Mahoney wanted to know. 'You said your husband was working on a book but that doesn't explain why *you* came to Dublin.'

'I wanted to find out what he was working *on*,' she said as the waiter removed the plates and tidied the table for the main course. 'The entries in his diary were all I had to go on. I think he was researching something, but I'm not sure what. That's why I had to find out who James Worsdale was.'

'And now you do?'

'I'm none the wiser, unless his work was something to do with the Hell Fire Club. It seems the most likely explanation now. Tell me what you know about them, Mr Mahoney.'

'Call me Gordon, please. I've never felt very comfortable with formality.'

She nodded and smiled.

'Gordon,' she said.

He raised his hands.

'There's so much to tell, Mrs Ward,' he began.

'Donna,' she told him. 'I thought we'd dispensed with formality.'

Mahoney grinned.

'The subject is vast,' he began. 'It depends what you want to know. It also depends on whether or not I can *tell* you what you want to know. I don't profess to be an expert.'

'You said you'd read a lot about them.'

'I've seen a lot of horse races but that doesn't make me a jockey, does it?'

She smiled again and reached for her handbag, sliding the diary free, laying it beside her as if for reference. The photo was in there, too, but she left it for the time being.

'I know more about the Dublin Hell Fire Club, obviously,' he continued. 'They were just one of the off-shoots. There were a number of branches affiliated to the main club in England. They had individual leaders at each club but one overall head. The affiliates were known as cells. As far as I can tell there were cells in London, Edinburgh and Oxford as well as here in Dublin.'

Donna swallowed hard, one hand involuntarily touching the diary. She remembered the entries.

Edinburgh.

London.

Oxford.

Her husband had been to all those places shortly before his death.

'Where were the meetings?' she wanted to know.

'In Ireland, usually at a place called The Eagle Tavern on Cork Hill. That's where Worsdale's painting was done. They also met at Daly's Club, College Green. That's where Parsons picked up his charming habit of setting fire to cats. He'd pour scaltheen over them first.'

'What's that?'

'It was a mixture of rancid butter and raw Irish whiskey, I believe. It's no wonder members of the Hell Fire Club were crazy if they drank that.'

The main course arrived and Mahoney sat back in his seat, seeing how intently Donna was looking at him, hanging on his every word. She glanced irritably at the waiter, barely resisting the urge, it seemed, to hurry him up so that her companion could continue. He finally left and Mahoney continued.

'Their favourite meeting place, though, was Mountpelier Hunting lodge near Rathfarnham. The ruins are still there today. Kids drive up there at nights and try to spot ghosts.' He smiled.

Donna didn't.

'How was it destroyed? You said there were only ruins there now.'

'One of the Hell Fire Club members, Richard Whaley, accidentally set fire to it one night. Well, he supposedly had drink spilled on him by a coachman so, by way of revenge, he poured brandy over the man and ignited him. Whaley got out but quite a few of the others didn't.'

161

'How difficult is it to reach?' Donna enquired.

'It's easy. You can drive up there. It's only twelve miles or so. They reckon on a clear day you can see the ruins from O'Connell Street.' He smiled again.

'Have you ever been up there yourself?' she wanted to know.

'When I was a student. Half a dozen of us went up there one night.' He shrugged. 'The only spirits *I* saw were Jamesons and Glenfiddich.' He chewed a mouthful of food.

'So what did they do at these meetings?' Donna persisted.

'Orgies, mainly. They drank a lot, they gambled, supposedly they practised the Black Mass. Their object was to undermine society, the Church in particular. But most of all it was just an excuse for an orgy.'

'What about the other clubs?'

'They were the same, but all the other cells were presided over by the man who founded the order at a place in England called Medmenham Abbey. They were called "The Monks of Medmenham". One man was responsible for starting the Hell Fire Club. A man called Francis Dashwood.'

Dashwood.

D.

Beside every entry. *D*.

'Dashwood was the President of the club. He used to travel around all the other cells to make sure they were carrying out their objectives.'

Mahoney chuckled. 'They had a nickname for him. They called him The King of Hell.'

Forty-Two

Gordon Mahoney held the brandy glass in his hand and swirled the amber fluid around gently before sipping at it.

The dining-room was almost empty; just one other couple occupied a table on the far side of the room now. Mahoney felt exhausted, as if he hadn't stopped talking since he sat down earlier that evening. Donna's questions had been unceasing, her curiosity boundless. He regarded her over the rim of the brandy glass, captivated by her looks. She certainly was a beautiful woman. As she drank her coffee Mahoney looked at her, studying the smooth contours of her legs, noticing the way the dress clung to her slim hips and waist. He felt an embarrassed stirring in his groin and shifted position in his seat.

'Did Dashwood ever come to Dublin?' Donna asked.

Mahoney sucked in a deep breath, preparing himself for the next round of questions.

'I would think so. Like I said to you earlier, he visited the cells all round the country. Parsons spent some time in England, too. They were powerful men. Dashwood was Postmaster-General of England at one time. Most of the members were wealthy young men. They were bored, I suppose. Nowadays the rich snort coke; in those days they got drunk and had orgies.' He smiled.

'What about the witchcraft side of it?' Donna wanted to know.

'They were perverts. It just gave them an excuse to do what they wanted in the name of the Devil. A lot of what went on was based on gossip, most of it spread by members themselves.' He drained what was left in his glass.

'What happened to Dashwood and Parsons?' Donna wanted to know.

'No one knows for sure. Parsons just disappeared, not long after the fire at Mountpelier lodge. Dashwood died, supposedly, of syphilis. The clubs broke up when too much political pressure was put on them, when it came out that some of their leading members were important social figures. The scandal ruined them.'

Donna nodded slowly, drawing her finger around the lip of the cup.

Mahoney watched her intently.

'Could there be a Hell Fire Club today?' she asked finally. 'Now, in the twentieth century?'

Mahoney shrugged.

'Anything's possible, but if there was I think *The News of the World* would have found them by now.' He chuckled.

'I mean it,' Donna snapped.

The Irishman was surprised at the vehemence in her voice.

'A group of men meeting together to get drunk and cavort with women? I should think that happens quite a lot, but I doubt they'd call themselves The Hell Fire Club. You can see that on any guy's stag night.' He shrugged. 'Dashwood and Parsons had political objectives; they wanted to do genuine damage to society. The clubs helped them recruit supporters.'

'So you're saying that couldn't happen now?' she said challengingly.

'No, I'm not saying that. All I'm saying is, I doubt if there are men practising the Black Arts and meeting on a regular basis for drunken orgies the way Parsons' and Dashwood's men did. I said it was unlikely; I didn't say it was impossible. Supposedly there was a Hell Fire Club in London in 1934, but what they were getting up to no one knows.'

Donna reached for her handbag and took the photo out. She pushed it across the table towards Mahoney.

'That's my husband,' she said, jabbing a finger at the image of Chris. 'I don't know who the other five are.'

Mahoney inspected the faces carefully, pausing at the two blurred images.

'Look,' said Donna, pointing at the first of the fuzzy figures. 'The ring on the left index finger. It's the same as the one worn by Parsons in that painting you showed me. The other man is wearing one, too.'

Mahoney frowned.

'They certainly look alike,' he mused.

'They're the same,' she snapped angrily.

'What are you trying to say, Donna?' he asked.

'Identical rings, one worn by a man in a painting done two hundred years ago, another worn by a man photographed less than six months ago. It's a hell of a coincidence, isn't it? I think that someone found the rings that belonged to Parsons and Dashwood. Those men in that photo. I think my husband knew that. I think he knew who they were. I'm sure that's what he was working on. All the places you mentioned that they used to meet, my husband had been there recently. I think he'd found a new Hell Fire Club.'

Mahoney didn't speak, mainly because he wasn't sure what to say. He could see the sincerity in her expression and hear the belief in her voice.

'I'm going to drive out to Mountpelier Lodge tomorrow,' she told him. 'Will you come with me?'

'What are you hoping to find there?'

'I don't know. Some answers?'

Mahoney exhaled.

'I told you, it's just a ruin,' he said wearily.

'Will you help me? Yes or no?'

He nodded.

'Pick me up at eleven,' he said. 'At the Gallery.'

'Eleven.' She nodded. 'Gordon, there's something else.' She licked her lips before she spoke. 'Were women allowed to join The Hell Fire Club as members?'

Could Suzanne Regan have introduced Chris to the others?

'No. It was strictly a male preserve,' he said, smiling. 'A couple of the high-ranking members like Parsons or Dashwood had what they liked to call "Carriers" but that was it. The carriers were women chosen to be impregnated, made pregnant by members. The children they bore would be used in ceremonies.'

'Jesus,' murmured Donna, taking a sip from her cup and discovering that the coffee was cold. She winced and pushed it away from her. She glanced up at the clock on the wall opposite.

It was 11.46 p.m.

'Gordon, I don't know how to thank you for your help,' she said.

'I could think of a couple of ways,' he said, smiling.

Donna looked at him coldly.

He raised his hands as if in surrender, then got to his feet.

'Shall I get them to call you a cab?' she asked.

'I'll be okay. The walk will clear my head.'

She walked to the main doors with him and said a quick 'Goodnight', reminding him that she'd pick him up at eleven the following morning.

167

Mahoney thanked her for the meal and left, stepping out onto the pavement. The fresh air hit him and he sucked in lungfuls and drank them down. After a few moments he began walking, pausing once to look up at the grand façade of the Shelbourne. He wondered which room she was in. Mahoney smiled to himself and set off. He should be home in less than thirty minutes.

Not once did he notice that he was being followed.

Forty-Three

Donna left the hazard lights of the Volvo flashing as she hurried up the steps towards the main entrance of the Dublin National Gallery. As she reached them she glanced back at the hire car, knowing that she couldn't leave it there for long. She hoped Mahoney would be ready to go.

She'd called Julie that morning to make sure she was all right, and that there had been no more trouble. Julie had told her she was fine. Donna, satisfied that her sister was well, asked the hotel to get her a hire car for the next couple of days. The Volvo had arrived less than twenty minutes later.

Now she reached the main doors and walked in, eyes flicking over the sea of faces in search of Mahoney.

He had told her a lot the previous night, too much for her to take in, but the salient points stuck out clearly in her mind. She had sat up that night in her room, sitting on the bed scribbling notes on one of the Shelbourne's notepads. She'd finally drifted off to sleep at about two, woken an hour later feeling cold and slipped under the covers, resting fitfully until room service brought her breakfast at eight.

She moved through the gallery quickly, looking for Mahoney but unable to find him. Finally she returned to the information desk where she'd first encountered him the previous day, and found a pretty young woman sitting there stacking up guide books on Dublin.

'I'm supposed to be meeting Gordon Mahoney here at eleven,' Donna said.

'He'll be back in a minute,' the young woman told her, still stacking.

Donna glanced agitatedly at her watch and walked to the main doors, trying to see the Volvo parked in the street beyond.

When she turned again she saw Mahoney approaching the desk. Donna smiled and approached him.

'Are you ready?' she asked.

He looked at her blankly.

'Can I help you?' he said flatly, his gaze barely meeting hers.

'Gordon, it's eleven o'clock. I've got the car outside. Come on.'

The girl stacking the guide books looked at both of them but said nothing.

'I can't go,' he said sharply. 'I'm working.'

'What the hell is wrong with you?' Donna demanded, irritated by his coldness.

'I'm busy.' He reached for a sheet of paper, picked up a pen and began writing.

'Was it something I said, last night?' she wanted to know. 'Why are you acting like this?'

'I don't know what you're talking about.' She could hear a note of disinterest in his voice, but something else too.

Fear?

'I've got work to do if you don't mind. I'm sorry,' he told her and continued writing.

The girl finished stacking the guide books and slipped out from behind the desk.

'I'll be back in a minute,' she said.

'Gordon, tell me what's wrong? Why are you doing this?' Donna said through clenched teeth.

Mahoney looked directly at her, his eyes blazing.

'Get out of here now,' he snarled. 'Leave me alone.'

Donna held his gaze, her own anger boiling.

'Get the fuck away from me,' he said vehemently. Then he looked around quickly. 'Get away from *me*, get away from this *place*, get away from *Dublin*.'

Donna frowned, opened her mouth to say something but was cut short.

'Go. Go now,' he said, still not looking at her. 'What do I have to say?'

She turned and walked briskly away from the desk, out of the main entrance and down the steps back to the car. She slid behind the wheel and started the engine, pulling away so sharply she caused the car behind to sound his horn as he braked to avoid her. Her mind still racing, she glanced down at the map on the passenger seat and then headed towards the road that would take her to Mountpelier Lodge.

Forty-Four

Perhaps it was her imagination, she thought.

Maybe she didn't really feel a chill in the air. After all, the sun was out and high in the sky. It was just her imagination working overtime.

Donna tried to convince herself of that as she walked slowly around the ruins of Mountpelier Lodge. Perched high on a hill, the remains of the place overlooked Dublin like some skeletal sentinel. The whistling of the wind was low, disappearing as quickly as it came, ruffling her hair. She pulled the collar of her jacket up. Evil places were said to retain an aura of Evil and, from what she had learned of this place from Mahoney, if ever that aura was present then it would dwell easily here.

171

The stone walls, what remained of them, were weather-beaten but untouched by overgrown weeds. In fact there were no plants anywhere near the ruins. Nothing grew in or around the stonework and, as she wandered around, she was aware also of the silence. A stillness which seemed to bear down on her like a physical presence.

No birds nested here.

Nothing living, it seemed, would come anywhere close to this long abandoned dwelling.

Mahoney had told her that the lodge had been built on the site of a demolished *cromlech*, a tower erected for the worship of native Irish Gods. Parsons and his followers had found it ironic that their place of depravity should be built on what had previously been Holy Ground.

As she walked, inspecting the ruins, she thought of Mahoney. Of their evening together, of how forthcoming he'd been with his information. How easy to talk to he'd been, generous in his desire to tell her what she wanted to know.

So why the change of attitude? What had happened to make him treat her so badly? It was another in a growing catalogue of mysteries and unanswered questions. Donna feared they might remain unanswered forever. At least some of them. One thing she *was* sure of was the purpose of her husband's visit here. Donna was convinced that he was investigating The Hell Fire Club or some organisation like it. What she didn't know was why.

Christ, there were so many whys and where-fores.

Why had he been having an affair?

There was always *that* question.

She crouched and picked up part of the brick-work that had crumbled away from a supporting pillar. Holding the stone in her hand, feeling its texture, she looked around the hilltop. Still she felt that breeze ruffling her hair, biting at her nose. Donna shivered and decided to head back to the car, not even sure why she had come here in the first place. Perhaps Mahoney might have been able to point out something to her, tell her more about the site. But Mahoney wasn't here, was he? She tossed the stone aside and headed back to her car, looking round again, even more aware of the silence and lack of birdsong. The only bird she saw was a crow flying high above, its black outline alien and unwelcome against the clear blue of the sky.

Donna slid behind the wheel of the Volvo and sat there for a moment, looking back at the ruins. She wondered exactly what kind of depravities had occurred inside that place when it was standing. She tried to imagine what an imposing building it must have been in its time. Ironic that so noble an edifice should house so vile an organisation.

She started the engine and swung the car around, catching a last glimpse of the place in her rear-view mirror.

Inside the car it seemed to warm up. In fact

the further from the ruins she got, the warmer she grew.

Imagination?

Donna adjusted the fan inside the car and headed back towards Dublin. She glanced into the rear-view mirror, convinced that hers was the only car on this lonely road.

Exactly where the black Audi had come from she had no idea.

There were numerous dirt tracks leading off from this road, but she didn't recall seeing it parked in any of them as she passed. All she knew was that the vehicle was behind her now. And, as she peered more closely into the mirror, she could see that it was drawing closer.

Accelerating.

Donna frowned and put her foot down, coaxing more speed from the Volvo, her eyes flicking back and forth from windscreen to rear-view mirror.

The Audi was still gaining on her.

She tried to look over her shoulder, to see the face of the driver, to mouth some kind of warning to him but she could see nothing. A combination of the sun on the windscreen and the tinted glass made it impossible.

The Audi was only yards from her now and Donna decided to pull in and let it pass.

It was then that it slammed into the back of her.

Forty-Five

The impact flung Donna forwards in her seat, the safety belt preventing her from hitting the windscreen.

She looked round, seeing the Audi reverse slightly.

'What the hell are you doing?' she screamed to the unseen driver as the black vehicle came hurtling towards her once more, this time clipping her offside light. She heard the crash of shattering glass as the cars clashed.

The Audi reversed a few yards. This time Donna stepped on the accelerator and the Volvo shot forward, dirt and stones spraying up behind it as she guided it back onto the road. She glanced in the rear-view mirror to see that the Audi was in pursuit.

She pressed down harder on the gas pedal, coaxing more speed from the car, trying to put more distance between herself and the maniac in the Audi, but whoever was driving the pursuing car had no intention of letting her get away. The black car swerved out in an attempt to get alongside her.

The road was scarcely wide enough to accommodate two cars travelling abreast but the Audi ploughed up a grass verge. Earth was sent flying upwards in a dirty wall as the wheels spun on the damp ground; puddles of water at the roadside splattered up the sides of the vehicles.

The Audi slammed into the side of the Volvo and Donna had to use all her strength to keep control of the car. Again she glanced at the windscreen of the other car but she could see nothing through the darkened glass. She spun her own wheel, smashing into the Audi. It skidded slightly and slowed down.

Donna accelerated, seeing a crossroads ahead.

She prayed there was nothing coming the other way.

The Volvo shot across the junction doing sixty.

The Audi followed.

Donna could feel perspiration soaking into her blouse and droplets beading on her forehead. When she turned her head her hair was matted to the nape of her neck. She gripped the wheel, looking alternately into the rear-view mirror and ahead, searching for a turn-off where she might be able to lose the chasing Audi.

The road forked about two hundred yards in front of her and Donna leant forward in her seat, willing the car to greater speed.

The Audi slammed into her again, the jolt almost causing the Volvo to skid, but she regained control and drove on. Her mind was blank. She was functioning on instinct alone. Self-preservation kept her going.

There was the renewed sound of breaking glass as the cars clashed again.

The fork was coming up.

Which way to go? Right or left?

She pulled hard on the wheel and took the left fork.

The Audi followed, spinning slightly on the wet road, the back end swinging round as the driver revved too hard. The momentary lapse gave Donna time to edge away and she pressed so hard on the accelerator she feared she might shove her foot through the very floor of the car.

The road was beginning to rise slightly, an incline that led to a gentle crest. Donna didn't slow up as she roared up the slope. She was doing seventy when she reached the top.

The Volvo left the ground for precious seconds, flying through the air before finally crashing back down to earth with a sickening jolt that jarred every bone in her body. She winced in pain as she felt a shock across her back at the impact.

The Audi came hurtling over the rise, too, one hubcap spinning away from it as it landed.

Donna grabbed the gear stick, simultaneously pressing hard on the brake.

The Volvo skidded for about fifty yards, its speed gradually slowing.

Donna jammed it into reverse. 'Come on you bastard,' she shouted and pressed down hard on the gas. The Volvo hurtled backwards and Donna gripped the wheel tightly, knowing that this particular ploy was going to stop the Audi or kill them both. She didn't know which.

The impact was massive.

The speeding Audi and the Volvo slammed into each other with sufficient force to buckle the Audi's grille and shatter both headlights. The Volvo fared little better but Donna closed her eyes tightly as the impact hurled her forward again and sent her crashing against the steering column with enough force to knock the breath from her. But she forced the Volvo into first, the engine screaming as she drove fifteen or twenty yards down the road. There was a loud crunching of gears as she forced it into reverse again, then sent the car hurtling again into the now stationary Audi, shunting it several yards further back. More glass covered the road; she heard it crunching beneath the tyres. There was steam coming from beneath the bonnet of the stricken Audi, water gushing out like blood from a wound. When the black vehicle tried to move away she heard a horrible clanking sound and saw the bumper come free.

The driver reversed and the whole thing came away, dragged for a few feet by the car.

Donna sent the Volvo crashing into the Audi again, then shifted up through the gears and drove off.

The Audi tried to follow but it could not muster its previous speed. Donna saw it in the rear-view mirror, convinced and elated that she'd done it crippling damage. She shouted defiantly for a second, tears forming in her eyes, tears of terror and relief. Her body was drenched with sweat; it was glistening on her legs and she felt moisture beneath her on the seat. Donna wasn't sure whether it was perspiration or if she'd wet herself in the hectic chase. For now, all she could think about was getting away. Getting back to the hotel. Calling the police.

She looked again at the rear-view mirror and saw that the Audi was turning into a side road, allowing her to go.

Her breath coming in short gasps, she drove on.

Forty-Six

The bathwater lapped gently up around her neck as she slid deeper.

Donna pulled the flannel from the water, wrung it out and placed it over her face. Her breathing was slow and steady, the only accompaniment being the slow dripping of one of the taps. Steam from the water had clouded the mirrors in the bathroom; condensation had formed a dewy veil over the tiles. It had run down in rivulets here and there like tears.

Donna pulled the flannel from her face and put it on the side of the bath. She felt drained.

How she had ever managed to get back to

the Shelbourne, she didn't know. It was as if her legs had turned to ice. She could barely feel the pedals beneath her feet. She'd left the smashed car outside and staggered inside, drawing disapproving glances from the other guests. Once inside her room she'd called reception and told them to get the police. She ordered herself a brandy and downed it a little too fast.

She'd been sitting on the edge of the bed when they'd arrived, two large uniformed men. One of them looked at her as if she were mad as she recounted the story. Donna smiled at the recollection. Why shouldn't he think her mad? The story sounded crazy enough. The entire scenario *had* been insane. Who would want to run her off the road the way the Audi had done?

No, he wasn't trying to run her off the road; he was trying to kill her. Don't fuck about. Face it. Whoever was driving the car had been trying to kill her, it was as simple as that. But why?

First the business with Mahoney, then the Audi. What was going on?

The police had apologized for the incident as if they were personally to blame, their apologies becoming even more profuse as they told her that, without a number plate (which she had been unable to remember) to trace, there was little chance of them finding the car, let alone the driver. Donna had nodded understandingly, anxious only then that they should go.

Alone in the room she had stripped naked and

run herself a bath, trying to wash away the sweat and relax after her ordeal.

She considered what she had discovered, her mind racing like a Roladex.

She was convinced now that her husband had been working on a book about The Hell Fire Club and . . .

And what?

That was it. The only other things she had were guesses and suppositions.

He *might* have discovered a modern-day equivalent of the Club.

It's *possible* they killed him (even though the police in England were convinced his death was an accident).

Gordon Mahoney had gone, overnight, from being helpful to being downright rude. *Why?*

Someone had tried to kill her that very morning.

Why?

Someone had broken into her house, apparently searching for something. *Why?*

Questions. But no answers.

Donna closed her eyes again.

Her husband had been having an affair with Suzanne Regan.

That was about the only other thing she knew for sure. She wondered how the other woman was involved in this chain of events. Had she been to these places *with* Chris? Had he shared information with her he wouldn't share with his own wife?

Donna clenched her fists beneath the water.

The knowledge of his affair still ate away at her, and it was knowing that she could never speak to him about the affair that hurt most.

No, not hurt, *angered* her.

He had escaped her wrath when he died. Both of them had. They'd been wiped off the face of the earth before they could taste her fury. That was what truly enraged her.

She sat up, splashing her face with water, catching a glimpse of herself in the steam-clouded mirror. Her reflection looked distorted. She hauled herself out of the bath, pulled on a bath-robe and wandered through into the sitting-room. She picked up the phone and reached reception, asking them for the phone number of the Dublin National Gallery.

Perhaps if she could speak to Mahoney again, tell him what happened out by Mountpelier that morning, he would tell her more.

She got the number, thanked the receptionist then jabbed the digits, reading them carefully from her pad.

A voice told her she'd reached her chosen number.

'Can I speak to Gordon Mahoney, please?' she said.

She was asked to hang on for a moment.

Donna shifted the receiver to her other ear and began doodling on the pad.

The other voice returned.

Gordon Mahoney had gone home about an hour ago.

'Could you give me his home number, please?' she asked.

The voice at the other end of the line obliged and Donna pressed down on the cradle to sever the connection before ringing the new number.

She waited for the phone to ring at the other end.

Waited.

It was finally picked up.

'Gordon Mahoney, please,' she said.

Silence at the other end.

'Hello.'

Nothing.

'Gordon, it's Donna Ward.'

She heard the click as the phone was replaced.

'Shit,' she murmured and punched the same digits.

Dead line.

She heard nothing but the endless whine over the wire. After a moment or two she replaced the receiver.

It was dusk by the time she checked out of the Shelbourne; night was approaching rapidly. The sun left a red stain behind as it retreated below the horizon.

The taxi took her to the airport. By the time the plane rose into the air it was dark.

Donna closed her eyes as it climbed through turbulence.

The flight to Edinburgh should take less than an hour.

Forty-Seven

The pistol was pressed against his cheek so hard that it almost broke the skin.

The sudden cold chill against his warm flesh woke him but, as Martin Connelly tried to sit up, shocked into consciousness by the sensation, the muzzle of the .45 was jammed against his face with incredible force.

In the darkness, and still half-asleep, he was unable to focus immediately on the figures standing around his bed.

All he was aware of was the deathly cold of the gun barrel. For a fleeting second he wondered if he might be dreaming, but this time he had woken *into* a nightmare.

Connelly blinked myopically, trying to clear his gaze, trying to figure out what the hell was going on. He felt his bowels loosen, felt the hairs on his neck and forearms prickle as he saw the face of the first intruder, the one who held the gun.

'Get up,' hissed Peter Farrell, stepping back. He kept the gun pointed at Connelly's head the entire time, the barrel never more than inches from his face. The muzzle seemed to expand, to grow into a vast black tunnel before his eyes.

'Move,' Farrell continued, grabbing Connelly

184

by one arm and jerking him towards the door of the bedroom.

The other man picked up the dressing gown lying on the end of the bed and threw it at Connelly. He looked at Farrell as if asking permission to put it on, to cover his nakedness; although, at the moment, decency was the last of his worries. Nevertheless he pulled it on and padded out onto the landing. Farrell kept close by, the gun still held at his head.

'I told you before I don't know anything,' Connelly said quietly, his voice cracking. His mouth felt dry, as if someone had filled it with sand.

Farrell grabbed the back of his hair and yanked his head back, forcing the gun hard against his temple.

'I didn't believe you then and I don't believe you now. I want some fucking answers,' he hissed.

'For Christ's sake . . .'

He was cut short by a shove in the back that nearly made him overbalance and fall down the stairs.

He shot out a hand and caught the banister, steadying himself. On shaking legs he began to descend.

Farrell and the other man followed him.

'Have you been in contact with the woman?' Farrell wanted to know.

'Which woman?'

'Ward's widow, who do you think?'

'Why should I have been?'

Farrell drove a foot hard into the base of Connelly's spine, the impact knocking him off balance. He toppled forward, pitching off the steps. He crashed against the wall then fell, rolled the last few stairs to the hallway.

Farrell was on him in an instant, dragging him upright, the gun held beneath his chin.

'Have you been in contact with her?' he repeated.

'No,' Connelly said, hurt by the fall. 'Look, I swear to you, I don't know anything.'

Farrell pushed the agent's head back sharply, banging it against the wall with a sickening thud. For a second Connelly thought he was going to pass out, but a hard smack across the face kept him conscious. Farrell grabbed him by the shoulder and pushed him towards a closed door leading off the hallway.

'What are you doing?' said Connelly, realizing which room he was being shoved towards.

'Move,' snapped Farrell.

Connelly was about to push the door when it was opened from the inside and he found a third man there.

Farrell pushed the agent inside and was joined by the other intruder.

All four men stood in the room and Farrell raised the pistol once more so that it was aimed at the agent's head.

'What the fuck are you playing at?' Connelly babbled timorously.

'We're not playing, Connelly,' Farrell told

him and pulled him across the hot and clammy room.

The kitchen was large but the air was warm and dry.

Connelly didn't know how long the rings of the electric cooker had been on but one of them was almost white-hot.

Forty-Eight

'No,' Connelly shouted as he saw the glowing rings and felt their heat.

Farrell took a step towards him and swung the butt of the .45 hard, catching him across the forehead.

The agent went down heavily, a gash on his head weeping blood down the side of his face. He rolled on the floor, moaning, and Farrell nodded to one of his companions.

'Shut him up,' he said. The second man reached into his pocket and pulled out a long length of what looked like ribbon. He slipped it around Connelly's chin and tugged it tight across his mouth, gagging him, then he dragged the agent upright. The other man moved over to join them, gripping Connelly's right arm so that his hand was groping at empty air. Farrell held the gun steady and looked directly at Connelly.

'I'm only going to ask you these questions once,' he said, 'so listen. When I ask you to answer, the gag will be removed. If you attempt to shout for help, I'll kill you. Do you understand?'

Connelly nodded, the action making his head ache. Blood had begun to run into the corner of his eye and he blinked to try and clear his vision.

The heat from the cooker was intense and sweat already beaded his forehead and face.

'Where is the book?' Farrell said.

The gag was pulled free.

'I don't know,' Connelly said, his eyes filling with tears of terror. 'I don't . . .'

The gag was pulled tightly back into position.

Farrell nodded.

The man holding Connelly's arm pushed it forward, forcing it down onto the largest of the electric rings, holding it there.

Searing, excruciating agony ripped through his hand and up his arm until it seemed to engulf his entire body. His scream was muffled by the gag; the sound was like a child shrieking inside a locked room.

As the hand was held on the blazing ring, the stench of burning flesh was clearly noticable in the hot air.

As the hand was finally pulled away, flesh stuck to the ring as if welded there by the heat. Tiny pieces of skin shrivelled and cooked on the red-hot ring and wisps of smoke rose into the air.

Connelly felt himself losing consciousness but he was aware of being slapped hard across the face, even if the pain of the blow was negligible compared to the mind-numbing suffering he felt from his burned hand. Blisters rose immediately, some of them in the shape of the ring. He felt as if his entire arm and hand were ablaze; as if someone had turned a blowtorch on them.

'Where's the fucking book?' Farrell snarled, moving closer. 'What did Ward do with it?'

'I don't know,' Connelly sobbed, tears mingling with the blood and sweat on his face. There was a dark stain on his dressing gown and he could feel urine running freely down his leg.

'Tell me,' Farrell said, glaring at him.

'He never told me about his work. I swear on my fucking life I don't know where it is.' His eyes bulged madly in their sockets, like bloodshot ping-pong balls threatening to burst from his skull. 'I don't know anything about the book, I don't even think he'd started writing it.'

Farrell looked puzzled but merely nodded to his companion.

The gag was tugged back into place, cutting off Connelly's exhortations for mercy. The muffled scream rose in his throat again as he felt the heat growing more intense, the closer to the blazing rings his hand was pulled.

Three inches.

He would rather died on the spot than endure that pain again.

Two inches.

The man tugged harder, using his immense strength to force Connelly's hand down towards the large ring.

One inch.

'Where's the book?' Farrell said again.

As his hand was crushed down onto the red-hot ring again, Connelly's body jerked convulsively and so savagely that the man holding him up was almost knocked off balance, but he stood his ground while his companion pressed down on the limb.

Blisters which had formed the first time now burst, weeping clear fluid onto the burner which hissed like an angry snake. The whole hand turned a deep shade of scarlet, the flesh itself heating up. Connelly, barely conscious now, felt as if his blood was boiling, as if his bones were calcifying under the incredible heat. Pain hit him in one intolerable wave and he blacked out.

The mercy of unconsciousness was denied him; as one of the men slapped him while the other threw water from the tap over him, also tugging his hair in an effort to bring him round.

He awoke to screaming pain in his hand, which hung uselessly at his side. The palm and most of his wrist were scorched black, the flesh seared into thick red welts. And again there was that sickly sweet stench of cooked flesh which clogged his nostrils and made him want to vomit. When his head lolled back, his hair was seized and tugged hard.

'Last chance,' Farrell said flatly. 'Where's the book?'

Connelly was sobbing uncontrollably now.

'You can't do this, please stop, Jesus fucking Christ, I don't know. Oh God,' he whimpered, tears pouring down his cheeks.

The man holding him tugged his hair and yanked his head back.

'Ward hadn't even written the fucking book, I swear to God.'

Farrell pushed his companion aside and grabbed the agent by the throat, almost lifting him off his feet, staring right into his bulging eyes.

'What do you mean he hadn't *written* the book?' he said.

'He was still researching it.'

'He stole it.'

'Stole what?' Connelly babbled frantically.

'He stole the book. He took it from us.'

'I don't know what you're talking about.'

'Liar,' snapped Farrell. He pushed Connelly's head towards the cooker, determined to push his face against the blistering rings.

'I don't know,' he shrieked, the screams cut off by Farrell's free hand. The muffled bellows were the only sounds he could make as his face was pushed closer and closer to the glowing rings. He could smell his own burned flesh on them, could see blackened streamers of skin sticking to the metal.

'Ward stole the book from us,' Farrell said. 'Where did he hide it?'

The heat was unbearable. Connelly used every ounce of strength he had to push himself away from the cooker, but Farrell was a powerful man and forced the agent's face ever closer to the ring. Another two inches and the burning cooker ring would be against his flesh.

'Tell me where he hid it,' Farrell urged.

One inch.

'He doesn't know,' said one of the other men, smiling thinly as he watched the agent struggle.

Connelly was fighting as hard as he could but it was useless. The heat made him feel faint; as his face was moved closer, he could actually feel the blistering heat drying his eye.

It was over now.

Farrell suddenly yanked him upright, away from the cooker. As he did he drove a fist hard into Connelly's face, the impact propelling him across the kitchen. He slammed into a wall, his head snapping back to crack against the plaster, then he fell forward.

'Bring him,' Farrell said, nodding towards the door.''We're taking him with us.'

Forty-Nine

At first he thought they'd blinded him.

Martin Connelly was sure that his eyes were open, yet he could see nothing. It took a few seconds after he regained consciousness to realize that he was blindfolded. The cloth had been knotted tightly round his head, cutting into his temples. But the discomfort was mild compared to the pain which engulfed the rest of his body, filling his veins like liquid fire. His head throbbed mightily from the blows he'd received, and the continuous agony of his burned hand made him feel as if the limb was swelling to gigantic proportions. Soon it would simply burst.

Connelly flexed his fingers and toes and felt renewed pain, a feeling of weightlessness. A terrible strain on his shoulders and neck. As if . . .

He was suspended in mid-air, dangling there like a useless, discarded puppet. He had no idea where he was and no idea how far off the ground he was. It could be two or three inches, it could be several hundred feet. Also, he was suddenly aware of the numbing cold. As a cool breeze swathed his sweat-drenched body he realized they had taken his clothes.

Martin Connelly dangled naked in the air, supported only by two thick pieces of hemp, wound so tightly around his wrists that they chafed the skin raw.

Help me.

He noticed the smell.

A rank, fetid odour clogged his nostrils and reminded him of bad meat. It seemed to be coming closer to him. Perhaps the mad fuckers had hung him in an abattoir. His mind began to race, all the possibilities hurtling through his consciousness. If he was hanging in a slaughterhouse, then might they not choose to use the implements of the slaughterer on him? The cleaver. The butcher's knife. The skewers.

Connelly felt sick and tried to twist himself free, his legs swinging helplessly beneath him. His ankles were unbound; it made him think he was higher off the ground than he would have liked. Perhaps they reasoned that even if he managed to slip clear of the ropes he would have so far to fall it wouldn't matter. The agent stopped struggling and hung there, aware of the pain in his wrists and the rasping against his skin, but even more conscious of the massive welts and blisters that covered his throbbing hand.

The silence was unbroken but for his own laboured breathing.

He let out an involuntary groan of pain and desperation.

'Where is the book, Mr Connelly?'

The voice lanced through the blackness, close to him and below him to the right.

He looked in that direction but the blindfold prevented him from seeing who had spoken.

'Where is it?'

Another voice. This time below to his left.

It was like the first. Slow, deliberate. Slightly mucoid. As if the speaker had a mouthful of phlegm.

'The book.'

Connelly felt a sudden stab of fear and also of

quite irrational embarrassment. The pain seemed to take a back seat momentarily, then he moved his right hand and it came thundering back into his mind.

'Christopher Ward took it from us, you know that,' the first voice said. Connelly was aware of that rancid stench growing stronger. It was closer to him now. So close, he could feel breath on his thigh.

On the thigh.

That meant that, unless the one standing to his right was abnormally tall, he couldn't be suspended more than about six feet off the ground. It was the only crumb of comfort he could salvage from the ordeal. He clung to it.

'We want to know what Ward did with the book. We want it back,' the second voice said.

'We *need* it back,' the first voice told him. 'Where is it?'

Connelly cleared his throat.

'I swear to you I don't know what book you're talking about,' he said. 'I know Ward was writing a book, but he hadn't even started it, he was still doing research.'

'We don't care about the book he was *going* to write,' the first voice snapped angrily. 'We want back what is rightfully ours.'

'He stole it and hid it somewhere. We need to know where so we can recover it,' the other voice added.

'Tell me about the book,' Connelly said, the last vestiges of reason working in his tortured mind. *Could he possibly talk his way out of this situation?* 'I may be able to help.'

'He doesn't know,' the first voice said.

'He's lying,' said the second.

'Ward was his client, he must have known,' intoned a third voice. A harsh voice that Connelly recognized as belonging to the tall man with the dark, close-cropped hair. 'He knows where it is,' Peter Farrell insisted.

'I don't know anything about a stolen book,' Connelly bleated.

'Then you are no use to us,' the first voice said.

'Wait,' Connelly said, panicking.

There was silence for a second, only his rapid breathing filling the air.

'His wife knows where the book is,' Connelly lied. 'Find her and she'll lead you to it.'

Would they believe it? Come on, convince them.

He realized that his last chance was to make his captors believe that Donna knew where the book they sought was hidden, whatever it was. If they thought that *she* knew, they might let *him* go. To hell with Donna. He had to save himself.

'Ward told her everything. He would have told her where your book is,' the agent continued, the lies falling easily from his lips. 'Find *her* and you'll find the book.'

'You're lying,' snapped Farrell. 'We didn't find it at Ward's house.'

'Well, he wouldn't keep it *there*, would he?'

Connelly hoped they couldn't hear the desperation in his voice. 'Besides, he owns another place, a cottage in Sussex. It could be there. Look, she's gone to look for it. His wife is searching for the book because Ward told her he had it. He told her he stole it. It's *her* you want, not *me*. She knows.'

'Where is this house in Sussex?' Farrell demanded.

Connelly searched his mind desperately, trying to remember. He almost smiled when he did, quickly imparting the information to them.

'It could be there but I doubt it. She was going to Ireland to find it. I asked her if she wanted me to go with her but she said no. She said she had to find the book, but that it was a secret between her and Ward. She's in Ireland now.'

'She *was*,' Farrell corrected him. 'She was seen near the lodge at Mountpelier yesterday.'

'I told you,' Connelly blurted.

'Shut up,' hissed Farrell, striking him hard across the stomach.

'Is this true?' the first voice asked. 'She was at the Lodge?'

'She left on a plane from Dublin last night. She's being followed,' Farrell explained.

Merciful fucking Christ, I think I've done it. They believe me, Connelly thought as he tried to suck in breath, tasting the rancid atmosphere as thickly as if it were smoke.

'I told you,' he said wearily. 'She knows where it is.'

'You would betray this woman to save yourself?' asked the first voice. A chuckle. It was a sound that made the hair at the back of Connelly's neck rise. 'You really have *no* honour, do you? I like that.' Another laugh. And another. The whole room seemed to be filled with it. Raucous, insane laughter that drummed in the agent's ears until he feared he would go deaf.

It gradually died away. His body swayed gently back and forth on the ropes.

'I've helped you,' he said. 'Let me go, please.'

'And if we do? We are to expect you to keep quiet? What do you think we are?' the second voice snorted. 'Your treachery is matched by your stupidity. If we release you, you will try to expose us the way Ward was going to.'

'How can I?' bleated Connelly. 'I haven't seen who you are. Please.'

He felt hands tugging at his blindfold.

'Look upon us,' the voice said and the agent opened his eyes.

'Oh God,' he whispered as he stared at his captors, his eyes bulging madly.

He gaped round the small room, realizing that he was suspended from a ceiling only fifteen feet high. There were a dozen or more people in the room, all seated, all staring at his dangling, vulnerable form.

'You have been a help to us and now we are

done with you,' said the first man, smiling up at him.

'No,' shouted Connelly.

He heard the sound of liquid slurping in a metal container as Farrell approached him from behind.

'What are you doing?' he shrieked, twisting about madly on the ropes that suspended him.

He felt cold, thick fluid being splashed on him.

He smelled the petrol as it covered his skin.

'No,' he bellowed. 'For God's sake, please don't. Please.' His voice cracked as it rose in pitch. More of the reeking petrol was doused over him. It matted the hair on his chest and ran down over his pubic hair and penis, dripping from his feet.

Tears of helplessness and terror welled up in his eyes.

'You can't do this, please,' he wailed.

The first figure struck a match and held it up in front of him, the tiny yellow flame glowing brightly.

'No,' Connelly screamed, his yell so loud it seemed his lungs would burst.

'Thank you for your help,' said the figure, and tossed the match at him.

The petrol ignited immediately, a loud whump filling the room as it consumed Connelly's body, which twisted insanely on the ropes as he screamed in uncontrollable agony.

From those watching there was movement.

They stood and, as one, began to applaud. There was some laughter.

Connelly's body continued to burn.

Fifty

It was raining outside, a thin veil of rain that was blown by the wind so that it appeared to undulate in the air like gossamer curtains. Droplets of fluid formed on the window and trickled down, puddling on the sills.

Donna Ward glanced distractedly out of the window for a second, her mind racing, her hand on her book.

The pages were stiffened with age and the tome smelt fusty, like a damp cloth left to dry on a radiator. Some of the words on the pages were faint, barely legible. Donna had squinted at them as she'd read. Some of the words did not even make sense to her but, through the confusion, she'd been able to salvage enough to piece together roughly the contents.

If not for the help of the librarian she might not even have found the book.

After checking into The Holiday Inn, Edinburgh, she had travelled to the library indicated in Ward's notes and diary, not really sure what she sought. The library was large and, rather than hunt through the endless rows of volumes dating as far back as 1530, she had sought the help of the librarian. The woman was in her mid-thirties, dressed in a black trouser suit and white sweater. She was a little overweight, her hands a touch too pudgy when she reached for various books and took them from the shelves. The badge she wore on one lapel proclaimed that her name was Molly. She seemed eager to help and selected half a dozen books for Donna to look at concerning The Hell Fire Club. She herself knew little or nothing about the organisation, and Donna wished she could have happened upon someone as knowledgeable on the subject as Mahoney had been.

This time she was on her own.

There were only a handful of other people in the library reference section; the normal air of peace and quiet one would expect in such a place seemed to have become an unnatural silence. Donna glanced round at the other occupants of the room but they were all hunched over their chosen books, seated at the wooden desks. Every so often the sound of a dropped pencil or pen would break the solitude, but apart from that the only sound was that of the wind outside, whipping around the building, hurling rain at the windows so hard it sounded as if thousands of tiny pebbles were being bounced off the glass.

Donna returned to the book, bending closer to make out the words:

Initiates into these clubs did undertake to join in deeds most foule to Christian Man. Some such as cannot bee described. The Acts demanded of them were as different as those Clubs themselves. Of the Clubs in existence there were the Mohocles The Blasters, The Bucks, The Bloods and, most vile of all The Sons of Midnight. These Heathen groups practised rites som would pray God not to here.

Donna flicked ahead a few pages but could see no way of hastening her search for the information she sought. She continued to read;

Those who joined were forced to fornicate in the presence of others. Some would beat the women afterwards. But these vile tasks were as welcome to them for they knew no love of God nor worship of Him. Only the pleasure of the flesh and pleasing their Masters was their joy. They killed too and found pleasure in it. After fornication with a woman then the one who would join would show his love of the Unholy by taking a child and killing it. The skull he would keep in his abode. A sign and an offering to those he wanted to join. Som would kill the unborn child or children of women and som ript open their bellys to take the child as offering. The skull of that child would always be theres. A sign of their villainy and proofe of their love of Evil.

Donna chewed her lip contemplatively as she read, forced to run her index finger beneath the words, so jumbled and irregularly formed were they on the faded page.

All these Evils are set down in great and Anciente Bookes called Grimoires. These books much prized by thes societys were filld with incantations and secrets known only to those who trod the dark pathes. Each club had a GRIMOIRE and where in every member would write his name as to show love of Evil and to show kinship with others of Evil.

Donna fumbled in her handbag, looking for a piece of paper and a pen. She found a notepad from the Shelbourne and scribbled the word Grimoire down.

She wondered where they kept the dictionaries.

The hand on her shoulder made her jump.

She turned to see Molly standing there.

'Sorry if I startled you,' she said, smiling. 'I just wondered how you were getting on.' She nodded towards the books in front of Donna.

'I'm okay,' she said, her heart slowing slightly. She administered herself a swift mental rebuke for nervousness. 'I need a dictionary, please.'

Molly nodded and hurried off to fetch one, returning a moment later. She handed it to Donna and stood by her as she flipped through it, running her finger down the columns of words until she found what she sought.

GRIMOIRE; *(Archaic) (Grim-wah) Old Norman French word*; (i) *A Book of Spells and invocations*.

(ii) *A book supposedly used for contacting Devils and Demons. Usually ascribed to Witches or Satanists*.

She re-read the definition, then closed the book and handed it back to Molly who smiled.

'Can I help you with anything else?' she wanted to know.

Donna ran a hand through her hair and sighed wearily. Her shoulders felt stiff and she could feel the beginnings of a headache gnawing at her skull.

'No thanks,' Donna said gratefully. 'I think I've finished.'

She glanced at the books in front of her, then at her watch.

It was approaching 4.15 p.m. She'd been in the library for close to four hours now.

All the reading and yet she wasn't even sure she'd made any progress. Because she wasn't sure what she was looking for. She knew more about The Hell Fire Club; she was certain that was what her husband had been working on. She knew that members had to fornicate and kill a child to gain entry. She knew that they relied on a book called a Grimoire for their contact with Evil.

Donna sat back.

In the cold light of day it all seemed so ridiculous.

Contact with Evil.

Hell Fire Club.

What had any of this to do with her husband's death or affair, she asked herself?

Perhaps she should be reading about infidelity instead of impiety. Widowhood instead of Wizardry.

And yet there were things wrong somewhere. Nagging doubts in her mind.

The police were convinced that her husband had *not* been murdered.

She *wasn't* convinced.

Why had masked men broken into her house? What had they been looking for?

Who were the men in the photo with Chris? Why did one of them look like a man who had supposedly been dead for over two hundred years?

Why had she been chased and nearly killed in Ireland?

Why had Mahoney withdrawn his offer to help so suddenly and unexpectedly?

Why? Why? Her life was turning into a series of unanswered questions.

Donna rubbed her eyes and got to her feet, picking up the piece of paper and putting it in her handbag.

On her way out of the library she thanked Molly for her help.

Donna hesitated on the steps of the library, looking out into the rain, seeing people caught in the downpour hurrying past. The cold wind closed around her like an icy fist, chilling her to the bone.

There had to be an answer to all this somewhere. She just wasn't sure where to find it.

Not yet.

Fifty-One

Julie Craig heard the car pull up in the driveway
and hurried across to the landing window to
look out.

She saw the Jaguar parked there but couldn't
make out the identity of its occupant. The
man was alone; he looked alternately towards
the house and then down, as if searching for
something on the dashboard.

She saw him rub one hand across his forehead,
as if wiping away perspiration. Still he remained
seated behind the steering wheel of the Jag.

Should she go downstairs, outside and ask him
what he wanted? No. Let *him* make the first
move. She was suddenly aware how ridiculous
she was becoming. Why should there be anything
sinister about him? She tried to think more
rationally, to dismiss the darker possibilities
from her mind, but after what had happened
here in the past week or so she found the
worrying thoughts came more easily. After all,
hadn't men broken into the house? He might
be one of them, come during the day to catch
her off guard.

She watched as the man swung himself out of the car.

He was dressed in a suit that looked as if it needed pressing. Indeed, as he shut the car door, he brushed at one sleeve as if to remove wrinkles as well as fluff. She watched as he stood beside the car for a moment looking up towards the house.

She stepped back a pace and watched as he looked across at the Fiesta then at the house once more.

He began walking towards it and she saw that he had one hand inside his jacket, as if reaching for something.

She moved to the head of the stairs and looked down into the hallway, listening to his footsteps approaching the front door.

He rang the bell.

Julie froze, gripped the banister tightly and waited.

He rang again and waited.

She moved quickly but cautiously down the stairs and stood close to the front door, edging towards the spy-hole, squinting through it.

The man she saw on the other side was in his late thirties, his hair receding slightly, but what hair he did have was thick and lustrous and reached the collar of his shirt. He was thin-faced, a little pale.

He shifted from one foot to the other as he waited for the door to be answered.

As Julie saw him reach for the doorbell a third time she opened the door and eased it back to the extent of the chain.

The man peered through the gap and smiled politely at her.

'Good morning,' he said. 'I'm sorry to disturb you. I was wondering if I could speak to Mrs Ward. Mrs Donna Ward.'

Julie eyed him suspiciously for a moment.

'My name is Neville Dowd,' he continued. 'Sorry, I should have introduced myself first.' He smiled warmly.

There seemed to be no threat in his manner.

Julie nodded a greeting.

'I was Mr Ward's solicitor,' he explained.

'Can I help you?' Julie wanted to know.

'I needed to speak to *Mrs* Ward, actually. I should have called round sooner but I've been on holiday and only returned yesterday to hear the news. It must be a very difficult time for her. I was going to call her into my office but I thought that would be a little heartless.' He smiled thinly, as if expecting praise for his gesture of concern.

Julie nodded.

'That's very good of you,' she said, some of her initial apprehension disappearing.

'May I ask who you are?' he said.

'I'm Donna's sister, Julie Craig.'

He extended a hand, tried to shake hers through the gap in the door. Julie slipped the chain and opened the door to its full extent.

'Sorry for the greeting,' Julie said, 'but you can't be too careful.'

'I agree. A woman here in a house like this, I

208

don't blame you being wary. Is Mrs Ward here, please?'

'She's away for a couple of days. Can I give her a message? I could get her to ring you when she gets back.'

Dowd looked perplexed.

'No, it's all right. Thank you, anyway. I don't want to keep intruding; she must have other things on her mind. It's just that there were some things I needed to clear up with her about her husband's estate. Some items I'd been holding for him. She should have them.'

'What kind of items?'

'I really shouldn't discuss that with anyone else but Mrs Ward. I'm sorry, I don't mean to be rude.'

'I understand.'

He looked down at his shoes which, unlike his suit, looked well-cared for.

'However, if you're not sure when she's going to be back . . .' He allowed the sentence to trail off. 'As long as she gets the items, that's all that matters. If you'd be so kind, you could pass them on to her from me. If she needs to get in touch with me for anything, she has my number.'

Julie nodded.

Dowd reached inside his jacket and pulled out a thick brown envelope. He handed it to Julie.

'Mr Ward said that this was only to be given to his wife in the event of his death,' the solicitor said.

'I'll see she gets it.'

Dowd extended a hand which Julie shook.

'Thank you for your help. Please pass on my condolences and tell her to call me if she needs any help.' He smiled, told Julie how delightful it had been to meet her and headed back to his car. She watched him slide behind the wheel of the Jag and start up the powerful engine. He turned the vehicle round in the drive and drove off. Julie closed the door again and slid the chain into place.

She lifted the envelope, testing its weight, then she moved across to the phone.

Running her finger down the notepad beside it, she found the number she sought and pressed the digits.

At the other end it began to ring.

Fifty-Two

6.46 p.m.

Julie cradled the mug of tea in both hands and looked at the wall clock on the other side of the kitchen. She checked her own watch.

'Come on,' she murmured irritably.

The phone on the wall close to her rang and she picked it up at the second ring.

'Donna?' she said.

'Yes,' the voice at the other end said.

'What kept you? I called this morning.'

'I've only just got back to my room and picked up your message. What's wrong?'

'Nothing, as far as I know. I've had a visitor today. Chris's solicitor, a man called Neville Dowd. Do you know him?'

'I met him a couple of times. What did he want?'

Julie looked at the envelope lying on the worktop. She told Donna about it.

'What's in it?' Donna asked.

'It's private. You didn't expect me to open it, did you?' Julie said, surprised. 'You'll have to look when you get back. How's it going, by the way?'

Donna told her sister what had happened in Ireland, the information she'd accumulated about The Hell Fire Club and also what she'd found in the library in Edinburgh. She explained a little about The Hell Fire Club itself.

'So that's what Chris was working on?' Julie said finally. 'Who the hell were the men who attacked you in Ireland?'

'I don't know. I don't know if it's linked to Chris's work either.'

'Can't the police do anything?'

'They can't act on maybes, Julie. I haven't got any concrete proof to show them.'

'Someone tried to kill you; how much more concrete does proof have to be?'

'Listen, I've been thinking about Chris's work. You know how deeply involved he got with it; he had on other books. I think he might have

211

discovered some kind of organisation *like* The Hell Fire Club. A modern day off-shoot of it. I'm not sure.'

'Then why didn't *he* go to the police if he had?'

'I don't know.' Donna sighed. 'I don't know what he was trying to do. I don't know if *she* was involved with it.'

'Who?'

'Suzanne Regan.'

'For Christ's sake, Donna, I thought you'd forgotten about that.'

'Forgotten about it? My husband dies in a car crash with his mistress and you think I can forget about it?'

'I meant about his love life. I thought you were supposed to be finding out what he was working on, not going on about what he might or might not have done with Suzanne Regan.'

'I think she was involved with it, too,' Donna said.

'How?'

'Some of the things I found out from books here today. I think Chris was using her to get himself accepted into the organisation, whatever it was.'

'You mean he was trying to join them?'

'It's possible. She could have been his way in.'

'What would he have gained by joining a group like that?'

'That's what I have to find out. I thought Martin Connelly might know, but I've phoned his office and his home a couple of times and there's never anyone there. Have you heard from him?'

'Why would he call *me*?' Julie said defensively.

'He might want to find out if *I* was back yet. If he *does* call, tell him I'll speak to him when I get back.' There was a pause, then the silence was finally broken by Donna. 'I think Chris was involved in something, Julie. Something dangerous. Perhaps that envelope Dowd brought round will answer some questions.'

Julie looked at the envelope lying on the worktop.

'There's nothing more for me here,' said Donna wearily. 'I'm coming home tonight. I'll get a shuttle flight.'

'Do you want me to pick you up from the airport?'

'No, I'll get a cab. I'll see you later. Take care.'

'You too.'

Donna hung up.

Julie gently replaced the receiver and walked across to the envelope. She picked it up, feeling the weight of it. It was packed tightly with papers and . . .

She ran her fingers gently over the manila surface and felt the outline of something small and cold inside. She pressed it with the tip of her index finger, trying to figure out what it could be. She frowned, gliding the pads of her fingers across the shape like a blind person reading braille, feeling every contour.

Fifty-Three

'She must die.'

The voice floated through the air like smoke, the words almost visible in the heavy atmosphere.

'Not yet,' another said. 'Not until we have the book.'

The room was large, the walls oak-panelled on two sides. The other two were dark brick. Paintings hung on them, large canvases in gilt frames. The room was lit by a number of small reading lamps, none powered by anything stronger than a sixty-watt bulb. It gave the room an artificially cosy feel, which was added to by the open fireplace and the array of expensive leather furniture that dotted the floor, spread out on thick carpet as dark as wet concrete.

The air was thick with cigarette and cigar smoke; a number of the twelve men seated there puffed away quite happily while they talked. They sat at different places in the room, most of them also with drinks cradled in their hands.

The house in Conduit Street was just two minutes walk from Berkeley Square in one direction and, in the other, the bustling thoroughfare that was Regent Street. The house and the room within were like a peaceful island in the sea of activity that constituted the centre of London.

The room was on the second floor of the three-storey building, its curtains drawn, its inhabitants hidden from those below. Windows like blind eyes reflected the lights of passing cars.

One of the men in the room got to his feet and crossed to a well-stocked drinks cabinet, refilling his glass, offering the same service to his colleagues.

They had been drinking for the best part of an hour but none were drunk. Even so, large quantities of brandy and gin were consumed as the men talked.

There was a large table in the centre of the room, made of dark polished wood. Two men sat at its head, their faces reflected in the gleaming surface. As the first of them drank, the gold ring on his left index finger clinked against the crystal.

'What if Connelly was lying?' said the one seated next to him. 'What if the woman doesn't know where the book is?'

'She knows,' the other said with an' air of certainty. 'She was at Rathfarnham, wasn't she? She went to the lodge at Mountpelier.'

'I want to know why she wasn't stopped there,' an angry voice from the other side of the room interrupted him.

'Those responsible for the mistake have been dealt with,' another said. 'Besides, we can't kill her until she's led us to the book or at least told us where we can find it.'

'If Ward *did* tell her about it then she might go to the police,' a third voice said.

'Let her,' chuckled another. Several others joined in the laughter.

One of the men at the head of the table brought his hand down hard on the table-top and the sound ceased.

'Enough of this. We need the book and we need it quickly. There isn't much time left.'

'We'll get it,' said another man, approaching the table. 'We'll get her *and* the book.'

The other occupants of the room gradually moved across to the table, each of them taking a seat around it.

'It must be in our hands within seven days,' one of the men wearing the gold rings insisted angrily.

'It will be.'

There was a note of certainty in Peter Farrell's voice.

'I hope for your sake that it is, Farrell. I hope for *all* our sakes it is.'

'What if *she* uses the book the way Ward was going to?' another voice added with concern. 'If she knew about the book, he may have told her about the contents, too.'

Farrell waved a hand dismissively.

'She's being followed now. There are two men on her. They'll find the book. They'll *make* her tell them where it is. And then they'll kill her. End of story.'

'What if they fail?' a worried voice interjected.

'They won't,' Farrell snapped irritably.

'You said that about the men who went to her house to search. *They* failed. Perhaps we underestimated her.'

'She's a woman,' Farrell chuckled. 'Just a woman.'

A chorus of laughter greeted his remark.

'So, we are agreed,' said one of the men at the head of the table. 'Once she tells us where the book is or she leads us to it, she dies.' He looked around at his companions. 'Yes?' He looked at each man in turn and waited for their compliance.

They nodded slowly, solemnly, like a jury passing sentence.

Farrell merely smiled.

'Perhaps we should have brought her here,' said one of the men. 'Let her enjoy our company for an evening.'

There was more laughter.

One of the men at the head of the table rose, his glass in his hand, the gold of his ring clinking against the crystal.

'A toast,' he said grandly.

'To the Death of God, the destruction of morality and to The Sons of Midnight.'

Francis Dashwood spoke the words with a grin on his wrinkled features.

Beside him, Richard Parsons echoed the toast, and so did the other men in the room.

'To The Sons of Midnight.'

Fifty-Four

The shuttle flights from Edinburgh to London were booked up right through until eleven that evening. Donna rang the station and discovered that there was a train to King's Cross leaving at 8.27 p.m. She booked a seat on it and took a taxi to the terminus.

Trains out of Waverley were running fifteen minutes late by the time she got there, but she didn't care. She wandered across the concourse to the Travellers' Fare buffet and sat warming her hands around a cup of coffee while she waited for her train to arrive.

She sat in the window, watching the streams of people coming to and from the trains. Taxis waited in a long queue to ferry them away, while others struggled up the stairs with cases or bags, determined to make their way by other means. She wondered how many of them were going home. Home to relatives, to loved ones. *To husbands?*

Donna felt a twinge of sadness and stared down into the depths of her cup, picking up the spoon and stirring unnecessarily, watching the dark liquid drip from the plastic utensil.

On the concourse people stood around gazing up at the departure and arrival boards, checking times of trains. She saw a young man squatting on a rucksack, eating a bar of chocolate and looking at the board. Close by a couple were kissing, holding each other close to ward off the cold wind that had sprung up. Donna watched them for a moment, then looked away.

One of the station employees was following a discarded wrapper across the concrete, trying to pick it up but thwarted every time by a fresh breeze that blew the litter out of his reach. Cursing, he continued his pursuit.

Donna finally got to her feet and wandered outside, glancing up at the board, noticing that her train was due in about five minutes.

She left the buffet and headed for the small John Menzies shop opposite.

She didn't notice the thick-set man dressed in jeans and a long dark coat get up and follow her out. He stood by the exit, watching, cupping one hand around the flame of his lighter as he lit up a Marlboro.

Donna glanced at the paperbacks on the bestseller stand as she entered the shop. Only six months earlier her husband's last book had occupied a prominent position on that stand and hundreds like it up and down the country. Again she felt that twinge of sadness. She selected three magazines, paid for them, then made her way back out onto the concourse.

The man outside the buffet sucked on his cigarette and watched her as she headed towards the gates and the platforms beyond. She paused to roll up the magazines and push them into her handbag, rummaging for her ticket.

The man in the long dark coat glanced at Donna, then back towards the Menzies shop.

Another man, dressed in a leather jacket and trousers that were too short, was walking briskly across the concourse, his eyes fixed on Donna. In fact so engrossed with her movements was he that he bumped into a young woman who was struggling with an impossibly heavy suitcase. He almost knocked her over but continued walking, ignoring her angry shouts. Other heads turned towards the commotion; indeed, even Donna looked round briefly. But she only saw the girl who had now returned her full attention to the case.

Other passengers for the train were forming a queue. Donna joined it, filing past the barriers, showing her ticket and heading down the platform towards the First Class carriages. As she passed the buffet car her stomach rumbled, as if to remind her she hadn't eaten since lunchtime.

She opened one of the doors and climbed up, selecting a double seat for herself, sliding her suitcase between two seats.

Further down the train the man in the long dark coat also climbed aboard.

The man in the leather jacket stood on the platform for a moment longer before stepping up into the carriage next to Donna's.

She spread her magazines out on the table and removed her shoes, massaging her toes as she waited for the train to pull away. There were perhaps half a dozen other passengers in the carriage, all spread out. Some read newspapers; one fiddled with a Walkman, adjusting the volume.

Donna shivered slightly, noticing how cold it was on the train.

The journey should take a little over six hours. She glanced at her watch as the train pulled away from the platform.

The man in the leather jacket walked to the door that linked the carriages and looked through, seeing where Donna was seated. Satisfied he knew her position, he returned to his seat.

There was plenty of time.

Fifty-Five

Apart from Donna there were only two other people eating in the train's dining car. They sat at the far end of the carriage, talking in hushed tones. Each man had a portable phone on the table beside him.

Donna enjoyed her meal, luxuriating in the warmth of the carriage. She felt tired and wondered if she might manage a couple of hours' sleep before the train reached London. It was about forty miles from York at present, so she had plenty of time.

She glanced up briefly as David Ryker passed

221

her, his leather jacket undone. As he passed by, Donna noticed that his trousers didn't touch the top of his shoes. She looked at his broad back, then at the short trousers, and smiled to herself, returning her attention to her coffee. When the steward returned with a steaming pot she had another cup.

Ryker passed her once more, glancing at her, cradling a plastic beaker of tea in his hand. As the train thundered over a set of points he steadied himself against her seat for a moment, then wandered off down the aisle.

Donna ordered brandy from the steward and sat gazing at the window of the train.

Apart from lights from distant towns, all she saw was her own reflection in the dark glass. The train sped along, countryside flying by in the gloom outside.

She moved across to the window, cupping one hand over her eyes so that she could see out, but there was little to see. They passed through a small station and she caught a glimpse of a couple of people standing on the windswept platform, but other than that there was nothing to see. She sat back and reached for her brandy. She closed her eyes and allowed her head to loll back against the pillow.

Was she any closer to a solution, to finding out why her husband had died?

He died because his car hit a wall.

But why? Was it *really* an accident?

The incidents in Ireland told her it wasn't, yet

she had no proof to support the fact that he had been killed. She was beginning to wonder if her trip had been worthwhile. She had also wondered if seeing the places he went might make her feel closer to him, but it hadn't. She was left with still more unanswered questions. Most of all, she was no wiser as to his involvement with Suzanne Regan.

Donna missed Chris badly. At nights, particularly, she had felt loneliness so great it was as if a hole had been torn in her soul, something irreplaceable had been ripped from her. Knowing of his involvement with another woman, however, had meant that that hole was in danger of being filled with hate, not sorrow. If only she'd had the chance to ask him why he'd had the affair.

She felt cheated, when she should have felt despair.

Just one chance to ask him.

One chance to say goodbye.

She sat forward and opened her eyes.

David Ryker's reflection filled the window beside her as he passed. For a second Donna thought he'd been standing there looking at her, this man in the leather jacket and trousers which were too short.

He retreated back down the aisle again.

Donna decided to take her brandy back to her seat with her. She paid the bill and walked back through the dining car, drawing glances from the two men at the other end with the portable phones. Both of them looked at her for a second, then continued their hushed conversation.

She made her way back to her seat, noticing that the man with the leather jacket was seated about five rows behind her.

Donna made herself comfortable and prepared to sleep, wondering, despite the fact that she was tired, whether or not the thoughts tumbling through her mind would be still long enough to allow her two or three precious hours' rest. She drained what was left in her glass and set it down.

'Mind if I join you?'

The voice startled her. She looked round to see Ryker standing there. His face was expressionless.

Without waiting to be invited he sat down beside her and crossed his legs, the trousers riding up almost to his calf.

'I saw you in the dining car,' he said. 'I thought you were travelling alone.'

'I prefer travelling alone,' Donna said, trying to be as tactful as possible. She smiled thinly at him.

'Can I get you a drink?' Ryker asked. 'I was going to have one.'

'No thanks, I *was* going to try and get some sleep,' she told him, an edge to her voice.

'I can't sleep on trains,' Ryker said.

And it doesn't look as if I'm going to be able to either, thought Donna irritably.

'I get bored,' he continued, looking up, noticing that another man was approaching.

224

A man in a long dark overcoat.

Donna saw him, too. Saw that he was looking at her.

She sat up, the puzzled look on her face turning to one of irritation.

The second man sat opposite her.

'I don't want to seem rude,' she said, 'but I was hoping to travel on my own. I . . .'

Ryker cut her short.

'Shut up,' he whispered. 'Just shut it.'

Donna turned to say something to him.

As he opened his jacket she saw his hand close over the hilt of a knife.

Opposite, the man in the long dark overcoat was smiling.

'We need to ask you some questions,' he said. 'We need your help.' He unbuttoned his coat and reached inside.

'And what if I call for the steward?' Donna said defiantly.

Stuart Benton pushed back his coat slightly so that she could see that he too carried a knife.

'If you do,' he said softly, leaning towards her, 'we'll slice you up like a joint of meat.'

Fifty-Six

'Who are you?'

Donna regarded the two men warily, her

gaze flicking from one to the other in quick succession.

'We need your help,' said Benton, staring at her. 'And you're going to give it. You're going to tell us what we want to know.'

Donna looked up and saw the steward coming up the aisle.

Could she alert him to her danger? *Should* she?

Ryker saw him too and nodded towards him.

Benton glanced over his shoulder and saw the man.

'Don't even think about it,' he said, his eyes blazing. 'I'll kill him, too.'

The steward smiled as he passed, glancing at the two men sitting close to Donna.

Benton watched him go.

'Well done, Mrs Ward,' he said, smiling.

'Don't patronize me, you bastard,' she snarled. 'And how do you know my name?'

'We've been following you since you left your hotel yesterday,' Ryker told her. 'The library, everywhere.'

'Was the book in the library?' Benton said.

'There's lots of books in libraries, you half-wit. You should try looking some time,' Donna said with gleeful malice.

'You fucking cunt . . .' Benton snapped, lunging forward.

Donna sat back in her seat, her heart thudding hard against her ribs. But it was Ryker who sat forward to restrain his companion.

'We can't hurt her,' he said quickly, hoping Donna hadn't heard. 'Farrell said not to hurt her yet.'

'Bitch,' hissed Benton. 'Fucking rich bitch.' He nodded slowly. 'Mouthy, just like your old man.'

'You knew my husband?' she asked.

'I saw him a couple of times. Flash cunt. Thought he owned the place. Too much mouth.'

'Did you kill him?' she wanted to know.

'No,' said Benton, 'but I wish I had. Perhaps I'll have to make do with killing his missus. Now, tell us where the book is. Are you going to pick it up now?'

'I don't know what book you're talking about,' she said.

The steward passed by again and Donna even managed to smile at him. She felt suddenly more secure despite the fact that she was flanked by men with knives. The train wasn't stopping until it got to London; there were other people in the carriage and surely these men wouldn't dare try anything here, now. If they harmed her there was no way they could get off the train other than jumping and, with it travelling at over ninety-five miles an hour, that didn't seem a very good idea. If she could call their bluff she might just be able to slip away.

Play for time.

She knew she had to keep her nerve.

Easier said than done.

'Do I take it that you work for the same

227

man as the two who broke into my house?' she asked.

Benton looked at his companion, who merely wrinkled his brow.

'I mean, they seemed to be incompetent morons like you. It's an understandable supposition. Don't you agree? Or would you prefer me to stick to words of one syllable?'

Benton leaned forward again, his face contorted with anger.

'I'm going to enjoy doing you,' he said angrily. 'I might even slip you one before I do.' He rubbed one hand across his groin. 'Right up your tight, rich twat.'

'And what do you think the other passengers are going to do? Just look the other way?'

'You think anyone's going to help you? Do you think anyone gives a fuck what happens to you? Nobody cares. They'll be too busy looking after themselves,' Benton hissed.

He and Donna locked stares for long moments.

'Where's the book?' Ryker said, jabbing her in the ribs with his elbow.

'Get off me,' Donna hissed.

'Where is it?' he asked, jabbing her again.

She tried to move away from him.

'Come on, bitch. Tell us.'

'Fuck you,' said Donna and kicked out hard under the table.

Her foot connected hard with Benton's right shin and he yelped in pain, reaching down to massage the throbbing limb.

Ryker jabbed her again with his elbow.

'Where is it?' he persisted.

'I'm going to fucking cut you,' Benton said, wincing in pain. 'I don't care what Farrell says.' He leaned closer. 'Get on your fucking feet, we're going for a walk.'

'I'm not moving from here,' Donna told him, meeting his steely gaze and holding it.

'Get up,' Benton repeated. 'I'll kill you, I swear I will.'

'You can't kill her,' Ryker reminded him. 'Farrell . . .'

'Fuck Farrell,' he grunted. 'We'll tell him she made a run for it, we had no choice.'

'He wanted her alive,' Ryker persisted.

Benton pulled the knife free of his belt, leant forward and touched the blade to Donna's left knee.

She felt the point against her stockinged leg.

'If you're not on your feet in five seconds I'll open your leg to the bone. You got that?'

Donna regarded him blankly for a moment, then nodded.

She stood up and squeezed past Ryker, picking up her handbag in the process. Throwing it over her shoulder, she set off down the aisle, the two men close behind her. As she passed the steward she nodded. He returned the gesture, looking at her two new companions.

Donna swallowed hard.

As long as she was on the train she was safe. Well, reasonably safe, anyway. There were other passengers around. What could they do to her?

The lights flickered briefly as the train entered a tunnel.

Donna kept on walking, aware that her two unwanted attendants were no more than a foot or so behind her.

The buffet car was up ahead; there was a young woman buying a drink and some sandwiches. Donna passed her, squeezing by. Ryker and Benton followed.

As they reached the area between two carriages Benton told her to stop. He pushed her towards the door, then reached into his coat pocket and took out a packet of cigarettes. He lit one, standing beside Donna, blowing smoke out of the window. Cold night air rushed in, ruffling her hair and making her eyes water.

What to do?

Ryker was standing by the door to the compartment, watching both ways for anyone approaching.

'Now, we'll start again,' Benton said, gripping Donna's wrist in one powerful hand. 'Where's the book?'

'I don't know,' she told him, trying to shake loose.

Benton leaned closer so that his face was only inches from hers.

'Have you ever seen anyone stabbed?' he said, spittle flying into her face. 'Do you know how much knife wounds can bleed?'

Donna pressed herself against the wall in a bid to move away both from his presence and his foul-smelling breath.

'I have to go to the toilet,' she said.

'What, so you can get in there and pull the emergency cord? Fuck off.'

'Then I'll have to piss all over your shoes, won't I?' Donna said defiantly.

Benton moved back slightly, then his lips curled into a crooked smile.

'You can go,' he told her. 'I'll stand in there with you. To make sure you don't come to any harm.' He chuckled and pushed open the lavatory door for her. 'Keep an eye open,' he told Ryker, pushing Donna into the small cubicle in front of him and pulling the door shut behind.

'Benton,' said his companion, grabbing the other man's arm. 'Don't kill her. I mean it.'

'I'll handle this.'

'Well then, *you'll* have to handle Farrell if you kill her. He said he didn't want her harmed until we find out what she knows about the book. Just go fucking steady, will you?'

Benton shook loose.

'And you just keep your eyes peeled. Right?'

There was scarcely room for one inside the cubicle, let alone two. Donna found the big man pressed close to her.

'What are you going to do? Stand there and watch me?' she demanded.

'I'm not going to turn my back on you, if that's what you were hoping. Go on, get on with it. Or do you want a hand?' He chuckled. 'I'll close my eyes, how's that?'

He did.

It was only a split second but it was all Donna needed.

She lashed out with her right foot, driving it into Benton's groin with all the power she could muster. She actually felt the bottom of his pelvic bone thump against her foot as she slammed his testicles up against the bone.

He howled in pain, the sound lost as the train hurtled into a tunnel.

Donna lunged at him, aware that his face was unprotected as he clutched at his genitals with both hands.

She raked his face with her nails, digging at his eyes, making him scream in renewed agony as she sheared a portion from his lower eyelid. Blood ran down his face. He tried to fight back, clutching at her throat and digging his thumbs into her Adam's apple, but she bit into his thumb until she drew blood, kicking again at the big man. She drove three kicks into his shins and smashed her handbag into the side of his head. Possessed of a strength born of fear and rage, she rained blows onto him, pushing him against the lavatory door, which flew open.

His face scratched and bleeding, contorted in a grimace of pain and anger, Benton toppled backwards, one hand reaching for the knife.

The train was still inside the tunnel, the wind howling like a mad banshee through the open windows. The lights flickered on and off.

Donna threw herself clear of Benton's groping hands.

She spun round and brought one heel down with tremendous force onto his outstretched hand.

The point of the heel crushed the tip of his index finger, splitting the nail as far as the cuticle. Blood burst from the shattered digit and Benton screamed again.

Donna turned as Ryker came at her, avoiding his clumsy attempts to grab her.

She was not so lucky with Benton, who sprang up and crashed into her, his arms locking around her waist, their combined momentum slamming them against the door.

The impact caused it to fly open. For what seemed like an eternity both of them were suspended in mid-air, filthy fumes pouring into the carriage from inside the tunnel.

Then the second passed.

Ryker tried to grab them but was too late.

They toppled out.

Fifty-Seven

She knew she was going to die.

In that split second, as she and Benton fell from the train, Donna *knew*.

The stench of the tunnel filled her nostrils; the roar of the train drummed in her ears. She felt weightless as they pitched into empty air.

Benton, in his terror, released his grip on her waist. His scream echoed madly inside the tunnel as he fell was slammed against the brickwork then bounced back against the speeding train, his body pulped by the impact.

Something inside Donna's mind, some shred of self-preservation, made her shoot out a hand.

She managed to grip the frame of the window on the door which was flying open now, banging against the side of the train.

Hold on, her mind screamed. *Hold on*.

She used all her strength to grip the frame, her body buffetted by the high-speed wind that swept against the train as it roared along. Her hair whipped around her face; she felt the icy chill filling her. Her fingers were beginning to go numb.

She was losing her grip.

The train burst free of the tunnel and Donna shouted in defiance, managing to get her other hand onto the frame, too. But all she could do was hang there from the side of the speeding train, unable to move, knowing her strength would eventually fade. It was only a matter of time before she fell.

'Grab my hand,' roared Ryker, extending a hand. 'I'll pull the door shut.'

He gripped the open door and pulled, one of his hands closing over Donna's.

She had visions of him slowly unpeeling her fingers, prising them from the door until she fell.

But instead he used all his strength to heave the door shut, battling against the onrushing wind as the train continued to hurtle along.

Donna felt faint; she thought her grip was failing.

HOLD ON.

Ryker pulled the door another few inches, pulled her closer.

If only she could hang on . . .

She felt her feet trailing through the weeds that grew at the side of the track, nettles and thistles tearing her skin as she was dragged through them at high speed.

'Take my hand,' Ryker shouted, bellowing to make himself heard. 'I'll pull you in.'

Donna didn't have time to think. She hadn't the luxury of considering her options.

She gripped his hand as tightly as she could, feeling a terrific wrench on her shoulders as he tried to haul her in, steadying himself against the door to ensure that he didn't end up suffering the same fate as his companion.

'Your other hand,' he shouted. 'Give me your other hand.'

She had one hand clamped in Ryker's, the other wrapped round the door frame. If she relinquished her grip on the door she was completely at his mercy.

'Come on,' Ryker screamed at her.

There was another tunnel approaching, looming large and dark, ready to swallow her and the train.

She heard a loud roar and realized that the 125 was sounding its air horn. A warning as it entered the tunnel.

She looked ahead, saw the yawning black mouth and the dark hillside around it.

Saw the lights.

Lights which got brighter as they came closer.

There was another train coming the other way on the track next to her.

It would leave the tunnel as her own train entered.

There would be less than five feet between the massive engines.

She would be crushed between them.

Donna let go of the door and allowed Ryker to grab her other hand.

He pulled as the two trains drew closer.

'Come on,' he screamed and heaved her upwards, clutching at her dress to pull her inside while she held his arms, squirming her legs through the window.

They both fell in an untidy heap on the floor.

The other train swept past with a roar and a deafening hiss of air. Then it was gone.

Donna rolled onto her back, her eyes half-closed, her limbs numb. She could feel nothing but the cold, that seemed to have filled every pore of her body. Her ankles and shins were scratched and bloodied, her stockings shredded by the trackside weeds and nettles.

Ryker knelt beside her, shook her, rubbed her arms as if trying to restore the circulation. She was still cold. Numbingly, almost painfully cold and some of it was shock.

'Why did you save me?' she said quietly, looking at Ryker.

'Because I need you alive,' he said, still rubbing her arms.

'I need information from you.' He looked worried.

'Who are you?' she slurred, close to fainting.

He struck her hard across the face to prevent that.

Then she felt his arms beneath her shoulders, lifting her, pushing her into the lavatory, locking it behind him. He sat her on the seat and stood looking down at her.

She glanced up and saw the knife hidden inside his jacket.

A thought occurred to her and she almost smiled.

Out of the frying pan into the fire.

Don't all laugh at once.

Donna rubbed both hands across her face, her body quivering as she began to regain some warmth, some feeling in her extremities. Her shoulders ached; her hands and legs were throbbing.

'I saved your life,' said Ryker. 'Now tell me what I want to know.'

She closed her eyes.

The banging on the door made her open them again.

Fifty-Eight

'Conductor,' the voice outside called.

Ryker shot an angry glance at Donna and mouthed something she couldn't make out. She held his gaze then called, 'Just a minute.'

Ryker looked at her with sheer hatred. For one terrible second she thought he was reaching for the knife.

'Open it,' she whispered, nodding towards the door.

'I'll kill you and whoever's outside that door,' Ryker said.

'You wanted me alive, you said,' Donna told him defiantly. 'Kill me and you don't get your information. Now open the door.' They glared at each other for a second longer, then Ryker turned the lock and pushed the door open.

The conductor looked in on them, eyebrows raised.

'What the hell is this?' he said irritably, seeing the two dishevelled occupants of the lavatory. 'What's going on?' He saw the cuts and scratches on Donna's legs. 'I've heard about this sort of thing before,' he said, as if realizing what he'd stumbled on, or at least what he thought he'd stumbled on. 'Very funny. I know what you've been up to. Another couple tried it on one of my trains a month or so ago. I caught them, too.'

'It isn't what you think,' Donna said, running a hand through her hair.

'No, I'm sure it's not,' the conductor said disbelievingly.

'I can explain,' Donna assured him.

Ryker said nothing.

'I fell, I hurt myself,' she said. 'This gentleman,' she nodded towards Ryker, 'he helped me. I needed to sit down for a minute. I must have fainted, I think. This was the nearest seat.' She smiled and patted the toilet beneath her.

The conductor looked at Donna, then at Ryker.

'Is this true?' he asked the other man.

'Yes,' Ryker said sharply, trying to hide his anger.

'Then why was the door locked?' the uniformed man wanted to know.

'I didn't want anyone bursting in and getting the wrong idea, like you have,' Donna said, smiling again.

'Well,' said the conductor, 'it does look a bit suspicious, you'll admit. Two people in one lavatory, I mean . . .' He allowed the sentence to tail off.

'I agree,' Donna echoed. 'If I could just go back to my seat I'll be okay. Could you help me, please?' she asked the conductor.

Ryker regarded her furiously as the uniformed man extended a hand to help her up.

'Are you two people not together, then?' the conductor asked.

'No,' Donna told him, smiling. 'It was just lucky for me this gentleman was passing.' She looked at Ryker. 'I hurt my ankle when I fell. The floor was harder than I thought.' She looked down at her scratched and grazed legs.

'Would you like me to see if there's a doctor on the train?' the conductor asked as he walked back through First Class with her. 'I can get them to call it out over the loudspeaker.'

'No thanks, I'll be fine.'

Ryker trailed along behind, his expression one of growing agitation. His chance, it seemed, was gone. How the hell was he going to get the information he required from her with the conductor prattling about? He clenched his fists in frustration and annoyance. *And fear?*

What would Farrell do if he failed?

The conductor saw Donna to her seat and ensured she was comfortable.

Ryker sat down opposite her, his eyes still blazing.

'Would you like a brandy?' the conductor said. 'It'll calm your nerves. I can get you one from the buffet car.' He winked. 'On the house.'

'That's very kind of you,' Donna told him. 'Thank you.'

He scuttled off to fetch it, leaving them to face one another across the table.

'I'm going to kill you,' Ryker hissed.

'You're not going to do anything,' Donna told him, anger in her voice. 'You said you needed me alive, that *you* wanted some answers. Well, so do I. I want to know who you are and who you're working for, and don't fuck me around or I'll have this train stopped. Tell the truth or the law will be here before you can make a move. I'll tell them you pushed that other bastard out of the train and tried to kill *me*.' She looked at him with a challenging stare. 'Who's Farrell? You said Farrell didn't want me harmed. Who is he? The man who sent you?'

'Fuck you,' Ryker said.

She leaned closer.

'No, fuck *you*. You're scared of him, aren't you, whoever he is? That's why you didn't want that other moron to hurt me. It's why you pulled me back inside the train when you could have left me to die. You're not going to get another chance to threaten me. This train doesn't stop until it reaches London now, and I'm not moving from this seat. If you want to risk killing me, that's fine, but you're going to have to kill the conductor and the other passengers in this carriage, too. Have you got the stomach for that, or are you only brave when you're threatening a woman?' She sat back, smiling. 'You blew it. You should have let me fall, like your friend. But you daren't, dare you? You gutless piece of shit.'

Ryker leaned forward menacingly, anger colouring his face.

241

'One brandy,' the conductor announced, returning with the drink and handing it to Donna.

She thanked him.

'Will you stay with me for a minute? This other gentleman is going back to his seat now,' she said, smiling at Ryker.

'I can stay,' he said through clenched teeth.

'No,' said Donna, making a great show of concern for him. 'I'll be fine now. Besides, I just need to relax. I might even get a couple of hours sleep before we reach London. Thank you for your help.'

Ryker hesitated a moment, then got to his feet. He paused, looked at her then stalked off down the aisle.

Donna took a sip of the brandy, feeling it burn its way to her stomach.

Most of the chill had left her now and, with Ryker's departure, she felt more comfortable. Nevertheless, she realized that she was only safe until the train reached King's Cross. Once in the capital, she was fair game once more. She had to find a way to escape him.

'Are there phones on board this train?' she asked.

'I'm afraid not,' the conductor said.

Donna felt her heart sink.

'I've got one of these bloody things, though, if you want to borrow it,' the uniformed man said, pulling a portable phone from his pocket. 'We use them for getting track information and arrival times, that sort of thing. I can speak to the driver on it if I want to,' he said, smiling. 'Not that I want to, miserable bugger.'

Donna felt her spirits rising again.

'The reception's a bit haywire sometimes, especially in tunnels, but it should be okay,' he reassured her.

'Thank you,' she said, taking the phone from him. He checked that she was all right, then told her he'd be back in a while and wandered off down the aisle.

Donna called to him.

'What time do we get to King's Cross?'

He checked his watch, then pulled a timetable from his jacket pocket. He ran his finger down the list of times.

'We've made up some time,' he informed her. 'As long as there's no hold-ups, we should be in about 1.30 a.m.'

She thanked him, then turned her attention to the phone, punching in digits.

She glanced at her watch.

10.16 p.m.

At the other end, the phone was picked up.

'Julie, it's me.'

'Where the hell are you? I . . .'

The line crackled.

'Just listen to me, I haven't got time to explain. I'm on a train from Edinburgh, it arrives at King's Cross at 1.30. Julie, you *must* be there to pick me up. Do you understand? You *must* be.'

'Donna, what's going on . . .?'

'I told you, I can't explain now. I'll tell you

everything when I see you. Julie, we've got to go to the cottage in Sussex. I want you to drive me from King's Cross down to the cottage, right? Just listen to me. Go into the wardrobe in our room, get the guns and the ammunition and bring them with you. Bring the letter from Chris's solicitor, too. Please, just promise me you'll do it.'

'Why can't you tell me . . .'

Donna cut her short angrily.

'Just do it, Julie. King's Cross at 1.30. For Christ's sake, be there.'

'I'll be there,' Julie told her.

Donna pressed the 'End' button on the phone and laid it on the table.

While she was on the train she was safe. Once they reached King's Cross she had no idea what Ryker would do. She looked at her watch again.

In less than three hours she'd know.

Fifty-Nine

Donna cupped one hand over her eyes and saw the lights of King's Cross through the window as the train slowed to a crawl, preparatory to gliding to a halt.

She was already on her feet, glancing back in the direction of the next carriage where Ryker was. There were a couple of men standing there by the door, waiting for the train to pull in and stop.

Of Ryker there was no sign.

She picked up her suitcase and made her way along the aisle, pausing to inspect the damage to her legs. She'd removed her ripped stockings earlier and now, as she looked down at the patchwork of scratches and grazes, she was relieved that there hadn't been more damage. There was one cut just above the ankle; it had bled only slightly. She shuddered when she thought what her fate might have been.

The conductor appeared, smiling broadly.

'Would you like a hand with that case?' he said.

She accepted the offer gratefully, feeling the train slow down even more as it cruised into the vast amphitheatre of concrete and glass that was the terminus itself. Other trains, some also newly arrived, stood emptily by platforms, their passengers long since departed. At this early hour there weren't that many people on the concourse. It wouldn't be so easy to melt into the background.

She glanced behind her to see if she could catch a glimpse of Ryker.

Still he was nowhere to be seen.

She looked at her watch; they were on time. She prayed that Julie was waiting for her.

The conductor was babbling on good-naturedly about long train journeys but Donna scarcely heard what he said. She smiled and nodded as he wittered on, moving towards the door as the train drew into the platform. The conductor pushed the

245

door open and peered up the train to see that others were doing the same.

It finally bumped to a halt. All the doors were thrown open and the uniformed man climbed down first, offering Donna his hand as she stepped onto the platform.

The first thing that struck her was the cold. It was freezing inside the huge building; it was as if someone had sucked every ounce of warm air from the interior and replaced it with icy breath. As she exhaled, her own breath clouded before her.

It was quiet, too, every sound echoing around the cavernous dome. Footsteps on the dark concrete platforms seemed to reverberate inside her head.

She walked quickly beside the conductor, who carried her case towards the barrier. There was no guard there to check tickets. Donna glanced around, looking for Ryker amongst the three or four dozen other people who had left the train along with her.

He was nowhere to be seen.

They were drawing closer to the barrier now and Donna began looking for Julie, praying that her sister was waiting, hardly daring to contemplate what she would do if she wasn't.

The conductor was still chatting happily. Donna didn't even bother to acknowledge his ramblings now, her mind was too occupied. Her eyes were too busy picking out faces amongst the other passengers.

Where was Ryker?

She glanced over her shoulder.

He was less than ten yards behind her, hands dug deep into his jacket pockets, walking fast, gaining on her. He pushed past an old woman in his haste to reach Donna, looking at the woman angrily as he nearly tripped over her suitcase.

Donna tried to quicken her pace, hoping the conductor would do likewise.

Ahead of her were half a dozen people, two of them pushing trolleys laden with luggage. Donna looked back at Ryker, then ahead once more.

She quickly slipped ahead of the trolley pushers as one of them blocked the exit, manoeuvring his way through. Those behind were prevented from going any further.

Including the conductor.

He walked to the barrier and handed Donna her case over the rail.

'I'll be okay from here,' she told him, seeing Ryker drawing nearer. 'Thank you for your help.' She took the case and spun round.

The first trolley was still stuck, its owner now flustered, aware that he was blocking everyone else's way.

Ryker pushed against the back of a man trying to get through and got an angry glare for his pains. He could see Donna on the other side of the barrier heading towards a dark-haired woman, whom she embraced.

They headed for the car park outside.

Ryker vaulted the barrier and ran after them,

slipping one hand into his jacket, touching the hilt of the knife.

He ran out through the main doors and looked to his right and left.

No sign of them.

He scurried over to the taxi rank. None of the vehicles had just picked up. There was no sign of Donna or the other woman. He stood on the pavement, hands on his hips.

'Fuck,' he rasped, knowing he'd lost them. He turned and walked slowly back into the station, heading for the payphones. He found one that took money rather than a card and dialled a number.

His hands were shaking.

It was picked up after a couple of rings.

'Farrell,' the voice at the other end said.

'It's Ryker,' he said, trying to control the anxiety in his voice.

'Well?'

'We lost her.'

At the other end the phone was slammed down.

Sixty

The headlights of the Fiesta cut through the darkness.

It was almost 2.45 a.m. The roads were all but

deserted south of London. The deeper into Kent Julie drove the more the two women began to feel as if they were the only people left on earth. Nothing was moving on the roads apart from them, it seemed.

Perhaps it was a good thing.

It was all Julie could do to concentrate on driving, as she listened incredulously to the chain of events her sister recounted.

Donna felt exhausted, drained both physically and emotionally. She lay slumped in the passenger seat, a jacket around her knees to keep her warm. The heating was on inside the car but it did little to drive out the chill that seemed to have settled in her bones. Recalling what had happened to her, especially on the train, served to intensify that cold.

She had come so close to death.

She shuddered.

Was that how Chris had felt seconds before he died?

She closed her eyes for a moment.

'We should call the police,' said Julie.

Donna ignored her.

She was thinking of what had happened on the train. About the two men, their threats. Their fear of the man who had sent them to find her. What had Ryker said his name was?

'Donna, I said we should call the police. This is too serious now,' Julie persisted.

Farrell. She opened her eyes, her tired mind gradually focusing on that name.

249

On that face.

'My God,' she whispered. 'It was the man at the house the day Chris was buried.'

'What are you talking about?'

'I told you that one of the men on the train kept saying that *Farrell* needed information from me, that *Farrell* had said I wasn't to be killed. That day at the house, the day of the funeral, I caught a man in Chris's office going through his papers. *His* name was Farrell. Peter Farrell.'

'It could be a coincidence.'

'It could, but I doubt it. He was looking for something that day; he said it was a book. Those men were looking for information about a book. Farrell sent them. It's the same man, I'm sure of it.'

'Even if it is, what does it prove?'

'It proves that Chris had something Farrell wanted. Something he thinks I've now got. Something which he was prepared to kill for.'

'Then call the police,' Julie insisted.

'They haven't been able to protect me so far,' Donna snapped.

'So what are you going to do with the guns? Shoot anyone who attacks you?'

'Did you bring them all?'

'Yes, and the ammunition. They're in the boot. You didn't answer my question.' She looked across at her sister. 'Donna, you can't take the law into your own hands. This isn't America. It's not some bloody film where the heroine straps on a gun and blows away the bad guys. This is reality.'

'And it was reality on that train when I was nearly killed,' Donna answered angrily.

'Who do you think you are? A female Charles Bronson? Call the police, for Christ's sake.'

'Julie, whoever those men are, whoever this Farrell is, they want something badly enough to kill for it. They might have killed Chris. They've *tried* to kill me. If they try again, they might not be too fussy about who they hurt in the process.' She looked at her sister. 'You're in danger, too. Perhaps it would be best if you left me at the cottage and went back to London. I've already involved you more than I should have. You should get out while you still can.'

'You really think I'd leave you now?' said Julie softly.

'I wouldn't blame you if you did.'

'I'm staying with you, Donna. No matter what. But I'll tell you something, I'm scared and I don't mind admitting it.'

'Join the club,' Donna said flatly.

They drove most of the remainder of the journey in silence, speeding through Kent into West Sussex, along roads flanked by hedges and trees, past isolated houses and farms.

It was approaching 3.15 when the headlamps picked out a sign that proclaimed:

WARDSBY 15 MILES

CHICHESTER 18 MILES

Donna instructed Julie to take the left-hand fork in the road.

Sixty-One

The ferocity of the assault lifted Peter Farrell off his feet.

He was slammed into the wall with crushing force and enough power to knock the wind from him. Reeling from the onslaught, he toppled forward but managed to keep his feet until a second attack pinned him to the wall and held him there.

'You said you would get the book,' snarled Francis Dashwood, gripping Farrell by the collar. 'We relied on you and you failed.'

Farrell recoiled, not from the verbal tirade but from the rank stench that wafted over him every time Dashwood spoke. It was a smell like rotting meat, a rancid, cloying odour that made him nauseous.

'I'm sorry,' he said breathlessly, trying to inhale as little of the fetid air as possible.

'Your apologies are no good to us,' roared Richard Parsons. 'We need the book, not your pathetic excuses.'

Dashwood let out a howl of frustration and hurled Farrell across the room. He crashed into a table, somersaulted over it and landed heavily on the carpet. He lay there for a moment before rolling over and getting to his knees.

The other two men advanced upon him.

'It has kept us alive for over two hundred years,' Dashwood told him. 'Get it.'

Farrell clambered to his feet, breathing heavily, forced to inhale the reeking smell. He looked at the other two men. There was a yellow tinge to their skin. Parsons' eyes looked sunken, with blue-black rings around them making him look badly bruised. The flesh of his hands appeared loose, as if it didn't fit his bones.

The skin beneath his chin hung in thick folds that swayed back and forth as he walked.

Dashwood looked even worse. A sticky, pus-like fluid dribbled from the corners of both his eyes. The orbs themselves were bulging in sunken sockets, criss-crossed by hundreds of tiny red veins, each one of which looked on the point of bursting. Like Parsons, his skin was sagging in places like an ill-fitting suit. In others it had begun to peel away in long coils. One of these coils hung from his left cheek like a spiral, frozen tear.

The stench inside the room was practically intolerable.

'Your men failed at the house and then on the train,' Dashwood reminded him.

'We will not tolerate another failure. *You* must get the book and bring it to us personally,' Parsons told him. 'Do you have any idea how important it is? Not just to us, but to everyone connected with this organisation?'

'If the contents were to be known, as Ward wanted them to be known, the results would be catastrophic,' Dashwood reminded him. 'Get the book.'

He shoved Farrell, who fell backwards, colliding with a chair and almost falling again.

'It isn't at the house,' he said, looking at each of the men in turn. 'We've already checked. She didn't have it with her . . .'

Dashwood cut him short.

'Are you sure of that?' he snapped.

'I'm not *sure*, but . . .'

Farrell was interrupted by a powerful blow across the face. As it landed he felt the repulsively soft feel of Dashwood's skin against his own.

'You know what will happen to us if the book is not found,' snarled Dashwood. 'You can *see* what is already happening.'

He grabbed Farrell again and pushed his face within inches. 'Look.' He touched the coil of rotting flesh with his free hand, pulling it slowly free. The skin tore slightly, leaving a red mark. Dashwood pushed it towards Farrell's lips, jamming the length of putrid flesh into the other man's mouth.

Farrell closed his eyes as he tasted the rotting matter on his tongue.

'Taste our pain,' hissed Dashwood, gripping Farrell's chin, forcing him to chew on the strand of flesh. As he spoke his foul breath swept over Farrell in a noxious cloud. 'Smell our suffering.'

Farrell knew he was going to be sick.

He felt Dashwood's index finger inside his

mouth, pushing the slippery piece of skin further into the moist orifice.

'Swallow it,' Dashwood demanded.

Farrell did as he was told and retched violently, falling away from Dashwood, feeling his stomach churn, eager to be rid of the disgusting matter inside it. He bent double and vomited, falling to his knees in the puddle of his own regurgitated stomach contents. The bitter stench mingled with the odour of putrescent flesh and he almost retched again but found that there was nothing left to bring up. His muscles contracted but could force nothing else out.

He sucked in deep, racking breaths and looked up at the two men.

Could the word be accurately applied to these two apparitions?

'Where is the woman now?' Parsons wanted to know.

'She hasn't been back to her house,' Farrell said. 'Someone picked her up at King's Cross. Another woman.' He wiped his mouth with the back of his hand. 'They could be anywhere.'

Dashwood took a menacing step towards him.

'My guess is they've gone to the other house,' he said quickly. 'The one Connelly mentioned before he died. If they have, we'll find them. *And* the book.'

'If you don't, it will mean *your* death as well as ours,' Dashwood told him. 'Now go.'

The stench of death hung in the air like an odorous, invisible cloud.

Sixty-Two

The cottage stood about two hundred yards back from the road, accessible only by a narrow drive flanked on both sides by stone walls. The walls extended round not only the front garden but the entire property, stark grey against the white walls of the cottage. The slate roof was mildewed in places and the guttering shaky, but otherwise the place was in a good state of repair.

Ward had bought it four years earlier with part of the advance on one of his books. He and Donna used it during the summer, making frequent week-end trips; Ward himself had written at least two books there. The cottage had no phone, something he had insisted on to prevent interruption when he was working. The nearest neighbour, a farmer well into his seventies, was more than five miles and a range of low hills away.

Donna guessed that it was more than two months since she had been to the cottage.

She wondered if he had ever brought Suzanne Regan here and found it more than usually difficult to wipe the thought from her mind. Even the stress of the past few hours had not removed the memories of his betrayal.

She stood in the small sitting-room and ran her finger along the top of a sideboard, drawing a line in the dust that had accumulated. The room was about twelve feet square, furnished with old, antique oak merchandise they'd bought from a shop in Chichester during their first visit to the place. It had few ornaments: a vase or two, an ashtray and a couple of ceramic figures. The windows were leaded.

The ground floor consisted of just the sitting-room and a large kitchen. The entrance hall seemed disproportionately large. There was a trap-door in the centre of the kitchen floor, which led down to a deep cellar. Ward kept old manuscripts down there. He also kept a substantial store of wine in the subterranean room. He had never been a great wine drinker, but on every visit to the Mayfair Hotel in London (which he used often) he was presented with a complimentary bottle of wine. He never drank them but always brought them home with him to add to the array in the cellar.

The floor of the lower ground room was of earth. Donna rarely ventured down the wooden ladder into it; it was not well lit and, despite Ward's attempts to convince her otherwise, she was certain that the entire cellar was seething with spiders, creatures she was frightened of.

A bare wood staircase led up to the first floor, which comprised a bathroom and two bedrooms. In the first bedroom a door opened onto a short flight of rickety steps that led to an attic. Ward had often threatened to have it converted into a work room but, as is the case with most attics, it remained nothing more than a storehouse for junk that wasn't wanted elsewhere in the cottage.

The obvious thing seemed to be to retire to bed; both women felt crushing exhaustion. But they seemed to have reached that point where they could not sleep despite their tiredness. Donna took a hurried bath, Julie made them some tea and, as the hands on the clock above the open fireplace crawled round to 3.56, they both sat down, one on either side of the table in the centre of the room.

In the centre of the table were two aluminium boxes resembling metal attaché cases.

Donna flipped the first one open and lifted the lid.

In the half-light cast by the lamps the metal of the Smith and Wesson .38 and the Beretta 92s gleamed.

Donna took each weapon from the case in turn, checked it and replaced it. She then opened the second case and performed a similar ritual with the .357 and the Charter Arms .22.

She flipped the cylinders from the revolvers and checked the firing actions, listening to the metallic click of the hammers on empty chambers. She worked the slide of the Beretta, then took fifteen rounds from the box of 9mm ammunition. She thumbed them into the magazine before placing it carefully back in the box with the weapon.

She loaded the revolvers, too, leaving the chamber beneath the hammer empty. Those two she replaced, then carried upstairs.

'I hope to God you know what you're doing,' said Julie when her sister returned.

'This is life and death, Julie,' she said solemnly.

'Then why don't you just call the police?' the younger woman said, agitated.

Donna didn't answer; she merely sipped her tea.

'I think you want it to come to this, don't you?' Julie snapped. 'You don't care if you kill them.'

'They tried to kill *me*.'

'And if you do kill anyone, *you'll* be the one who'll go to prison.'

'I'll take that chance.'

'Let's just hope it doesn't go that far.'

'It already has.'

They regarded each other for long moments, then Julie reached into her handbag for the envelope. She handed it to Donna, who turned it over in her hands, seeing Ward's handwriting on the front. She smiled thinly and ran her index finger over the Biro scribble.

I miss you.

'It can wait until morning,' she said quietly. 'We should get some sleep.'

Julie agreed.

Donna took the envelope upstairs with her and laid it on the bedside table. Before she got into bed she touched it once, running her fingertips over the smooth manilla package. Then, naked, she slipped between the sheets.

Her last waking thought was of her dead

husband. As she drifted off to sleep, a single tear rolled from her eye.

I miss you.

Sixty-Three

The book is called Domus Vitae, which is translated as 'The House of Life'. It was written by a man called Edward Chardell in 1753. Only one hundred copies were printed. The copy I discovered is, as far as I know, the only one in existence. It is vital to the members of The Sons of Midnight. Vital to their survival and also to their protection.

Every member of the club, from its formation back in 1721 right up until the present day, is forced to write his name in the book. I have those names. I know those names. That is why I stole the book and that is why they want me dead and why they need the book back. If its contents were released then they would be destroyed; but also the repercussions would be enormous.

The actual content of the book itself consists of a series of spells and invocations designed to be used at meetings of the club, just as similar books were used at meetings of The Hell Fire Club all over Britain and Ireland. Each club had one of these books which they called Grimoires, and the loss or destruction of these Grimoires has accounted for the disappearance of other branches of The Hell Fire Club over the years. The Sons of Midnight are the only remaining group I know of, still linked to the original Hell Fire Club. I have researched everything about them, their customs, their members and their motives. They trusted me enough to allow me into their ranks, but when I saw what they were planning I knew that the only answer was to destroy them, expose them.

They must be stopped. Their aims are sedition. They have infiltrated everywhere. Every branch of the Media, Politics and the Church. They are more powerful than anyone can imagine, more dangerous than anyone could realize. Perhaps I might be able to stop them by exposing them but I don't think they will allow that to happen. However, I have made contingency plans. Even if they kill me there are still ways to stop them.

Destroy the book. Destroy that and you destroy them. Especially Dashwood and Parsons. They need the book to live. Its very existence guarantees them life. Without it they are dead.

But don't look to anyone for help. They have members everywhere. No one can be trusted. Fight them alone. I tried and I would have succeeded. I hid the book from them, I covered my tracks as well as I could.

The location of the book I felt was too important to put down in this note. The key you will find enclosed fits a safety deposit box in the Chichester Branch of Lloyds Bank. Take the key and remove the contents of the box then find *the book. Directions and instructions and also a description of the Grimoire itself are contained in there. The bank manager, Maurice Langton, is under orders not to allow anyone to open the door except you, Donna. Take this letter with you when you go there.*

I pray that it is you reading this, my darling. If not then nothing I have written before matters. If it is you, then do this for me.

I love you. I will always love you, more than I thought it was possible to love anyone.

Christopher Ward.

Sixty-Four

Donna put down the note and ran her hands over the paper, as if trying to smooth out the creases. She was shaking slightly. Julie could see the tears in her eyes as she re-read the sheet of paper, touching her dead husband's name with her fingers as she read.

'Oh, Chris,' she murmured quietly, wiping one eye with the back of her hand.

He loved you. Then why did he have an affair?

Jesus, even now it plagued her. She lowered her head.

'Donna, are you all right?' Julie asked, slipping one arm around her sister's shoulders.

Donna nodded.

'We have to go,' she said, sucking in a deep breath, folding the note again. She looked at the small key on the table, then dropped that into the envelope with the note.

'No one can be trusted,' Julie said, echoing the words on the paper. 'You were right not to call the police.'

'Is my paranoia catching?' Donna laughed humourlessly. 'I've said it to you before, but I'll say it again. If you want to leave I'll understand, but you're the only one I can trust now.'

Julie touched a hand to her cheek.

'We'll do it together,' she said softly, holding Donna's gaze. The older woman stood up and the two of them embraced, holding each other tightly, neither wanting to let go, united in their grief and also in their determination.

'Come on,' said Donna finally. 'Let's get to that bank.'

In the daylight Julie could see the holes in the road which, the previous night, she'd only been able to feel. The surface was badly pockmarked and the car bumped and bounced over the uneven thoroughfare, its journey only becoming smoother as they reached the main road that would lead them into Chichester itself.

Along the way they passed through one or two collections of houses masquerading as villages. The sun managed to escape the shackles of dark cloud every now and then; when it did, glorious golden light fell across the countryside.

But for the most part the land remained in shadow.

As they drew close to the outskirts of Chichester itself rain clouds were gathering. As Julie finally found a parking space close to the bank the first droplets of rain were striking the windscreen of the car, like oversized tears.

The two women hurried across to the main doors of the bank. It was quiet inside. At the 'Enquiries' desk a young man with a strange, flattened haircut looked up from behind the counter. He smiled, ran swift appraising eyes over both women and coloured immediately.

'Can I help you?' he asked.

'I want to see the manager, please,' Donna told him.

'Can I ask what it concerns?'

'Could you just fetch him, please? It *is* important. Tell him my name is Donna Ward. My husband was Christopher Ward.'

The young man nodded and scuttled off, returning a moment later with a much older man in tow. The older man regarded the two women expressionlessly for a moment, then stepped forward. Donna made quick introductions. The man told her in a broad Scots accent that he was Maurice Langton, the manager. Then he invited them both through into his office.

'I was very sorry to hear about your husband, Mrs Ward,' Langton said, closing the door of his office and ushering them towards two chairs.

'My husband kept a safety deposit box here,

didn't he?' Donna said. She reached into her handbag and took out the key. 'I need to see the contents.'

'There are one or two forms to be signed first . . .' Langton began but Donna cut him short.

'That's all right,' she said briskly. 'It's important.'

Langton looked at her for a moment, then reached into his desk. He produced the necessary documents and handed them to her, pointing out where she should sign. She did so and handed them back to him, her irritation scarcely hidden.

Langton realized her impatience and ushered them out of the office towards another door, which he opened with a heavy key he took from his pocket. Beyond it fell a flight of stone steps which led down to the bank's vault. The walls on either side of the stairwell were dazzling in their brightness. Led by the bank manager, the two women descended to a corridor and more antiseptically white walls that seemed to crowd in on them like banks of snow. Langton led them through two more doors, finally coming to a small room with a desk and two chairs. To the right was another door; beside this one stood a uniformed man in what looked like a Securicor outfit. He looked impassively at the trio of visitors as they approached.

Julie waited outside while Donna and Langton passed through the last door into the vault itself. She saw hundreds of drawer facings, row upon row of safety deposit boxes. Langton led her to the one she sought.

'Your key, Mrs Ward,' he said.

Donna just stared at the box.

'I need your key,' he said, almost apologetically.

She nodded, handed it to him and watched as he put her key into one of the locks and the duplicate he carried into the other, turning both simultaneously. He pulled the drawer free and carried it outside for her, setting it on the desk.

'Just call me when you've finished,' he said and stepped back.

Donna sat looking at the box for long moments. Then, finally, hands quivering slightly, she reached for the contents.

All it contained were two envelopes.

Two flat, white envelopes.

'What the hell is this?' said Julie. '*This* is the big secret?'

Donna slipped the envelopes into her bag and called Langton back over.

'Did you know what was inside the box?' she asked him.

The manager looked aggrieved at the suggestion he might be privy to the contents of one of the high-security lockers.

'You knew there were just two envelopes in there?' she continued.

'I had no idea what was in there,' he said.

'Was my husband alone when he brought them

in?' Donna wanted to know. *Or did he have another woman with him?*

'Most certainly,' Langton told her. 'Is there something wrong, Mrs Ward?'

She shook her head, thanked him for his co-operation and then headed for the way out. Julie followed closely behind. They passed back the way they had come, past the gleaming white walls and up the stairs. Donna thanked Langton again and the two women left the bank.

Inside the car, Donna glanced at the two envelopes then slipped them into her handbag.

'Get us home,' she said, 'as quick as you can.'

Sixty-Five

By the time Julie parked the Fiesta outside the cottage the sky was a mass of dark cloud. Rain was falling fast now, drenching the countryside, turning the road that led to the cottage to mud, puddling in the ruts.

The two women jumped out and sprinted for the front door of the cottage, Donna struggling with the key. She finally pushed the door open and they both tumbled gratefully inside. Donna hurried through into the kitchen and sat down at the wooden table, pulling the envelopes from her handbag. For long moments she stared at them, as if reluctant to open them. She knew for sure that

267

one contained the means to finding the Grimoire. The contents of the other was a mystery.

'Open them, Donna,' said Julie, her impatience getting the better of her.

Donna looked at her sister reproachfully.

'Give me time,' she said quietly.

A part of her didn't want to; in some strange way it meant severing her links with Chris. As long as there had been secrets, she had felt close to him but now, with the opening of these two slim packages, the last of those secrets would be gone. Just like *he* was gone. Her hands were shaking as she reached for the first of the envelopes.

It looked relatively new. The paper was untainted by age. She wondered how long they had lain in the safety deposit box.

There was a single sheet of paper in the first one.

It bore a name and an address.

'George Paxton,' she read aloud. 'Wax Museum.' And then an address in Portsmouth.

'That must be where he hid the book,' said Donna. 'He wrote a novel about a waxworks a few years ago. Chris said he'd become friendly with the owner; that must be who this Paxton character is.'

'Why hide it there?' Julie wondered.

Donna could only shrug.

'We don't even know what the bloody thing looks like,' Julie added. 'It could be anywhere there. Paxton might even have it himself. How the hell are we going to find it?'

There was more writing at the bottom of the sheet.

'The Crest on the Grimoire is a hawk, family crest of its author,' she read. She looked at Julie, her eyes alight. 'A hawk?' Donna reached into her handbag and pulled out the photo of Ward and the five other men. She looked carefully at the picture, studying the rings on the index fingers of the two shadowy figures.

They too bore engravings of some kind.

She squinted more closely.

'A hawk,' she said triumphantly, jabbing the picture with her index finger. 'The crest on those rings shows a hawk. You can see the wings.'

Julie squinted at them.

'Jesus,' she murmured.

Donna was already opening the second envelope.

It was another single sheet of paper, this time with typed letters on it:

RATHFARNHAM, DUBLIN.
BRASENOSE COLLEGE, OXFORD.
REGENCY PLACE, EDINBURGH.
CONDUIT STREET, LONDON.

Dublin, Oxford, Edinburgh and London. *And beside each entry D.*

'Chris was at all these places shortly before he died,' Donna said. 'They must have been meeting places for The Hell Fire Club he discovered.'

D for Dashwood?

'We have to get to Portsmouth,' Donna said, 'and find that book.'

'We can't go in this weather,' Julie said, looking out of the window. The rain was coming down in a solid curtain. It was as if God had kicked a bucket of water over. 'We'll be stranded, with the state of the roads around here.'

'As soon as it stops,' Donna said.

'If it stops,' Julie added quietly, gazing up into the heavens.

The rain continued to pour down.

7.08 p.m.

The sky still wept.

The ceaseless deluge had turned the small front yard of the cottage into a swamp. Water poured through the guttering and splashed noisily from the eaves. It was falling so fast that rivulets of rain streaming down the window-panes made it difficult to see out at all. Darkness had come prematurely with the deluge, the gloom summoned early by such an abundance of black cloud. The sky looked like one massive mottled rain cloud.

Donna sat in the sitting-room, glancing endlessly at the sheets of paper they'd picked up from the bank that day and also at the notes Ward had left. She knew the words off almost by heart.

'*Destroy the book and you destroy them.*' She exhaled deeply and massaged the back of her neck with one hand.

'*They must be stopped.*' A throbbing headache was beginning to gnaw at her.

'*They have infiltrated everywhere.*' Donna closed her eyes for a moment.

'*No one can be trusted.*'

'Donna.'

Julie's shout caused her eyes to snap open. She looked round and saw her sister standing at the window, gazing out.

'Come here,' the younger woman said, a note of urgency in her voice.

Donna did as she was asked and stood beside her sister, peering through the rain and darkness.

Two cars were moving towards the house, both with their lights turned off.

'Who are they?' Julie wanted to know.

Donna was reasonably sure she knew. When she spoke, her voice was low.

'Lock the doors and windows,' she said. 'Hurry.'

Sixty-Six

The cars stopped about twenty yards from the front of the cottage. One of them parked across the narrow track leading away from the building; it acted as a barrier.

Donna saw men scuttle from the vehicles, two of them running towards the house, slipping in the mud but keeping their balance.

271

She recognized one of them as Peter Farrell.

Julie was busily locking the doors and windows, sliding bolts and turning keys. Donna seemed transfixed by the approaching men. She saw two more of them move towards the sides of the cottage. She turned and ran upstairs.

'What's happening?' Julie asked breathlessly, hurrying to secure a window-lock on one of the kitchen windows.

The face loomed up out of the darkness and leered at her through the rain-soaked glass.

Julie screamed and took a step back.

The man held something in his hands.

Something he was swinging towards the window.

The iron bar struck the frame and the glass simultaneously, shattering the glass, sending shards spraying into the kitchen.

Julie screamed again and threw herself to one side, hissing in pain as a silver of broken glass sliced through the flesh on the back of her left hand.

The man outside struck at the window again, smashing more of the wooden frame, then he dropped the iron bar and snaked one hand inside, trying to slip the catch.

'No,' shouted Julie. She picked up a knife lying on the draining board by the sink, and drove it towards the man's hand. She heard him shriek in agony as the blade pierced it, cutting through the web of skin between his thumb and index finger. Embedded in the wood, it momentarily skewered him to the window-frame. Julie saw blood pumping thickly from the wound.

With a shout of pain he tore his hand free, the flesh ripping as he dragged himself away from the knife, leaving it embedded in the wood.

Julie snatched at the knife as the man disappeared back into the blackness outside. Rain now poured in through the broken window, the wind also whipping through, buffeting Julie as she moved across to the back door.

The impact against it was enormous.

It seemed to bow in the centre; for one terrible second she thought that it was going to split.

The second blow sent the door flying open. For fleeting seconds Julie found herself staring into the rain-soaked face of the intruder. He fixed her in a maddened stare and she saw the blood running from his gashed hand.

'Fucking bitch,' he hissed and lunged towards her.

On the cooker to her right stood a frying pan the two women had used for their meal less than an hour ago.

Julie snatched up the heavy skillet and swung it with all her strength.

It smacked savagely into the man's face, flattening his nose. The bones splintered under the force of the blow and blood spilled down his chin and the front of his jacket. He staggered.

She struck again, wielding the frying pan like a club, bringing it down hard on the top of his head with a blow hard enough to cut his scalp.

He dropped to his knees and tried to scramble away but Julie hit him again, kicking him hard in the ribs as he fell to the ground.

She dropped the frying pan and used both hands to push the back door shut, heaving with all her strength as the man tried to block it with his body.

She pulled the door back a foot or so then slammed it forward, catching him between the heavy wooden door and the frame. He grunted in pain.

She slammed it on him again.

And again.

He let go and ducked back into the driving rain.

Julie banged the door shut and slid the bolts into place.

Donna had been rummaging beneath the bed upstairs, where she'd pulled out both of the metal cases. She flipped one open and took out the Beretta and the .38, jamming one into the waistband of her jeans. Then she rushed back towards the stairs, almost falling in her haste to get back to the ground floor.

As she dashed into the sitting-room she heard movement outside the front door and immediately swung the automatic up into firing position.

It had been a while since she'd fired a pistol and the initial retort took even *her* by surprise. In the confines of the cottage the noise was thunderous.

The 9mm bullet left the barrel travelling at over

1,200 feet a second and cut a hole through the door. She fired again, and again.

Movement by the window.

Donna fired.

The glass exploded outwards and rain suddenly came pouring in through the hole. The curtains billowed madly as the wind caught them and Donna dashed across to the light switch and slapped it hard, plunging the room into darkness.

With her ears ringing from the massive blast of the weapon she threw herself down and crawled across to the wall by the front door, able to see back through the sitting-room to the kitchen.

She could see Julie also crouching down, one hand closed around the handle of the frying pan.

Outside she heard footsteps in the sucking mud.

The lights upstairs were still on; if she could only get to a window she might be able to see what the men outside were doing.

Rain continued to sweep into the cottage, driven by the strong wind that screamed around the building.

For interminable seconds the only sounds were the wind and rain and the heavy beating of her own heart.

Donna crouched where she was, the Beretta held close to her, the stink of cordite strong in her nostrils.

The attackers had obviously been surprised by the ferocity of their defence. Perhaps, she reasoned, they had left, not expecting to be greeted with guns.

There was no sound from outside, although it was difficult to pick out anything in the torrential rain that battered both cottage and landscape.

Donna got to her feet, still keeping low, and moved towards the small round window close to the front door in the hall.

If only she could get a look, see what they were up to . . .

It was pitch black; she could scarcely see a hand in front of her. Her breathing was deep and she tried to control it, tried to stop herself hyperventilating. She gripped the pistol more tightly as she reached the wall beneath the window and rose slowly.

Just one quick look.

Her heart thudded madly against her ribs and the blood sang in her ears.

She steadied herself, ready to look through the window.

Then the first burst of gunfire tore across the front of the cottage.

Sixty-Seven

The roar of the UZI sub-machine gun was deafening. In the howling wind and driving rain the burst of 9mm fire looked and sounded like man-made thunder and lightning. The muzzle flash illuminated Farrell and the yard around him for several feet as he raked the sub-gun back and forth, spent cartridge cases spewing from the weapon; smoke and steam rising into the damp air.

Windows were blasted inwards by the fusillade. Bullets drilled into wood or stone or sang off the walls with a loud whine. Lumps of plaster were torn free. Part of the guttering at the front of the cottage was blown away.

The hammer finally slammed down on an empty chamber. Farrell angrily ripped the empty magazine free and rammed a fresh one in.

A dark figure appeared at his side, limping.

'She locked the back,' said Frank Stark, wiping blood from his broken nose away with the back of his hand.

'I didn't expect her to have a gun,' said Brian Kellerman, peering at the cottage, shielding his eyes from the driving rain.

'I don't care if she's got a fucking cannon in there,' Farrell snapped, pulling back the slide on the UZI. 'Get inside.'

He fired another short burst from the sub-gun, blowing in an upstairs window.

Fragments of glass and shattered window-frame fell. He raised his eyebrows.

The porch was directly beneath the window. Anyone managing to get on top of the porch could easily clamber up through that bedroom window.

Farrell grabbed Kellerman and pointed at the window.

'You and Stark get in through there,' he said. 'Ryker, you go round the back again. Listen, all of you, we need Ward's wife alive, got it?'

'What about the other woman?' Stark wanted to know.

'Who gives a fuck?' said Farrell and opened fire.

More bullets spattered the front of the cottage, drilling lines back and forth in the stonework. Dust was washed away as the rain continued to pelt down.

Stark and Kellerman ran towards the house, keeping low, as anxious about Farrell's erratic covering fire as they were about Donna's possible retaliation.

Three bullets suddenly hit the ground only inches ahead of Stark.

The muzzle flash that accompanied their arrival came from inside the house.

He pitched forward, throwing himself down in the glutinous mud, covering his head with his hands as Farrell replied, bullets slicing through the air and singing above the prone man's body, missing him, it seemed, by mere inches. He kept his face pressed to the muck as bullets drilled holes in the wall and door. Lumps of wood were blasted free.

More shots from the Beretta came back, one of them striking the car. The 9mm slug exploded one of the Orion's headlights, smashing the housing and causing Farrell to jump back and seek cover behind the vehicle.

Kellerman reached the porch and hauled himself up onto it, hoping that the wooden canopy would take his weight. He looked down and saw his colleague still lying in the mud, not daring to move. Kellerman wondered if he'd been hit. He turned and saw that the window ledge was about three feet above him. He steadied himself, then shot out both hands and gripped it, hauling himself up the wall to the beckoning entrance.

Farrell saw him and smiled.

Donna scrambled through the hall to the sitting-room, the automatic smoking in her hands.

'How many of them are there?' Julie asked frantically.

'It's hard to tell,' Donna said breathlessly. 'I think I might have hit one of them.' She crept towards the shattered front window and peered out.

Stark was no longer lying in the mud.

'Shit,' snapped Donna, sinking back down to the floor.

Rain was still driving through the broken window.

'Oh God,' gasped Julie, pointing towards the kitchen.

Donna saw it too and her eyes widened in panic.

One of the men had set fire to the kitchen curtains.

Flames were licking hungrily at the material; it was blazing fiercely. She could smell petrol.

'Put it out,' she screamed at Julie as another burst of fire from the UZI spattered the cottage.

Donna sucked in a deep breath and headed for the stairs, intent on getting a clearer look at what was going on outside. From a vantage point up high she would be able to see their attackers.

Julie meanwhile was filling a saucepan with water, trying to stay clear of the flaring curtains. Thick black smoke spread through the room, thousands of tiny cinders filling the air like black snow. She coughed as she felt the heat searing the air in her lungs. It made her eyes water but she stayed where she was until the saucepan was full, then tried to douse the flames. One curtain went out, extinguished by the shower of water. Julie tugged hard at the remains of it and pulled it down. The other one continued to burn. She refilled the saucepan, sweat soaking her body despite the cold wind and driving rain blasting through the smashed window.

Ryker loomed at her through the flames and she hurled the water both at him and at the fire.

He grinned. She dropped the saucepan as she saw him raise the pistol and aim at her.

He fired twice and Julie threw herself down as bullets ploughed into the kitchen table. Another hit a vase on the sideboard. It promptly disintegrated in a cloud of dust, pieces spinning in all directions.

He fired again.

Julie rolled over, finally propping herself against the back door, touching the bolts there to reassure herself that it was locked.

She almost screamed when she felt the blows raining against it.

Donna emerged on the landing, momentarily frozen, unsure what to do. She had heard the shots from downstairs, heard Julie's shouts, but what to do? Go back downstairs or try and get a better shot at one of the bastards from up here?

She chose to move on.

The door to her left was open slightly; she could feel cold air blowing through.

Donna shoved the door open, steadying herself against the frame, the Beretta raised.

Stark was caught completely by surprise.

For one moment he looked as if he was raising his hands in surrender, then he leapt forward.

Donna got off two shots before he crashed into her.

The first missed and blasted a hole in the far wall.

The second caught Stark in the left shoulder. The bullet ripped through his deltoid muscle and pulverized part of the scapula as it exited, the impact enough to spin him almost three hundred and sixty degrees.

He yelled in pain, then crashed into Donna, both of them falling, hitting the floor with a thud that knocked the wind from her.

The Beretta flew from her hand, bounced against the wall and skidded down the stairs.

She reached for the .38 jammed into her waistband, trying to pull it free as Stark grabbed for her throat.

Donna didn't manage to get her finger around the trigger but she did pull the weapon clear, closing her hand around it and using it as a club.

She drove it into the side of his head as hard as she could, hearing a crack as she smashed his temporal bone.

Stark fell to one side and Donna scrambled out from beneath him. He tottered drunkenly to his feet and reached inside his jacket. She saw his fingers close around the butt of a .45.

Donna fired twice.

From point-blank range the first bullet hit him in the stomach, doubling him up as it punched a hole just to the left of his navel, ploughing through intestines before lodging close to his spine.

The second hit him in the right shoulder, the impact lifting him off his feet and sending him toppling towards the head of the stairs.

He threw out a hand, clutching at empty air, then fell backwards, tumbling head over heels down the steps, finally crashing to a stop at the bottom, where he lay in a spreading pool of blood.

Downstairs, Julie looked across and saw Stark hit the floor, her attention diverted only momentarily from the blows still raining against the door.

She felt sure that, any second, the wood must splinter and the attacker would be inside.

She looked around desperately for something to defend herself with.

The tool box was lying in one corner of the room, close to the cellar hatch.

Jesus, the cellar.

That was it.

She crawled across the floor in the darkness, her body drenched in sweat, her eyes stinging from all the smoke.

She grabbed a hammer from the tool box and crawled back towards the cellar hatch. Lifting it, she peered down into the blackness below, feeling the first rung of a rickety ladder as she dangled her foot into the yawning gap.

She eased herself down a few rungs, praying it wouldn't collapse under her.

The stench of damp that enveloped her was noxious; she tried to take short breaths. Gripping the hammer in one fist and propping the hatch up with her free hand, she crouched low so that she had about an inch gap through which she could see the back door.

The door was starting to split from its merciless battering.

One of the hinges was coming loose.

Julie gripped the hatch and waited. She almost screamed when she felt something soft touch her face.

A spider the size of her thumbnail dropped past her in the gloom, its legs brushing her cheek.

She gripped the hammer and waited.

The door was practically off its hinges now. One more blow and the attacker would be inside.

Julie swallowed hard, closing her eyes.

There was a final crash and the door, and Ryker, hurtled into the kitchen.

Upstairs, Donna heard the sound of forced entry, her eyes still fixed on the barely moving form of Stark.

Had she turned round quicker, she might have seen Kellerman advancing upon her.

Sixty-Eight

The attacks happened simultaneously.

Kellerman launched himself at Donna.

Ryker crashed into the kitchen, looking for Julie.

Donna heard a grunt as Kellerman grabbed her, pinning her arms by her sides, lifting her off her feet. She could not raise the pistol to use against him.

She found herself looking directly into his face as his arms tightened around her in a bear hug that threatened to crush her ribs.

With horror she realized he was carrying her to the top of the stairs.

Donna twisted in his grip but could not free herself.

She screamed loudly, but it was a bellow of rage not helplessness.

Kellerman grinned at her but the gesture faded instantly as Donna spat in his face, the mucus sliding down his cheek thickly like gelatinous tears. She snaked her head forward and bit hard into his nose, biting down with all her strength, ignoring his shrieks of pain, trying not to gag on the blood that filled her mouth.

He let go of her and staggered back, reaching for his gun.

She ran at him now, driving one foot up, kicking him with all her force between the legs.

He groaned and dropped to his knees, grabbing her other leg and pulling hard enough to send her flying. She hit the floor with a bone-jarring thud and lay there, momentarily dazed. Kellerman leapt on her, his weight pressing down. She jabbed two fingers into his eyes and he screamed and rolled off her, trying to rise to his feet, blinded by her attack. Her stabbing nails had torn his left upper eyelid and blood from the wound dribbled down the side of his face, some of it running across the orb itself, turning one half of his world crimson.

Donna tried to raise the .38, anxious to get a shot at him, but he knocked her hand down and the gun discharged into the floor. The thunderous retort deafened them both momentarily. He struck out again, this time with the back of his hand, catching her a blow across the face which split her top lip and sent her reeling. But she still held the gun and, as Kellerman turned on her, Donna shook her head clear and fired at him.

Luck playing a somewhat greater part in the matter than judgement, the bullet struck him in the calf, tore through the muscles there and exited, spattering the wall behind with blood and pink tissue.

He screamed and almost lost his footing as he made for the stairs.

Donna, her head spinning, tried to follow but he was halfway to the bottom before she managed to get off another shot. The heavy-grain slug powered into the wall inches above Kellerman's head. He looked up at her, teeth gritted, his face a mask of blood from his injuries.

She saw him stop and slide an arm around Stark's waist, carrying his companion towards the front door, both of them leaving a trail of blood behind.

Donna tasted her own blood as it ran into her mouth from the cut on her lip.

She tried to follow and almost fell down the stairs, gritting her teeth to prevent herself passing out.

She had to get to Julie.

As Ryker came careering into the kitchen, Julie threw back the cellar hatch and came hurtling forth like a maddened trap-door spider, brandishing the hammer.

So startled was he by this sudden onslaught, Ryker momentarily froze, rooted to the spot.

Julie swung the hammer with all her strength and caught him in the mouth with its gleaming head.

She heard teeth shatter under the impact, saw one of them driven through his top lip. Saw blood burst from the cut.

He reeled backwards, one smashed incisor falling from his bleeding, pulped gums.

Julie struck again, this time catching him just above the right eye, tearing the flesh. The hammer carved through his eyebrow and opened up a cut as deep as the frontal bone it cracked.

Julie spun the weapon, bringing the clawed part down on his hand as he raised his fists in defence.

The metal tore into his flesh, ripping it away, slicing effortlessly through skin and muscles, exposing a portion of the middle-finger knuckle.

Ryker ran for the shattered back door, out into the driving rain and the darkness, which suddenly seemed welcoming.

Julie stood by the back door, rain drenching her, mingling with the tears of rage and fear on her cheeks. She tasted blood and thought that it was Ryker's, but then realized that her own face was gashed just below the left eye, she guessed by flying glass.

Panting breathlessly, she turned from the door and moved through to the hall, where Donna was trying to make her way down the stairs.

From outside, they both heard the sound of car engines.

Julie, still gripping the bloodied hammer, looked cautiously through the window by the front door.

She saw two cars disappearing down the dirt track, away from the cottage, their tail-lights gradually swallowed by the gloom and the relentless downpour.

'Donna,' she gasped.

Donna said nothing; she just dropped to her knees, the .38 still gripped in her fist, face bruised, her lip bleeding.

Julie dropped the hammer and found she was sobbing uncontrollably. She was standing in a pool of blood.

Sixty-Nine

It wasn't a matter of *if* they would return; it was merely a question of *when*.

Donna sat at the sitting-room window, the Beretta on the sill in front of her. On the coffee table to her right lay the .38 and the .357. All had been reloaded.

On the sofa behind her Julie was sleeping fitfully, a blanket covering her, her face pale and drawn, dark rings beneath her eyes. The cuts on her hands and arms had been cleaned and bathed, then covered with plaster. She'd been fortunate to escape more serious injury from the flying glass.

Donna herself touched her lip tentatively with one finger, feeling how it had swollen. There was a dark bruise surrounding it; she hoped that the discoloration wouldn't last too long. Her sides ached when she inhaled, and when she moved too quickly she felt a sharp pain in her lumbar region. As the night wore on it began to diminish. There were more bruises on her arms and legs, and some on her shoulders.

The house had been cleaned as well as was possible. The broken windows had been boarded up with pieces of wood from the attic. Donna had re-attached the back door to its frame as well, while Julie mopped up the blood in the hallway – although she finally passed out during the task. Donna had helped her onto the sofa, woken her gently but then realized that she was becoming hysterical. She had been forced to slap her face to quieten her. Tears had followed, both women understandably shaken by their ordeal, by the knowledge of how close to death they had come.

And of how close they might come again.

Donna felt herself dozing and sat upright, shaking her head free of the crushing tiredness that threatened to envelope her. Another fifteen minutes and she would wake Julie. They had agreed to keep the vigil between them. One would watch for two hours while the other slept.

Donna reached out to touch the butt of the automatic, as if the feel of the cold steel would somehow shock her from her lethargy.

How easy it would be to surrender now, she thought, not only to sleep but also to the demands of these men. How easy to give them the book they sought, to be done with the entire affair.

And just walk away?

Donna knew that was impossible. Even if she did tell them the whereabouts of the Grimoire, there was no way they were going to spare her *or* Julie. Too much damage had been done; she knew too much about them now. They would have to kill her.

As they had done her husband?

She still didn't know for sure if Chris had been murdered. The police had been convinced it was a genuine accident that took his life

(and that of his mistress)

but after what she'd been through, after what she had discovered, Donna could not believe that men willing to kill for the possession of a book had not taken the life of the man she'd loved.

Once loved? Before his affair?

She administered a mental rebuke. She and her sister had almost been killed only hours earlier and all she could think about, it seemed, was her dead husband's infidelity.

No one can be trusted.

How prophetic had been those words he'd written. How apt. How irritatingly, fittingly, fucking appropriate. She gritted her teeth in anger and pain.

And frustration?

No. She would not give in to these men. She would not let them have the Grimoire.

She wanted it. Not because she needed it, but because she was determined no one else should have it. It was like a prize. This hunt for the book had become a contest and Donna intended winning.

Life and death.

Win or lose.

There was no turning back now, even if she wanted to.

Life or death.

She looked at the guns.

Seventy

'Farrell, he's dying.'

'What do you want me to do about it?'

'Help him.'

Brian Kellerman looked down at Frank Stark, then at Farrell.

Stark was lying on his back in the motel room, his shirt open to reveal the bullet wound close to his navel. Blood pumped slowly from the hole, which was tinged black and purple at the edges.

Kellerman himself looked bad. His nose was little more than a bloodied lump and the bruising around his left eye was so severe he could barely see out of it. He had two or three minor cuts and grazes on his cheeks; they looked as if someone had pulled a fork through the flesh.

On the other bed in the double room of the Travelodge David Ryker sat, head bowed, hands clapped to both sides of his skull. Every now and then he would spit blood onto the carpet. He had bandaged his cut hand so tightly his fingers were beginning to go numb. He touched his shattered front teeth with his other hand, feeling part of one smashed incisor come free. He spat out enamel and blood.

Farrell was sitting at the table in the room, thumbing 9mm bullets into two magazines for the UZI. Each held thirty-two rounds.

Fucking women, he thought, pushing the high calibre shells into the box magazine. Fucking bloody women. They were spoiling everything, those two troublesome cunts. He gritted his teeth, loading the bullets more quickly. Jesus, he'd make them pay. Especially Ward's wife. That fucking bitch would wish she'd never seen the book or *him* or anything to do with it. He'd put a bullet in her brain himself. No, he'd put several in. Hold the UZI against the base of her skull and let rip. Blow her fucking head right off. Turn her face and head into confetti. He slammed the full magazine into the weapon and gripped it for a moment, the veins in his temple throbbing angrily.

On the bed Stark groaned loudly and clapped hands to the wound.

'We've got to do something about him,' snapped Kellerman.

'Have you got any suggestions?' Farrell wanted to know 'Do you want to call the ambulance yourself? Why not call the police, while you're at it? Tell them how he was shot. What he was doing when that crazy mare put three fucking bullets in him. Go on, call them.' He banged his fist down on the table and glared at Kellerman.

'We'll have to leave him here,' said Ryker, probing another loose tooth.

'And when he's found?' Kellerman asked. 'What then?'

'We'll be long gone,' Farrell said. 'There's nothing to link him to us. We'll take his ID with us so they won't be able to identify him.'

Stark coughed, a sticky flux of phlegm and blood spilling over his lips. The movement made the pain worse and he groaned even more loudly.

Farrell regarded the man impassively.

'I didn't expect them to have guns,' said Kellerman, gazing down at his stricken companion.

Farrell didn't answer.

Ryker got to his feet and wandered into the bathroom. He inspected the damage to his mouth again, wincing as he saw just how much destruction Julie had wrought with the hammer. His lip was torn, a flap of skin hanging uselessly from it. The area between his gashed top lip and his nose was heavily bruised. Blood had congealed on his other front teeth; when he licked his tongue back and forth he could taste the coppery tang. He

293

allowed a long streamer of mucus to hang from his mouth, watching as it struck the white enamel of the sink and trickled slowly into the plughole, leaving a crimson slick behind it.

'So we leave him here?' Kellerman protested. 'Just leave him to die . . .'

'Do you want to stay with him?' hissed Farrell, turning the UZI on Kellerman. 'Do you?'

Kellerman looked at the dying man, then stepped away from the bed.

'What about the women? Do we go back there? Try again?' Ryker asked, returning from the bathroom, wiping his mouth with the back of his hand.

Farrell shook his head.

'We follow them. Let them lead us to it. Then we'll take care of them.' He stroked the short barrel of the sub-machine gun. His eyes strayed to the telephone. The other two men saw him looking at it.

'What makes you think they'll try to get it?' Ryker asked. 'After what happened tonight they might have had enough.'

'This isn't over until we've got that book. Besides, Ward's wife will want to get her hands on it. She's stubborn, like her fucking old man was. She won't give up now.'

He looked at the phone again then lifted the receiver, aware that his hand was shaking.

He dialled the number and waited.

Seventy-One

Julie Craig sat at the wheel of the Fiesta, her head bowed. She sucked in a deep breath then looked up, squeezing her eyelids tightly together as if to clear the fuzziness which clouded her vision. But it wasn't her vision that was affected, she realized; it was her mind. She felt as if someone had wrapped her thoughts in a blanket. Reasoning seemed difficult; actions were a major effort.

'Do you want me to drive?' Donna asked, looking across at her sister.

'No, it's okay,' Julie replied, starting the engine.

The rain slowed to a fine drizzle which hung over the countryside like a dirty curtain. The yard in front of the house and the dirt track were little more than liquid mud. The rear wheels of the Fiesta spun, trying to gain purchase in the sucking ooze. Finally Julie stepped harder on the accelerator and the vehicle moved off. She flicked on the windscreen wipers. One of them squeaked but neither woman seemed to notice the irritating sound. Both kept their eyes fixed firmly ahead.

Donna dared not settle herself too comfortably into her seat in case she dozed off. She doubted she'd had more than three hours sleep the previous night, and Julie only a little more. It showed, too; despite their make-up, they both looked pale and wan. Donna had managed to disguise the worst of the bruising on her top lip beneath some foundation cream and a little rouge had given at least some artificial colour to her cheeks, but as she pulled down the sun-visor on the driver's side and peered into the mirror she realized she *looked* as tired as she *felt*.

She had no idea how long the drive into Portsmouth would take. Two hours, perhaps less? The road conditions and Julie's emotional state weren't going to help. Again Donna asked if *she* should drive but Julie merely shook her head.

'This man at the waxworks,' she said. 'What's his name? Paxton? Have you ever met him?'

'No, but Chris got on well with him. He helped him a lot with research about the history of the building, how the models are made, that sort of thing.' She sighed. 'Chris must have trusted him in order to hide the Grimoire there.'

No one is to be trusted.

'But he didn't say whereabouts he hid it?'

'No. I doubt if Paxton knows either,' Donna said, looking at the piece of paper she'd collected the day before. Beside the address of the wax-works, it also had two phone numbers. One she guessed was the owner's home number; as it was Sunday, she might well need it. Off season, she doubted if the attraction would be open. It was hardly the weather to attract day-trippers, either.

'So what do we do when we find it?' Julie asked.

'I wish I knew,' Donna confessed. 'Read it?' She smiled thinly.

She glanced at the dashboard clock.

1.56 p.m.

By the time they reached the outskirts of Portsmouth the rain had practically stopped, but the sky was still slate grey and threatening. There wasn't much traffic on the roads until they approached the city centre, and then roads became a little more clogged. Julie had cold air blowing into the car in an effort to keep them both alert. The crushing weariness was a formidable enemy, though, and she felt her eyelids drooping as if they'd been weighted.

'I'm going to have to stop for a while, Donna,' she said finally. 'I'm practically driving asleep.'

'I know how you feel,' her sister said, pointing at something up ahead. 'There's a café there. Let's get a coffee.'

Julie checked the rear-view mirror and prepared to swing the car across the road into a parking space. At the last moment she stopped the manoeuvre and drove on instead.

Donna looked at her in bewilderment.

'I thought you were stopping,' she said.

Julie didn't answer, but drove on towards the traffic lights, glancing again in the rear-view mirror. They were amber as she swung the car round to the right and through them, heading down a side street, taking another right then another until they were back on the street where they'd started.

297

'I appreciate the tour of the block,' said Donna, smiling, 'but what's wrong?'

'We're being followed,' Julie said flatly.

Donna's smile faded immediately. She sat forward so that she could see into the Fiesta's wing mirror.

'How can you be sure?' she wanted to know.

'Because whoever's driving went through a red light to keep up with us.'

'Which car?'

'The Granada,' Julie said, and Donna saw the dark blue vehicle behind them.

'What shall I do?' Julie asked.

'Pull in,' Donna said unhesitatingly. 'See what he does.'

Julie nodded, indicated again and this time swung the car into a gap in front of the café.

The Granada drove past, disappearing around a corner.

'They spotted me,' Brian Kellerman said into the two-way radio.

'Where are they now?' Farrell wanted to know.

Kellerman told him.

'All right, we'll follow them from here. You keep out the way. I'll let you know where we're heading, but keep back. If they spot you again we might lose them.' Farrell switched the two-way off and jammed it into the seat pocket beside him. He gave Ryker directions, then sat back in his seat.

'Now we'll see,' he murmured.

Seventy-Two

They sat at a window table in the café looking out, watching every car that passed.

Donna warmed her hands round her tea and glanced at her watch again.

4.26 p.m.

They'd been in the café for over thirty minutes now, with only the sound of a fruit machine and the loud chattering of a group of youngsters in their late teens for company. A couple were playing the fruit machine; every so often, a cacophony of bells and buzzers would go off. The place smelt of damp clothes and cigarette smoke. There were a few curled-up sandwiches in a glass-fronted cabinet beneath the counter and a cheese roll that looked like it had been hewn from granite rather than baked with dough. Bottles of Coke, Tizer and Pepsi were lined up, along with a few token bottles of Perrier and Evian. The Formica-topped tables were scarred with cigarette burns and discoloured by spilled coffee. A woman in her forties was busily scrubbing tables at the far end. Donna thought she would need more than hot, soapy water to remove the accumulated grime.

Julie did not take her gaze from the window. Every vehicle that passed she scanned, every passer-by she scrutinised.

The Granada hadn't been past. But it could be lurking up ahead somewhere, Julie reasoned, waiting to continue its pursuit. Or worse.

'We can't sit here forever,' Donna said finally. 'Come on.'

'They could be waiting,' Julie said warily.

'We'll take that chance.' As she opened her handbag to retrieve her purse, Julie saw the Pathfinder .22 nestling inside.

Donna paid for the teas and the two women walked out to the Fiesta and got in.

Julie's hand was shaking as she pushed the key into the ignition but she sucked in a deep breath and started the car, checking her rear-view mirror both for approaching traffic and, more particularly, for that Granada.

'How much further?' she wanted to know.

Donna consulted the directions on the sheet of paper and realized that they must be pretty close to their destination. She checked street names carefully, peering at a sign indicating an approaching roundabout. She pointed to the turn-off they should take.

'We're close now,' Donna said.

They were still on the outskirts of the city centre itself and Donna wondered what something as strange as a waxworks was doing so far from the city centre, even what it was doing in a place like Portsmouth. She could understand the existence of such an attraction at a seaside resort, but this traditionally nautical stronghold could hardly be classified as such. She wondered how Paxton made it pay.

'There,' Donna suddenly shouted, jabbing a finger against the glass.

Julie looked to her left and caught a glimpse of what looked like a large terraced house fronted by a blue and white canvas awning. There was a small paved area in front of it and a low wall. The paved area had several figures on it. A ticket booth was guarded by two of these figures dressed as policemen.

HOUSE OF WAX proclaimed the sign on the awning.

The shutters were firmly closed at the ticket booth, the waxwork policemen staring with sightless eyes at passers-by. The street was more or less deserted.

There were more shutters at the windows of the building, only one of which was open. Leaning out of it the figure of Charlie Chaplin waved to anyone who cared to look up, frozen forever in that pose.

'Now what?' Julie asked, seeing that the place was closed.

'Let's find a phone box,' Donna said. 'I'll call Paxton.'

They finally found one two streets away. Julie pulled in and her sister ran across to the two booths, pulling the piece of paper from her handbag, finding Paxton's number. She touched the .22 Pathfinder for reassurance as she removed the sheet.

The first phone was broken and the second took only phone cards. Donna rummaged in her purse and found hers. She pushed it into the slot and dialled, dismayed to see she only had six units left. She hoped he picked up the phone quickly. She hoped he was there. The phone continued to ring.

'Come on,' she muttered.

Another unit was swallowed up.

The phone was picked up.

'Hello,' the voice said.

'Mr Paxton? George Paxton?'

'Yes. Who's this, please?'

Another unit disappeared.

'I'm in a call box, I can't speak for long, just listen to me, please. My name is Donna Ward, Chris Ward's wife. You knew my husband very well; he wrote a book about waxworks and you helped him with his research. He left something inside your waxworks. He hid something. A book.'

Silence at the other end as another unit was consumed.

'Mr Paxton, I need your help, please. It's very important.'

'Where are you?' he wanted to know.

'In a call box, I told you.'

'Meet me outside my waxworks in an hour, Mrs Ward,' he said.

Donna hung up, left the phone card in the box and hurried back to the car.

Julie drove off.

* * *

'We've got them,' said Peter Farrell into the two-way. He gave Kellerman the location. 'Get here as quick as you can, but stay out of sight. We don't want to fuck it up now.' He looked at Ryker and nodded in the direction of the Fiesta. 'Don't lose them, but be careful.'

Ryker guided the Orion into traffic, keeping well back from the Fiesta.

Farrell watched as the smaller car parked across the street from the waxworks. He saw the two women sitting there as the Orion glided past and disappeared up a side street. Satisfied that they were staying put, he flicked on the two-way again.

'It's Farrell. We've got them under surveillance. They won't get away this time.'

'We'll be there in about thirty minutes,' the voice on the other end said, then there was a sharp hiss of static followed by silence.

Farrell reached inside his jacket, his fingers touching the butt of the .45 in his shoulder holster.

No escape, he thought, smiling. Not *this* time.

Seventy-Three

The office was small, less than fifteen feet square, dominated by a large antique desk piled high with correspondence. A glass paperweight in the shape of a tortoise held the letters down. Framed photos on the walls showed the front of the waxworks. Set out in chronological order, the first picture had been taken in 1934, then, every ten years until the most recent one. The building itself had changed little, apart from a lick of paint here and there; it still reminded Donna of a huge terraced house.

There were cabinets set against one wall, each filled with photos and biographical details from figures in history and the media, politics and sport – everyone from Clement Attlee to the Greek god Zeus.

'My grandfather started the museum,' said Paxton. 'He saw a number of them in America when he visited during the Thirties. When he died it was passed on to my father and then to me. It doesn't make much money now, just enough to keep it running, but we break even every year. I wouldn't want to close it down.' Paxton smiled affectionately and touched the picture of the Wax Museum taken in 1934.

He was a tall, attractive man in his mid-forties, the grey hair at his temples giving him a distinguished look. More so than the bald patch at the back of his head. He wore an open-neck shirt and trousers that needed pressing, but he'd apologized for his 'unkempt' condition when he'd first greeted them, explaining that he'd been decorating at home and had pulled on the first things to hand in his haste to get to the waxworks.

'We used to make all the figures here ourselves,' he said. 'There was a workshop in the basement.

My father employed three people to create them. I don't need them any more. I simply write to Madame Tussaud's and put in a list of requests for figures.' He smiled. 'They send me the ones I need. They sometimes suggest figures I should have here. You know, the 'Famous for fifteen minutes' type. The pop stars, the TV celebrities or sportsmen. I put them in my Warhol Gallery. That's what I call it.' He smiled again. 'Everyone will be famous for fifteen minutes,' he mused. 'I usually replace them after a month or so.'

'Mr Paxton, how well did you know my husband?' Donna asked.

'How well do *any* of us know someone else, Mrs Ward?' he said philosophically. 'I got on well with Chris while he was here doing his research. He spent about a week with me, learning about the running of the place, things like that.'

'How much did you know about the book he hid here?'

'Nothing at all. He rang me one day and asked if he could bring something down. He wouldn't even tell me what it was over the phone.'

'How long ago was that?'

Paxton shrugged.

'Six or seven weeks,' he said. 'All he told me was that the book was important to him and to some other people.'

'He didn't say which people?' Donna interjected.

'No. He just asked if he could hide it in the museum. I agreed. He said he'd pick it up in a month or so. Then, of course . . .' He allowed the sentence to trail off.

'Did you see the book? Do you know where he hid it?'

'I haven't got a clue. It could be anywhere in the museum.' He paused for a moment, looking almost apologetically at Donna. 'Would it be rude of me to ask who he was hiding it from?'

'I'm not completely sure,' Donna told him, 'but I need to find it.'

She felt it unneccessary to mention some of the incidents that had taken place over the last few days, least of all the confrontation at the cottage the previous night. She merely told him that the book bore a crest, an embossed crest of a hawk. It was very old, too, she said.

'I know that's vague,' she said, 'but it's all I know.'

'I'd like to help you look if I can,' Paxton volunteered.

Donna smiled.

'That's very kind of you. Thank you.'

Paxton slid open a drawer in his desk and took out what looked like a floor-by-floor plan of the three-storey building. He laid the diagram out on the desk-top, weighting each corner down with a pile of papers.

'The museum is divided into galleries,' he said, jabbing the plan. 'It makes it sound grand, doesn't it? Museum.' He chuckled. 'My grandfather thought that wax museums should be places of learning, too. Three-dimensional temples of knowledge, he used to call them.'

Donna and Julie were more interested in the layout of the building than in Paxton's nostalgic musings.

'Is this the ground floor?' Donna asked, prodding one part of the map.

'No, that's the basement. It's where we keep our Chamber of Horrors. No waxworks is complete without one. It's always the most popular area, too. It brings out the morbid streak in all of us, I'm afraid.'

'And you've no idea where Chris could have hidden the book?' Donna repeated.

'None at all.'

'We'll have more chance of finding it if we search separately,' Donna suggested. 'Julie and I will start on the top floor, then work our way down.'

'I'll meet you on the second floor. If we miss each other we'll meet back in this office in three hours.'

'Miss each other? Is that likely?' Julie wanted to know.

'There are two sets of stairs into and out of every gallery,' Paxton explained, 'So that if we get too many visitors it doesn't get too congested as people move around. It's quite possible we could pass each other and not even realize it. It's dark in the galleries, too, apart from the lights on the figures.'

Julie felt her heart beating faster.

'If one of us finds the Grimoire, we call out to let the others know, then bring it back here to this office,' Donna suggested.

Paxton nodded.

He left the office first, waiting for the two women to follow him out before closing the door again.

There was a flight of stairs directly to their right.

'Follow the stairs straight up to the third floor,' he said. 'I'll go that way.' He nodded in the direction of an archway. Through it, Donna could see the first of many wax tableaux showing famous film stars. The atmosphere was thick and gloomy. She hugged her handbag tightly to her sides, comforted by the thought of the Pathfinder inside.

Two or three feet away, standing by the entrance to the waxworks, were the figures of Laurel and Hardy. In the darkness they seemed not the amusing and loveable clowns they were meant to be but somehow menacing. Their glass eyes regarded the group blindly. Julie again felt a shiver run up her spine. She glanced up the stairs; the top of the flight almost disappeared into the dimness.

'Back here in three hours,' said Donna, her voice sounding loud in the unyielding silence. 'Unless one of us finds the book.'

Paxton nodded.

They set off.

The hunt began.

Seventy-Four

Marilyn Monroe gave him no clues. John Wayne offered no help. Neither did Marlon Brando or any other member of the Corleone family.

Paxton stood in the middle of the tableau entitled:

THE GODFATHER

and moved between the figures of James Caan, Al Pacino and Marlon Brando, all of them identified by name plates at their feet.

In the display the Godfather's desk had a number of books on it; the waxworks owner reached for them one by one. They were encyclopaedias or dictionaries with the dust jackets removed. Not wax but real books.

The figure of Robert Duvall was holding a briefcase; he glanced inside but found nothing but a sheet of blank paper. He moved on, past Indiana Jones and Rambo until he came to a display of THE EXORCIST.

It featured a bedroom and figures of Max Von Sydow, Jason Miller and Linda Blair in her possessed incarnation. The waxwork of Von Sydow held what was supposed to be a Bible but Paxton wondered if Ward might have substituted the Grimoire for the Holy Book. After all, he had no idea how big it was. He stepped in amongst the figures, moving around the bed until he reached the kneeling wax effigy.

The book it held was indeed a Bible.

Paxton moved on.

It wasn't just the silence Julie found overwhelming, it was the claustrophobic atmosphere of the place. The solitude and the almost palpable darkness combined to create the feeling that they'd been drapped in a blanket. The carpeting of the floors served to enhance the illusion; they could not even hear their own footsteps as they moved around.

Julie walked quickly, keeping within two or three feet of Donna. Even so, her sister was a barely glimpsed shadow most of the time.

They passed through an archway into a display of great sporting figures. The waxworks were arranged in groups beyond a rope, which was supposed to separate them from their admirers. In a mock-up of a boxing ring stood Henry Cooper, Mohammed Ali and Mike Tyson. At the edge of the ring Joe Louis and Rocky Marciano glared glassily at her. Julie found herself drawn almost hypnotically to the blank stares. She could see herself reflected in the glass orbs, a distorted image.

Ahead, Donna was standing beside Pelé and George Best. Kenny Dalglish and Eusebio looked on impassively. Johan Cruyff, one foot perched on a football, regarded her with the same emotionless expression as the rest.

Further along there was a model of Sir Francis Chichester; on what was supposed to be the deck of his yacht lay a number of books. Donna climbed into the exhibit and began inspecting them. She found to her annoyance that they were all books about sailing.

She pressed on.

Julie followed, her passage unnoticed by Lester Piggot and Willie Carson.

A flight of three steps led up into another gallery, this one depicting great artists.

They moved on.

Sean Connery, George Lazenby, Roger Moore and Timothy Dalton stood around Paxton as he searched through the drawers of M's desk, but the James Bond tableau was no help to him either.

So many places to look. So many places Ward could have hidden the book.

As he walked among the figures Paxton wondered what could be so important about this missing book. What could be so vital to send him and two women trekking around the place?

Opposite him a display showed Gene Kelly, Fred Astaire and Ginger Rogers all dancing together, watched by a group of admiring figures. One of the figures was of a child; at its feet were a set of school books. He strode across to it, climbing into the little set-up. The child was Shirley Temple and the books were spilling from her satchel. He began sorting through them.

Danny Kaye, Liza Minnelli and Judy Garland

looked on blankly as he sifted through the books. Again he found nothing.

The hand grabbed his hair.

So surprised by the movement he felt as if his vocal cords had frozen, Paxton hardly moved as his head was yanked hard backwards.

The knife flashed in the spotlight, glinting viciously before the razor-sharp blade was drawn across his throat.

Blood erupted from the wound that opened like a grinning mouth, spewing crimson over the lifeless figures.

Peter Farrell held tightly to Paxton's hair, careful to avoid the jetting blood. He heard the soft hiss as the waxwork owner's sphincter muscle collapsed. Then he allowed the body to drop to the floor, watching it twitch for a second before stepping back into the shadows from which he'd emerged. He pulled a two-way radio from his pocket and flicked it on.

'I'm on the ground floor,' he whispered into the machine. 'Paxton's dead. Split up and find the other two.' He paused a moment, still looking down at the body, the head in the centre of a spreading pool of blood. 'Keep them alive until I get there,' he added as an afterthought.

He put the two-way back in his pocket and slipped away, swallowed by the gloom.

Behind him, Paxton's body lay amongst the frozen dancers and entertainers smiling down blankly as if welcoming him.

Blood from the hideous wound washed over.

the title plate of the tableau, which proclaimed happily:

GOTTA DANCE.

Seventy-Five

Second floor.

The top storey had yielded nothing. Outside, the rain which had been falling when they entered the building seemed to have eased. Night had invaded the heavens, closing around the waxworks like a black fist as impenetrable as the umbra that seemed to fill every inch of the museum. The exhibits were small islands of light within a sea of shadows.

Donna paused at the bottom of the flight of steps and looked to her right and left.

To her right was a gallery featuring GREAT EVENTS IN WORLD HISTORY; to her left, THE ENTERTAINMENT WORLD.

'Do you want to check one side and I'll check the other?' she asked Julie.

'No. I'm staying with you,' the younger woman said, horrified at the thought of being alone in one of these darkened rooms. Donna gripped her hand briefly to reassure her, but the gesture did little to ease Julie's fear. Donna, too, felt the hairs on the back of her neck rise as they moved into the right-hand gallery.

A mock-up of the front benches of the House of Commons displayed a dozen of the country's most important politicians. Behind them were older, more famous ones. Gladstone, Disraeli and Lloyd George all stood in judgement, silent and unmoving as the two women passed by.

The next exhibit showed Napoleon's final trip to St Helena. He was in a cabin on board the ship with several figures standing around him.

There were books on the desk at which the effigy of the Emperor sat.

Donna wasted no time checking them out.

Julie, meantime, took a couple of paces across the gallery towards a group of world leaders, past and present, gathered around a desk.

She shivered as she felt so many sightless eyes boring into her.

A board creaked beneath her feet and she sucked in a startled breath.

Adolf Hitler stood, arms folded, beside Benito Mussolini. Stalin and Trotsky stood to their left.

Julie could see bookshelves behind them.

The Grimoire could be there.

'Donna,' she whispered.

No reply.

She looked round to where her sister was searching through the other books.

'Donna,' Julie repeated.

There was no sign of the older woman.

Julie felt as if someone had suddenly pumped her full of ice water.

'Oh, Jesus,' she murmured, fearing she was alone. 'Donna.' She raised her voice slightly.

There was a chipboard wall between the exhibits and Julie turned and moved towards it.

She could hear sounds on the other side.

The breath was stuck in her throat and her mouth felt dry.

It was if someone had filled it with sand. In the deafening silence inside the gallery she could hear her heart thumping madly against her ribs.

'Donna,' she said again, the word sounding thunderous in the solitude.

Close by a floorboard creaked.

Julie swallowed hard.

'It's not here.'

Donna stuck her head out from behind the chipboard wall.

Julie just managed to stifle a scream. She raised a hand to her forehead and let out a breath which seemed to empty her lungs.

'For Christ's sake,' she murmured.

Donna saw the exhibit her sister had been looking at and crossed to it. She looked up at the books on the shelves and reached for the closest.

She flipped it open.

Blank paper.

So was the next.

And the next.

Every book on the shelf was a volume of blank sheets.

Donna sighed wearily and prepared to continue the search.

Julie suddenly grabbed her arm.

'Listen,' she whispered, her eyes bulging in their sockets.

'What . . .'

'Just listen.'

They stood as motionless as the wax figures surrounding them, ears alert for the slightest sound, eyes roving around the darkened gallery for any trace of movement.

Donna heard it too.

The unmistakable creaking of floorboards.

Someone was on the floor above them.

'It must be Paxton,' Donna said quietly.

'He was below us,' Julie protested.

'He said that we could pass each other without knowing. Perhaps he went up to double check, in case we missed something.'

The footsteps receded.

The two women remained motionless, gazing up at the ceiling as if to trace the source and direction of the footsteps.

There was one more protesting creak, then silence.

'I'm sorry,' said Julie none too convincingly. 'This place . . .' She allowed the sentence to trail off.

Donna squeezed her hand and nodded.

They paused a moment longer, then moved further down the gallery, inspecting each exhibit, checking any books which could be the hidden

Grimoire. Finally satisfied that these tableaux held no secrets, they turned round and headed back towards the gallery marked THE ENTER-TAINMENT WORLD.

At the top of the stairs between the two galleries Donna paused and peered into the thick shadows, listening for movement from either above or below. She heard nothing. She wondered if she should call out to Paxton, just to find out where he was. She decided against it and walked through the archway to be confronted by the figure of Elvis Presley.

Julie followed, past the cast of *Dallas*, glancing at figures of Rod Stewart, Tina Turner and Madonna.

So many eyes watching them.

These exhibits were mostly just single figures, not set out in any kind of tableau, but isolated in their stage clothes with just a name plate for company.

Kate Bush stood defiantly before them, her hair frozen in an imaginary breeze, curling in the air like the deadly locks of a Gorgon.

Bob Hope was leaning on a golf club.

Frank Sinatra was holding a microphone.

Donna moved quickly through the gallery.

'There's nothing in here,' she said. 'Let's try the next floor. Perhaps Paxton's found some-thing.'

'He would have called, wouldn't he?' Julie enquired.

'Perhaps we didn't hear him.'

317

At the top of the stairs just beyond the archway at the exit from the gallery stood figures of Michael Jackson and Stevie Wonder.

The former of the two was in a glass case.

Donna moved close to it, peering in at the finely sculpted features, momentarily distracted by the sheer artistry of the effigy.

She and Julie moved nearer to the glass.

Julie touched it.

The figure turned and looked at them.

Seventy-Six

Julie could not suppress a scream this time.

Her shriek of surprise echoed around the building, drumming in their ears, amplified by the stillness.

The figure turned stiffly and fixed them in a sightless gaze.

It took Donna a moment or two to realize that it had been activated by some kind of electric eye. When the glass was touched, the mechanism was set in motion. The figure swayed slightly on its base, then was still.

Julie ran a hand through her hair and closed her eyes, her heart racing.

'Oh God,' she murmured.

Donna too felt her heart thumping; the sudden shock made her tremble. She squeezed Julie's hand and motioned for her to follow down the stairs that led to the ground floor.

They were halfway down when the thought struck her.

Why had Paxton not come to find the source of the scream? Why, at least, had he not called out? There was no question of him hearing the noise in the stillness of the waxworks. Where the hell was he?

Perhaps they had been his footsteps they'd heard above them earlier. But even so, why had he not come running to find out what was happening?

Donna licked her tongue across her dry lips and stopped at the bottom of the stairs. Julie joined her.

'What now?' Julie wanted to know.

Donna glanced across into the gallery on the ground floor then at another doorway ahead of them marked PRIVATE.

She crossed to the door and found that it was unlocked. It opened out onto a narrow flight of stone steps. There was a cloying fusty smell rising from below, like drying clothes. It was cold in the narrow stairwell; the metal banister was freezing when she touched it.

'Come on,' she said. 'This must lead to the basement.' She began to descend, and Julie followed. They trod carefully on the bare stone until, finally, Donna pushed open the door at the bottom and stepped out.

The smell here was even stronger. The odour

of decay as well as damp was strong in her nostrils. She looked round.

The door from which they had emerged was also marked PRIVATE.

To the left was a light, well-illuminated area that contained various electronic games and fruit machines.

To the right, a set of steps led down into what looked like seething blackness. The darkness was so total that she wondered if they would even be able to proceed without the aid of a torch. There was a sign on the wall beside this entrance:

ALL THOSE WISHING TO LEAVE THE WAXWORKS HERE, KINDLY USE THE APPROPRIATE EXIT. IT IS RECOMMENDED THAT YOUNG CHILDREN OR THOSE OF A NERVOUS DISPOSITION LEAVE NOW.

Donna took a step closer to the top of the steps and peered down.

There were five stone stairs leading down to a wooden floor and a narrow stone corridor.

The smell of damp and rot seemed to waft from the doorway as if expelled from putrid lungs. There was a sign just inside the doorway, suspended from the ceiling by two rusty chains. Donna read it aloud.

'Abandon hope, all ye who enter here.' She smiled. 'It would have been just like Chris to hide the Grimoire down there,' Donna said, pointing towards the abyss beyond the steps. 'It would have appealed to his sense of humour.'

'What is it?' Julie wanted to know, wrinkling her nose at the smell.

Donna raised her eyebrows.

'The Chamber of Horrors.'

Seventy-Seven

It was like stepping into empty space.

Donna, who couldn't see her feet beneath her, moved cautiously for fear of slipping on the stone steps. Julie followed behind, steadying herself against the wall, recoiling slightly as she felt the moistness of the stone.

Paxton must have had the place treated with something, Donna thought. She was sure the basement that housed the waxworks' grisliest exhibits was not naturally damp and decaying. Part of the process of making the viewing experience all the more real and eerie was the smell which went with the darkness and unbearable silence. There were companies in the film business who made fake blood; why not someone to recreate the smell of damp and neglect? Perhaps that odour could indeed be bottled and sold. Paxton must have bought a crateful.

Fake cobwebs had been sprayed over the walls, too, although how much of the gossamer-like material was real and how much was fake she wasn't sure. There would be no need to clean this part of the waxworks. Grime and the odd spider could only serve to enhance its appearance.

The figures of the murderers themselves were arranged behind what looked like rusty prison bars. These too were covered by cobwebs both fake and genuine.

Dependent on their stature or the nature of their crimes, figures were enshrined within their own individual displays. Others were grouped together, usually with a newspaper of the day framed beside them proclaiming their arrest or, in the case of those before 1969, of their execution.

How perverse, Donna thought, that there should even be a hierachy amongst killers. Men like Denis Nilsen, Peter Sutcliffe and John George Haigh were presented in tableaux of their own, while those who had killed only once or twice, or who were there more for their notoriety than their savagery, merited a smaller setting where they were crowded together. Ruth Ellis, Lee Harvey Oswald and the Kray Twins stood together.

Christie was displayed surrounded by his nine victims, portions of them visible from gaps in the walls and floor of the mock-up of his front room at Ten Rillington Place. Behind him stood Timothy Evans, the man wrongly hanged for a murder Christie committed.

If the atmosphere in the rest of the waxworks had been unsettling, in this odorous basement it was close to oppressive. These glass eyes stared out with a venom and hatred that matched those of their inspirations. Julie felt her skin crawl.

Nilsen stood at the cooker where he'd boiled down the remains of his victims.

Sutcliffe gripped a claw hammer and a screwdriver, his face twisted into a half-smile.

Haigh, dressed in a leather apron, was in the process of dissolving one of his victims in an acid bath.

Julie tried to swallow but felt as if someone had blocked her throat.

Beneath the model of Eichmann were newspaper cuttings about Auschwitz; yellowed with age like some of the other clippings, they were still as abhorrent, even after all these years.

Dr Crippen was standing by a desk on which lay a pile of books.

Donna looked for a way in to the exhibit. The only door was in the side of the cage-like display, at the end near the exit. In order to reach the figure of Crippen she would have to pass the other figures, too. She turned and headed for the door immediately, relieved that it was open when she pushed. She stepped inside.

Julie gripped the bars, wincing as she felt how cold and wet they were, watching as her sister drew closer, pausing to look at the tableau of Christie. There were many cupboards in the display; Ward could have hidden the Grimoire in any one of them.

Donna opened them but found that they were

empty. She glanced at the figure of Christie and walked on. Past Haigh. Past Nilsen.

The figure of Peter Sutcliffe was standing over the body of a woman, old newspapers beneath his feet. Donna paused to lift the newspapers and look beneath them.

Julie sucked in an anxious breath, her eyes fixed on the model of Sutcliffe.

The head moved a fraction.

She opened her mouth to shout but no sound would come.

Donna was still at his feet.

Julie blinked hard and looked at the waxwork again.

This time she saw no movement. A trick of the light? A trick of her mind? A little of both, she fancied.

'Come on, Donna,' she said, her breath coming in gasps.

Her sister nodded, got to her feet and finally reached the Crippen figure. She looked at the books on the desk: a medical book and a book on anatomy.

The third had a picture of a bird on it. *A hawk?*

Was this the Grimoire?

Her hands were shaking as she lifted it.

A *picture* of a hawk, not an embossed crest.

Could it be . . .

She opened it.

Blank pages.

'Shit,' she muttered angrily and replaced the

book. She hurried out of the cage and rejoined Julie. Ahead of them was another wall with a small gap in it; barely five feet high and three across, it formed a doorway into the last part of the exhibit. The Torture Chamber.

Donna advanced towards it.

There was a red light over the narrow opening. As she waited for Julie to join her, the light bathed her in crimson so that it looked as if she'd been drenched in blood. She looked down into the Chamber and saw that the same inky blackness awaited them. Only the models were lit, but this time by even weaker beams from hidden spotlamps in the low ceiling. This was the only entrance in *and* out. Donna led the way, glancing at several severed heads arrayed before a guillotine. Nearby a wax body dangled from a hook embedded in its side. Behind them a display featured a man with rats trying to eat their way through his stomach while imprisoned in a red hot cage.

Burning out the eyes.

Driving needles beneath the fingernails.

Tearing off the nose with red-hot pincers.

The horrors came thick and fast, vying with each other.

A man being boiled alive in what looked like a massive metal bowl.

A man with a steel ring through his tongue, the ring attached to a metal ball by a chain.

The revulsion Donna felt was tempered by her recognition of the skill with which these monstrosities had been constructed. They were obscenely realistic.

The two women turned a corner and Julie groaned aloud.

THE MURDER OF SHARON TATE proclaimed the plate on the bars of the enclosure that housed one of the most horrendously realistic exhibits in the building.

In front of the tableau a newspaper of the day headlined the slaughter of the Hollywood star and four others by members of the Charles Manson family. The figure of Manson himself, eyes wild, hair flying behind him, watched over the scene. It showed the living-room of the Tate residence with the film star's killers, armed with knives and guns, and the other people who died with her. Whoever had modelled it had certainly been painstakingly accurate in the depiction, anxious to show that Sharon Tate had been eight months pregnant when she'd been hacked to death, her blood used to write the word PIG on the wall.

'Jesus Christ,' Julie whispered, her attention drawn to the vile display.

Donna had her eye on something else.

Further down the corridor another, larger exhibit showed the Spanish Inquisition. It featured several hooded figures and a victim being racked, while another was being hung from the ceiling on chains, his glass eyes fixed on a cowled figure carrying what looked like a set of rusty garden shears. The intention was castration.

Another hooded figure sat at a desk, a book open before it.

A book of Latin phrases. An old book.

Donna looked round frantically for the entrance to the exhibit and found it nearby in the form of a metal door. She opened it and stepped inside, making for the book. She pulled it towards her and flipped it over, looking at the cover.

The crest showed a Hawk.

The cover felt cold and clammy, as if the book had been in a damp hole for months, years even. The pages were stiff with age, some of them split at the edges. Some of the writing was in Latin, the rest in the same quaint script she'd seen in the book in the library in Scotland.

'Julie,' she called.

Her sister hurried over.

'I've found it,' Donna said triumphantly. 'This is the Grimoire.'

It was then that the hooded figure at the desk leapt to its feet.

The cowl slipped away to reveal the face of Peter Farrell.

Seventy-Eight

Farrell lunged at her, his face contorted in an expression of pure hatred.

His grunt of anger mingled with Donna's own shout of surprise and Julie's scream.

Donna jumped back, pulling the book with her, allowing it to fall to the floor with a crash.

Farrell leapt over the desk, not sure which to grab first, Donna or the Grimoire. He launched himself at Donna, who managed to avoid his rush, seeing him crash into the figure holding the castrating irons. An arm broke off and the metal implement went skidding across the dusty floor. Donna snatched it up as she saw Farrell reaching inside his jacket, pulling the .45 free.

She swung the castrating iron with all her force and caught him across the back of the hand, the clang of metal on bone reverberating through The Torture Chamber.

The gun flew from his grasp, but instead of trying to retrieve it Farrell came at her again.

Donna swung the iron again. This time she caught him in the face with it.

The blow split his cheek almost to the bone and blood burst from the wound and ran down the side of his face. Grabbing the book, Donna dashed past him towards the door where Julie was waiting.

'Get them,' roared Farrell. As if from nowhere, Ryker and Kellerman appeared from the shadows. Like two spectres rising from the umbra they rose up before the women.

Donna pulled the .22 Pathfinder from her handbag, thumbed back the hammer and fired twice. The first shot carved a path through the shoulder of Ryker's jacket without touching flesh; the second missed both men and blew the head off the model of Torquemada.

Ryker dived to one side but swung his foot at Donna and managed to trip her.

She pitched forward, the gun falling from her grasp and skittering across the floor. As she hit the ground, she fell on top of the Grimoire.

Ryker leapt on her, trying to wrestle the book from her grip.

Julie kicked out at him, catching him in the groin, but then she felt powerful hands fastening around her throat as Kellerman grabbed her.

'You cunt,' he hissed, squeezing until his fingers pressed deep into her windpipe.

White stars began to dance in front of Julie's eyes; no matter how she scratched at his hands she could not break his grip.

She was helpless, supported by the hands but dying because of them.

Donna pushed Ryker off her and scrambled to her feet, seeing that Farrell was now about to free himself and join the fight, blood pouring down his face. But it was Julie she was concerned with.

Kellerman was tightening his grip on her throat, squeezing until Julie's eyes bulged madly in their sockets as she fought for breath.

Donna looked around for the gun and saw it. She dived onto the floor, snatched up the Pathfinder and rolled over. She fired once, and more by luck than judgement the bullet hit Kellerman in the shin, just below the left knee. The sound of the pistol was deafening inside the chamber, but even above the roar she could hear the strident crack of splintering bone as the tibia was shattered by the bullet.

Kellerman shrieked and released his grip on Julie, clapping his hands to the wound. Blood ran through his fingers as he crashed to the ground, clutching the ragged hole.

Julie, too, had fallen to the ground, barely conscious. Donna tried to help her up but felt herself grabbed from behind by Ryker.

She pushed herself backwards and both of them went hurtling over the low chain that separated them from the exhibits. Donna landed on top of Ryker, winding him as he took her elbow in his chest. Again the gun slipped from her grasp.

Farrell was out of the cage by now, racing towards Julie, the .45 out and lowered at her.

He grabbed her around the waist and lifted her to her feet, the barrel of the pistol pressed to her temple.

'No,' Donna shouted, trying to struggle away from Ryker, 'leave her alone.'

Kellerman was groaning loudly, his lower leg smashed by the bullet.

Ryker made a grab for the book but missed and overbalanced, crashing into the guillotine display. He cracked his head on one of the sharp corners and went down in a heap, clutching his throbbing skull.

'Stop.'

The voice boomed out, filling the chamber.

Both Donna and Farrell turned towards the entrance.

Francis Dashwood moved slowly into the chamber, closely followed by Richard Parsons.

Dashwood was smiling.

Seventy-Nine

The stench was appalling.

Donna noticed it as soon as Dashwood and Parsons entered the chamber. The unmistakable rank odour of death.

'You have something which belongs to us,' Dashwood said, jabbing a finger towards the book she held.

'Your husband stole it from us,' Parsons added.

'Return it.'

Donna swallowed hard, her stomach somersaulting as she inhaled the rancid stench that emanated from the two men.

'Who are you?' she asked, seeing the pallid skin that hung in festering coils from their faces. Dashwood's forehead was dotted with boils, one of which had recently burst. Thick pus seeped down towards his eyebrow.

'Friends of your husbands,' Dashwood told her, smiling, lips sliding back to reveal blackened teeth. 'Now give me the book.' The smile faded to be replaced by a look of anger. He held out a hand.

Donna kept a tight grip on the Grimoire.

'I'll blow her fucking head all over the wall,' hissed Farrell, pushing the barrel of the .45 forcefully against Julie's temple. 'Now give him the book.'

'Fair exchange, Mrs Ward,' Dashwood said. 'You have something *we* want. We have something *you* want. Give me the Grimoire.'

'If I do you'll kill us both,' Donna said, trying to swallow.

'And if you don't, Farrell will shoot you. *Then* we'll take it,' Dashwood told her.

'Fair exchange. Her life for the Grimoire,' Parsons added, nodding towards Julie.

'Why does it mean so much to you?' Donna asked, taking a step backwards, the book in her arms.

Dashwood advanced a pace, his eyes fixed on the Grimoire.

'Give it to me,' he rasped. She heard the anger in his voice but there was something else there, too.

Fear?

'Give him the book or I swear I'll kill her,' Farrell said, looking first at Donna, then at Dashwood.

Donna moved back another step.

'Tell me why it's so important,' she demanded, opening it at the first page, smelling the musty odour that rose from the parchment-like paper. She closed her hand on the top sheet.

'Don't damage it,' shouted Dashwood. Now Donna was sure it was fear she heard in his voice. He moved closer to her but she merely held her ground, one hand poised to rip the page free. 'Don't damage the book,' Dashwood repeated. 'You can both go, just don't damage the book.'

'Let her go, or I'll rip this page out and all the others,' Donna said defiantly, looking at Farrell.

He kept his grip on Julie, the gun still pressed to her temple.

'Shoot her,' Parsons snapped.

Dashwood shot up a hand.

'No,' he hissed.

'I'll destroy the book,' Donna threatened. 'Let her go.'

'You couldn't rip up a dozen pages before I killed you both,' Farrell said, not impressed by her show of bravado.

'Let her go,' snarled Dashwood, glaring at Farrell.

He hesitated a moment then released his grip on Julie, pushing her away from him. She stumbled and fell to her knees, one hand massaging her bruised throat.

'Drop the gun,' Donna said.

Farrell did as he was told.

'Now back off, all of you,' she continued, moving across to her sister, the Grimoire still held in her hands.

Dashwood didn't move but his rheumy eyes followed the book.

Farrell, Ryker and Kellerman, still clutching his knee and the wound just below it, moved out of the chamber, leaving the two women to face Parsons and Dashwood. The stench seemed to grow in intensity.

'We made a bargain,' said Dashwood. 'Give me the book.'

Donna glanced quickly to one side and saw the .45 that Farrell had dropped. It was a couple of feet to her right.

'Give me the book and I'll tell you why it's so important to us. You said you wanted to know.'

She edged closer to the automatic.

Julie was leaning back against the wall, her head spinning, her eyes filled with tears of pain and fear.

'A bargain, Mrs Ward,' Dashwood continued.

Donna dropped to one knee, snatched up the .45 and then straightened up with the barrel pointed at Dashwood.

He chuckled.

The sound echoed around the chamber. Donna felt the hairs on the back of her neck rise.

'Take the fucking thing,' she hissed and hurled it at Dashwood.

He grabbed it and pulled it close to his chest, his eyes blazing.

Donna raised the .45 until it was level with his head and steadied herself to fire.

'Stay back,' she said, teeth gritted, her finger resting on the trigger.

'I have what I want now,' Dashwood told her, moving towards the exit.

'They'll kill us,' Julie croaked.

'No, not *us*,' Dashwood smiled. '*We* will not touch you.'

Donna frowned.

What the hell did he mean?

She had the sights directly over Dashwood's forehead; all she had to do was tighten her finger and she'd spread his brains all around the chamber.

Perhaps she should.

He was still hugging the book to him as if it were a nursing child.

'Your husband was inquisitive, too,' he said, smiling, showing his array of blackened teeth. 'Perhaps you're like him. You want to know about the Grimoire?'

She nodded slowly.

'Then I'll tell you.'

Eighty

Kill him.

Donna felt as if a tiny voice were whispering in her ear. She kept the automatic raised as Dashwood ran his hand over the cover of the Grimoire.

Blow the fucker's brains out.

'You killed my husband,' she said quietly, the words sounding more like a statement than a question.

Dashwood shook his head.

'It was none of our doing,' he said. 'He brought about his own death because of his betrayal.'

'You murdered him.'

'Is that what the police told you? That he was murdered?'

'They said they were reasonably sure he *wasn't*. That his death *was* an accident.'

'Then why don't you believe them?' Dashwood asked, smiling thinly.

'I don't know what to believe any more,' she said, keeping the gun trained on the other man. 'All I know is his death is linked to that book.' She nodded towards the thick volume.

'Possibly. As I said to you, it *is* very important to us.'

'And just who are you?' she wanted to know.

'Surely you must know by now. We are The Sons of Midnight.' He spoke the words with reverence. 'And always will be.' Again that smile. 'At least now we have our Grimoire back we can be safe again. Safe from men like your husband, who sought to expose us.' He eyed Donna impassively. 'Do you have any idea of the power this book contains? No, you couldn't. Your mind isn't capable of comprehending such power. The power of life. The power to *give* life.'

He looked down at the cover of the Grimoire and touched the crest lovingly. Even in the darkness Donna could see his eyes blazing with a ferocity that belied the appearance of the rest of his body.

'Edward Chardell, the author of this book, believed that life was immortal. Not so much in *time*, as in *essence*. This book,' again he held it up, 'was published as Chardell was dying. It contains his theories and his researches. The sum total of knowledge he'd spent years accumulating. He says that life exists outside and independent of Creation, and independent of birth too.'

Donna looked puzzled.

'He says that life can, and does, attach itself to inanimate as well as animate objects. Organic life can exist, can be *made* to exist, anywhere and within everything. Within the bricks and mortar of a house. Within a jewel.' He smiled. 'Within a car.' He paused a moment. 'Do you believe in ghosts, Mrs Ward?'

Donna shrugged.

337

'As far as Chardell was concerned, a ghost was merely living consciousness without a body to house it. The body can function without consciousness, in a state of coma or sleep. Why should consciousness not function without a body? It becomes a separate entity, able to enter objects at will, or if guided. Guided by men like myself. I'm not saying I can bring the dead back to life; there are limits even to *my* abilities.' He chuckled. 'But I have studied the words within this book and I can bring life to what were otherwise lifeless objects.'

He pointed at the gun.

Donna felt something pulsing in her hand, as if she held a beating heart. The sensation was vile. As she looked down she saw the .45 moving slightly, the butt throbbing in her grip.

She did see it, didn't she?

The barrel seemed to twist, snake-like, the muzzle opening up like a mouth, growing wider.

Donna dropped the weapon and stepped away from it.

The .45 lay at her feet.

She blinked hard and looked at it again.

'No, you didn't imagine it,' Dashwood said. 'The Church would call it a miracle.' Both he and Parsons laughed aloud. 'Fascinating, isn't it?' Dashwood said, smiling. 'Your husband thought so, too. That was why he sought us out, why he wanted our knowledge.'

'He was going to destroy you,' Donna said. 'He

338

knew you needed the book to survive; that was why he took it from you.'

Dashwood raised his eyebrows questioningly.

'He wanted knowledge. He wanted to learn and he would do *anything* in order to gain that knowledge. He threatened to expose us, yes, but in order to expose us he first had to join us. To learn about us. The best way to destroy is from within. Your husband knew that.'

Donna felt her heart beating more rapidly.

No, this couldn't be.

'He wanted what we had,' Dashwood said. 'He wanted to *be* one of us.'

'No,' Donna murmured, shaking her head.

'How well did you know your husband, Mrs Ward?'

Donna was quivering.

'How do you think he knew so much about us? Why should we consider him such a danger unless he could damage us?'

'He took the Grimoire. That was why you wanted him dead,' Donna said.

'But how do you think he got close enough to take it in the first place?'

Donna shook her head.

'What did he tell you?' Dashwood asked. 'Did he tell you he was one of us?'

Donna didn't answer.

'No. He didn't, did he?' Dashwood said, smiling.

'He couldn't have been,' she shouted. 'I know about you. I know about what you do. You kill.'

'Some things are worth killing *for*,' Dashwood told her. 'Some knowledge has a high price.'

'He wasn't one of you,' she said defiantly. 'He wouldn't have done the things he . . .'

'What things, Mrs Ward?'

'The initiation rites. I read about them.'

'What *wouldn't* he have done?' Dashwood chided.

'He wouldn't have killed . . .' The sentence trailed off.

'Killed a child?' Dashwood smiled broadly. 'He wouldn't have killed a child, is that what you were going to say? He wouldn't have fornicated in front of us, he wouldn't have taken the life of a child, he wouldn't have urinated on the cross. You think he wouldn't have pissed on Christ.' Dashwood bellowed the final words, the noise echoing around the chamber. 'How well did you know your husband, you bitch? How well did you know him? Could you see into his mind? You ignorant, stupid bitch.'

Donna leapt forward, grabbing the .45.

She rolled over, aiming it at Dashwood, squeezing the trigger.

Nothing happened.

He merely stepped back, away from her through the exit.

As he did she saw him raise his hand, the index finger pointing at something behind her.

Donna kept squeezing the trigger until, finally, she hurled the automatic away with a wail of despair.

The door of the chamber was slammed shut. She and Julie were trapped.

They ran to the door but it was firmly closed, unyielding despite their frantic efforts to open it. Julie turned, sliding exhausted down the damp wood, her back to the door. Donna continued thumping at the recalcitrant partition.

'Donna.'

Julie could scarcely force the word out. She grabbed her sister's leg, waiting until she'd turned before pointing at something inside the chamber.

'Oh, Jesus,' Donna whispered.

Was this imagination? Or madness?

The wax figures in the tableau of Sharon Tate's murder were moving frenziedly.

Rooted to the spot, their limbs jerked insanely, as if charged with some kind of kinetic energy. Arms and legs thrashed wildly.

Then the sounds began.

Screams of pain and terror rose from frozen throats and drummed in the ears of Donna and Julie.

Those who'd died that night in 1969 were dying again, their agony finding a new voice.

Donna watched, her eyes bulging in their sockets, her throat constricted.

Julie too found that she was paralysed by the sight.

Only when the figure of Charles Manson turned and looked at her did she finally allow her own scream to escape. It mingled with

the others in a hideous cacophony of suffering.

The figure took a step towards them.

Eighty-One

In some obscene parody of a child's first steps,
the Manson figure lurched from its position on
the display, steadying itself against a wall.

From the tableau itself the large figure of the
man who had been known as Charles 'Tex'
Watson also struggled free and turned on the
two women. Both the effigies held knives.

Donna, her mind still reeling, looked around
for the discarded .22 Pathfinder.

It lay ten or twelve feet away, beneath the rack
of the Inquisition victim.

To reach it she would have to pass the figures
of Manson and Watson.

Donna ran towards the weapon, but Manson
moved towards her. The waxwork moved with
surprising speed; Donna felt cold hands grabbing at her.

The knife slashed down and carved through
the air only inches from her face. She turned and
lashed out, feeling her hand connect with the hard
wax of the face. The eyes fixed her in their glassy,
stare, the eyes of a dead fish on a skillet.

The screams continued, over and over again.

Manson grabbed her by the wrist and pulled her towards him.

Towards the knife.

Donna managed to twist in his grip and drove a foot into his midriff, knocking him backwards. He crashed into the effigy of a torturer burning the eyes from his victim.

Donna lunged towards the gun and scooped it into her hand, rolling over in time to see Watson bearing down on Julie.

The younger woman avoided the knife-thrust and hurled herself to one side, rolling beneath a table on which a man was being subjected to the Chinese Water Torture.

The dust and grime was thick beneath the table and Julie coughed as it clogged in her throat and nostrils.

Watson turned and came at her again, his movements thankfully slow.

Donna rose to one knee and swung the Pathfinder up into position.

She fired twice, the retort, even from a pistol as small as a .22, quite deafening within the confines of the chamber.

The first bullet struck him in the back of the head, the second in the side of the face, blasting most of the area from the temple to the chin away. Fragments of wax flew into the air.

Watson continued moving towards Julie.

Donna thumbed back the hammer and pumped two shots into Manson with similarly useless results. She saw the body quiver, saw the burns on the shirt of the mannequin. She even heard the sharp crack as the slugs thumped into the hard wax. The figure did not pause, merely raised the knife and lunged forward.

Donna rolled away beneath the table and came up on the other side.

The Manson figure made a sudden movement and the knife came hurtling down, burying itself in the wood, missing her hand by inches.

Donna made a grab for the knife but Manson's hand closed over hers. Again she felt the clammy chill of wax; it was like being touched by a dead man. She struggled to escape the grip. Using the pistol as a club she slammed it into the side of the figure's head with such force that one of the glass eyes popped out, the wax around it splintering.

The grip on her hand was released and she backed off.

The Manson figure kept coming.

Julie scrambled to her feet, pushing other figures over in an effort to halt the inexorable progress of Watson, who had the blade brandished high.

The screaming continued, great racking caterwauls of agony that deafened the women as surely as the retorts of the pistol. The backdrop of sound was intolerable.

Donna ran towards a scene showing the execution of Mary Queen of Scots. As the Manson figure advanced on her, she dragged the axe from the frozen grip of the headsman. It was heavy, the razor-sharp blade comfortingly lethal.

With all her strength she swung it, burying the blade in Manson's chest.

The figure wobbled.

Donna struck again, her own shouts of defiance and fear mingling with the screams all around her.

The next blow sheared off an arm.

Manson still advanced.

'Bastard,' roared Donna and struck his head from his shoulders.

The effigy flew into the air, the wax head spinning, the fake hair flowing out wildly.

The waxwork toppled over and lay still.

'Donna,' shrieked Julie, and she looked over to see her sister trapped in a corner, the Watson figure only a couple of feet away.

Watson swung the knife, the cut slicing through the material of Julie's shirt and gashing her forearm. She looked up into the sightless glass eyes, unable to move as the knife was raised again.

Donna ran at the figure, bringing the axe down with manic force. The blow was so powerful it cleft the wax head cleanly in two and bit into the torso as deep as the shoulders.

Watson swayed uncertainly for a second then fell backwards, the axe still embedded.

Donna sucked in the stale air, perspiration soaking her T-shirt, matting her hair at the nape of her neck.

Julie shook her head, the tears running down her cheeks. Donna dropped to her knees and the two women embraced, blood from the wound on

Julie's arm smearing Donna's clothes as they held each other tightly.

The screams continued to echo around them.

Eighty-Two

She woke with a start, looking around her frantically, disorientated, unsure of her surroundings. She felt her heart beating madly; the fear she had come to know only too well enveloped her like a cold glove.

Julie Craig sat forward on the sofa and rubbed her eyes, still trying to shrug off that twilight state between dreams and awareness.

'Shit,' she murmured, exhaling deeply.

Her faculties seemed to return slowly. She shook her head, as if that simple action would clear her mind. Immediately she became aware of a dull ache in her right forearm and looked down to see the bandage wound round it from just above the wrist to the elbow.

'You okay?' Donna asked her quietly.

'I dropped off. I'm sorry,' Julie apologized, rubbing both hands across her face, pulling her long dark hair back from her forehead. 'What time is it?'

'Just after one,' Donna told her. 'I flaked out, too, when we got back.'

They had returned to the cottage almost two

hours ago, exhausted, drained and frightened. Both of them had fought against the sleep they so desperately craved, but eventually it had overtaken them. Through that troubled sleep the events of the night returned to them. The drive to the Wax Museum, the slow exploration, the meeting with Dashwood and Parsons and the terrifying aftermath. All of it was re-run through their subconscious like a video recording. Their escape from the waxworks, through a small window which opened out into a side alley, and then the long drive back to the cottage.

Donna wondered if, indeed, she had just awoken and the entire bizarre chain of events had been the product of her fevered mind.

If only that were the case.

She need only look at the cuts and bruises on her own body and on Julie's to know that the events had been all too real.

'We have to leave here tonight,' Donna said.

'We need to rest,' Julie protested.

'We can rest when we get back to London. I don't think they will, but if they come looking for us and find us here . . .'

She allowed the sentence to trail off.

Julie closed her eyes for a moment.

'The police will come,' she said.

'That's another reason we have to get out of here,' Donna said.

'Why? When they come, you can tell them what happened. Tell them everything. Like you should have done in the first place.' There was a trace

347

of anger in her voice. 'Let *them* take care of this business now, Donna.'

'No. It isn't *their* business. Besides, if they find out what happened there'll be problems. How the hell are we supposed to explain what happened at the waxworks? They'll lock us both up. They'll think we're insane, and I wouldn't blame them if they did.' She regarded her sister for long moments then spoke again. '*We* have the advantage now. Dashwood and his men think we're dead. They won't be expecting us to go after them. They think they've got rid of us. They'll be off guard.'

'What the hell are you talking about, "Go after them"?' Julie said incredulously.

'Like I said, they think we're dead. They won't be expecting us,' Donna said almost excitedly.

'You're mad,' Julie said quietly. 'Donna, for God's sake, they've already tried to kill you Christ knows how many times, and you're still not satisfied. Do you *want* to die?'

'I want *them* to die,' she rasped.

'Forget it, it's over. They've got the bloody book, that was what they wanted. Let them have it. Let them keep it. We're alive, that's all that matters.' The anger had turned to desperation.

'It's not about the book, Julie, it never was.'

'No, it's about revenge. Your need for revenge. It's become an obsession with you, Donna. It's eating you away and you don't even know it. First it was Chris's affair, and now it's that book, and even after everything we've been through that's

348

not enough for you. You won't be happy until you've got us both killed.'

'You don't know what I'm feeling,' she said angrily. 'It was bad enough knowing about the affair, then being involved in something which could have caused our deaths, but now I find out my husband could have been a murderer, too. You heard what Dashwood said tonight. Chris was *one* of them.'

'And you believe that?'

'I'm going to find out and I'm going to wipe those bastards off the face of the earth.'

'You can't even *see* what it's doing to you, can you? You can't see what it's made you. All that matters to you is this ridiculous need for revenge. You couldn't have it against Chris or Suzanne Regan so you used the hunt for the book, instead. And now that's gone you've found another excuse to carry on.'

'Perhaps that's all I've got left, Julie.'

'Well, I won't help you. I'm sorry but I can't take any more. I'm not going to be there when you get yourself killed. I won't watch you die, Donna.'

'Part of me died when I found out about Chris and Suzanne Regan,' Donna said. 'And perhaps you're right, perhaps this whole thing has been about that, an extension of the anger I felt. Somebody had to pay for it. Somebody *will* pay for it. And if *you* won't help me, then I'll do it alone. I can't stop now. Not until this is over.'

'It *is* over,' Julie shouted, tears running down

her cheeks. 'Jesus Christ, how many more times? How much more pain can you stand? You were looking for the truth and you thought you'd found it. Well, you didn't.' She sniffed back more tears. 'He wasn't having an affair with Suzanne Regan. He was having an affair with *me*.'

Eighty-Three

Silence.

The words Julie had spoken brought only silence from her sister. For dreadful seconds Donna was reminded of her first sight of the policeman on her doorstep bringing her news of her husband's accident. How long ago was that? A month? It felt like years. Suffering had a way of distorting even time.

Now she looked blankly at her sister, momentarily unsure she'd heard right. The words gradually found their way into her consciousness. They began to take on their full meaning.

She swallowed hard.

'I don't believe you,' she said finally, her voice a hoarse whisper.

Julie sucked in a weary breath.

'It's true. Do you want dates, times, places? What do I have to say to convince you?' Julie answered wearily. She sank back on the sofa, one hand over her eyes.

She waited for the explosion of rage and recrimination.

It never came.

Donna sat at the other end of the sofa, hands clasped around one knee.

'How long had it been going on?' she wanted to know.

'Nine or ten months.'

Donna felt as if she'd been struck by an iron bar. Her head was spinning.

'Jesus,' she murmured, trying to recover her wits. 'Why?'

'I don't know. It just happened, I . . . We never intended it to happen.' She looked at her sister, her own shame intensified by the confession. 'I'm sorry.'

'So am I,' Donna said. Then, more vehemently, 'Did you love him?'

'I don't know.'

'I wouldn't have thought that was a multiple-choice question, Julie. You either did or you didn't.'

The younger woman shook her head.

'Did *he* love *you*?' Donna persisted.

'No.'

'You sound very sure. Ten months is a long time; are you telling me you never felt anything, either of you?'

Julie didn't speak.

'It was just sex then, was it?' Donna hissed. 'No love, just plenty of fucking. Was that it?'

'Donna, he loved *you*. I knew he'd never leave you, he always made that clear.'

'Did you want him to leave me? Were you trying to get Chris away from me?'

'No, I would never have done that. It was *his* decision. Like I said, he loved you.'

'But you hung around, just in case he changed his mind, right?'

'It wasn't like that.'

'Then tell me what it *was* like, Julie,' Donna hissed.

'We were more like friends.'

'Friends don't fuck each other.'

'Sex wasn't important.'

'But when you did it, was it good? Did you enjoy it? How did you rate him? Did he do things to you other men hadn't? Did he make you come? Was he considerate, caring? Tell me, Julie.'

The younger woman had no answers.

'What attracted you to him in the first place, or did *he* make the first move?'

'I had an exhibition of some of my photographs in a gallery in Knightsbridge. Chris came along, we chatted. He took me for a coffee.'

'And that was when you decided, was it? That was when you thought you'd start fucking your sister's husband. Well, was it? Come on, I'm curious. Did he suggest going back to your place or did you tell him to come round when he felt like it?'

Julie was about to answer when Donna's face darkened.

'Did you ever fuck him in *our* house?' she demanded, anxious that the betrayal should not have entered her most private domain.

Julie shook her head.

'It was usually my flat, sometimes my studio,' she said. 'Like I said, Donna, it wasn't that often.'

'It doesn't matter if it was once or a hundred times, you still did it.'

'He was an attractive man, for Christ's sake,' Julie said irritably, as if that were some excuse to explain what had happened. 'He was hard to resist. We'd always got on well, you know that. I admired his attitude to life, perhaps that was what attracted me to him. He didn't give a fuck about anyone or anything. If he wanted something, he got it. I'd never met a man so ambitious, so determined.'

'Yes, Chris always got what he wanted. Did that include *you*?'

'I know it was wrong and if there was anything I could do to change things I would, Donna.'

'Would you really? Are you trying to tell me you regret the affair? Or are you sorry Chris is dead because *you* lost him as well as I did? *Do* you regret it?'

'I regret hurting you.'

'Then why tell me? Was your conscience pricking you? I find that difficult to believe, after ten months. I would have thought you'd have come to terms with the guilt by now. Pushed it to the back of your mind. Did you ever think about me

353

when you were with him? Did you ever once stop and think what you were doing?'

'No,' Julie said flatly.

'Ever since Chris died my life has been one continual round of suspicion, mistrust and deceit. And now I find out that it extends into my own family. With my own fucking sister.' Donna looked at the younger woman with an expression that combined rage and bewilderment. 'How long would it have gone on, Julie, if he hadn't died? A year? Three years? The rest of our lives? Or just until I found out?'

'It would have petered out. Like I said, we didn't love each other.'

'There must have been something between you to keep it going for ten months. Don't tell me it was just because Chris was good in bed.'

'*We didn't love each other*. How many times do I have to say it?'

'It's easy to say that now, because it's over. But if it had gone on you might have. Then you might have tried to get him away from me. But that's something we'll never know, isn't it?'

The two women faced each other for long moments.

'Did anyone else know what was going on?' Donna said finally, angered by the fact that the secret might have been shared.

'Martin Connelly knew,' Julie confessed. 'Chris took me out for dinner one night and Connelly was in the same restaurant. He didn't say much. I don't know what Chris told him.'

'I wish you could feel what I'm feeling now,' Donna said vehemently. 'Anger, sadness – and I feel like a fool, too. I feel as if you've been laughing at me. I feel as if everyone's been laughing at me. Was it because your own marriage failed, Julie? You couldn't stand to see anyone else happy after what happened to you? Was that it?'

'I've told you the reasons and I know it's pointless to say it but I'm sorry, Donna.' She got to her feet. 'I'll go now. You won't see me again, I promise you.'

'No. You're not walking out on this, Julie,' Donna rasped. 'You say you're sorry.'

'I am. I know you don't believe me, though. You never will.'

'Make me believe.'

'How?'

'Stay and help me destroy The Sons of Midnight.'

'I can't.'

'You mean you *won't*?' Donna glared at her sister. 'It would be so easy for you to walk out, wouldn't it? Well, if you want to show me you're sorry then you'll help me.'

'That's emotional blackmail.'

'Too fucking right it is. Anyway, you're not giving yourself an opportunity to get over your guilt if you walk away. Stay and help me.'

'We could both be killed.'

'Look on it as paying back a debt,' Donna said, her eyes narrowed. 'You *owe* me that.'

Eighty-Four

The .357 bucked violently in her fist as the hammer slammed down.

The retort was massive. Even with her protectors on, Donna could still hear the dull ring as the heavy grain slug struck the back wall of the range travelling at over 1,450 feet a second. As another bullet left the barrel she felt a spattering of tiny metal fragments bounce off the wooden wall of the booth and pepper her hand. The smoke from the round cleared. She jabbed the red button on the control panel beside her to retrieve the target. It whirred back up the range towards her. As it drew close she laid the Magnum down and leant forward to inspect the grouping of her shots.

On the man-sized target she had put three shots through the centre, two in the outer ring and one low, in the groin.

Donna shook her head, reached for the roll of sticky white spots and covered each hole, jabbing the red button once more to send the target back up the range.

She pushed six more of the hollow-tipped shells into the cylinder and steadied herself, squinting down the sights.

These next six she fired off quickly and brought the target back, her hand still slightly numb around the base of the thumb where the recoil of the Magnum had slammed the butt repeatedly against her palm.

All six shots were in the central area.

Donna nodded and removed the target, selecting another and pinning it to the black rubber backboard.

She was the only one in the range. She usually was during the day; the clock outside, beyond the double-thickness bullet-proof glass panels, showed that it was just 11.15 a.m.

She had risen early that morning, despite not getting back to the house until almost four. Sleep had eluded her for all but a couple of hours. Despite that, she felt fresh and alert. She turned to look out at Julie and caught a glimpse of her own reflection in the plate glass. There were dark rings beneath her eyes and her skin was pale. She might not *feel* tired but she looked as if she'd been without sleep for days.

Julie.

Donna had given up even trying to suppress her anger towards her sister. They'd exchanged words only briefly that morning, most of them unpleasant.

Now Donna turned back to face the counter where the .357, the .38, the Beretta and the Pathfinder were laid out. She selected the .38 and began thumbing in bullets from the box to her left.

She still felt numb from the revelations of the previous night.

Her own sister involved in an affair with Chris.

Donna shook her head.

Perhaps it *would* have been easier just to let Julie walk away. Walk out of her life. If she did, there would be no one left for her. Better the company of one she hated than complete loneliness.

Donna snapped the cylinder shut.

Did she hate Julie? Hatred was a very strong emotion. Stronger, she was beginning to think, even than love. But did she truly *hate* the younger woman?

She raised the .38 and took aim, firing off the six rounds evenly.

No one is to be trusted.

Christ, how prophetic the words in Chris's letter had proved to be.

She brought the target back and looked at the damage. Two in the centre, two in the head. Two in the groin. She covered the holes with white spots, sent the target away again and began pushing 9mm shells into the magazine of the Beretta.

How many times had she done this when Chris had been with her?

She almost smiled.

They'd been coming to the shooting club in Druid Street for almost three years. As she thought of her husband she felt a familiar but fleeting twinge of sadness but it was rapidly replaced by anger.

She hated Julie for what she'd done. She hated

Chris for his part in the deception. She hated The Sons of Midnight for what they too had done.

Someone had to pay for her anger; someone must be forced to suffer for her pain. It would be that organisation. Those who had tried to tell her that not only was her husband a liar and adulterer, he was capable of murder too.

Adulterer.

The word seemed peculiarly archaic.

Murderer *didn't*.

That was one of the things which *really* troubled her. She didn't find it easy to dismiss the suggestion as effortlessly as she would have liked. Why would Dashwood lie? Some kind of psychological trick? But why taunt her about facts she could never prove or disprove? Why?

Why?

There were so many questions; she knew that she would never know answers to most of them.

She continued thumbing bullets into the magazine.

Why had Chris decided upon an affair with Julie?

There were ten in the magazine now.

What had been so wrong with their marriage to make him do such a thing?

Eleven. Twelve.

Had Dashwood been telling the truth? Had her husband not merely wanted to expose The Sons of Midnight? Had he joined their ranks?

Thirteen.

Had the man she'd loved been capable of murder?

Fourteen.

And there still remained the mystery of Suzanne Regan. If it had been Julie embroiled in the affair with Chris, then why had Suzanne Regan been with the writer when he died?

Was there no end to these mysteries? No end to the pain?

She pushed in the last bullet, slammed in the magazine and worked the slide, cocking the weapon. She raised it, drawing a bead on the centre of the target.

If there were answers she would find them.

And then?

What was there to live for after that?

Donna gritted her teeth and tried not to think about it. For now she had something to drive her on.

The desire for vengeance. And she would not stop until it was hers. Someone was going to suffer for her torment and she didn't care who it was.

She fired off all fifteen rounds with remarkable rapidity and accuracy, the shots shredding the centre of the target, the pistol bouncing in her grip, empty shell-cases flying from the weapon until finally the slide shot back, signalling the weapon was empty. Donna lowered it, her breathing heavy, the stench of cordite strong in her nostrils.

Dark smoke surrounded her like a dirty shroud.

Eighty-Five

'It has to be the place in Conduit Street.'

Donna prodded the sheet of paper with the locations on, her eyes moving swiftly back and forth over the names:

RATHFARNHAM, DUBLIN.

BRASENOSE COLLEGE, OXFORD.

REGENCY PLACE, EDINBURGH.

CONDUIT STREET, LONDON.

The meeting places of The Sons of Midnight.

'How can you be sure?' Julie asked. 'What about Oxford?'

'London would have been easier for them to reach after leaving Essex but,' she exhaled deeply, 'I can't be *sure*. All we can do is check it out. If they're not there, we'll keep looking.'

Julie regarded her impassively across the table. The tension between the two women was almost palpable.

'Didn't Chris ever mention them to you?' Donna asked, not looking at Julie. 'Did he ever talk about his work to *you*?'

'No. He wouldn't discuss something with me that he refused to discuss with you, would he?'

'I don't know. I thought I knew him up until the last few weeks. Now I'm not sure of *anything* he would or wouldn't do.' She looked at Julie irritably. 'I thought I knew *you* too, Julie. Looks like I was wrong about both of you.'

'Why do you want me around, Donna?' Julie demanded. 'You can't stand me near you any more because of what happened. It would be best for both of us if I left.'

'I told you why. You *owe* me your help, *because* of what happened between you and Chris.' Her eyes narrowed. 'Don't think I enjoy looking at you and imagining what you and he used to get up to, but I'm damned if I'm going to let you walk away from what you did. You'd like that, wouldn't you? To think it was over and you'd escaped the consequences.'

'I'm not proud of what I did, Donna. If you think I am then you're even more fucked up than I imagined.' She spat out the words angrily.

Donna allowed her fingers to touch the butt of the .357 that lay on the table but she kept her gaze fixed on Julie.

'Why don't you use the bloody gun on me,' Julie said challengingly. 'That'd solve your problems, wouldn't it?'

'Don't think I haven't thought about it,' Donna told her. 'Don't think I haven't imagined how much I'd enjoy killing you.'

'I can understand that. Revenge seems to be the most important thing in your life now, Donna,' said Julie sardonically.

'Perhaps it's because there's nothing else in my life any more,' Donna told her. 'Chris is gone, even my memories of him might as well be gone.

You destroyed them, Julie. When I think of him I think of him with you. I think of his deceit. *Your* deceit. I *shared* him for ten months with you.'

'I saw him once a week, if that,' Julie said. 'In all that time, if you add up the hours I spent with him it's probably no more than two weeks.'

'And that's supposed to make it more acceptable, is it?'

'Look, Donna, I thought you wanted to destroy this group of men. I thought you wanted revenge on them. That's your *mission* now, isn't it?' She made no attempt to hide the sarcasm in her voice. 'Then concentrate on *that*.'

'And forget everything else?' She smiled thinly.

They sat in silence for what seemed like an eternity.

'So what do we do?' Julie asked finally.

'We find them. All of them.'

'And then?'

Donna looked down at the .357.

'Kill them.'

'I think the police might have something to say about that,' Julie observed.

'To hell with the police,' Donna snapped.

'Wasn't there something in Chris's notes about destroying the book?' Julie asked.

' "Destroy the book and you destroy *them*",' Donna muttered, as if she'd learned the words by heart. 'And you think they're going to let us walk in and do that without a fight?'

The two women regarded each other across

the table. Julie's eyes roved over her sister's outfit. The two shoulder-holsters she wore looked strangely incongruous.

Beneath one arm she carried the Beretta. As Julie watched, she slid the .357 into the other holster.

'Mrs Rambo,' Julie said almost scornfully. 'Do you have any idea how ridiculous you look?'

Donna eyed her malevolently.

'People are going to die, Julie,' she said quietly. 'Maybe you and me, too.' There was angry resignation in her voice. 'But who cares?'

She got to her feet, glancing at her watch.

It was 7.46 p.m.

Eighty-Six

The drive into Central London took less than fifty minutes. Traffic was relatively light, even in the centre, and Julie parked the Fiesta on the corner of Conduit Street and Mill Street.

'It's not too late to stop this bloody insanity,' Julie said, looking at her sister.

'We'll leave the car here,' Donna said, ignoring her.

She reached beneath her jacket and gently touched the butts of each gun in turn.

'We don't even know which house it is,' Julie protested.

There weren't many to pick from. Most of the buildings that occupied the street were shops or offices, their stonework grimy with years of accumulated muck. Donna gazed at the frontages of the buildings, her eyes finally coming to rest on a dark brick edifice sandwiched between a jeweller and a travel agent.

'From Chris's notes, it has to be that one,' she said.

The house had three stone steps leading up to its black front door. There were two windows downstairs, three on the first floor. Shutters were pulled tight across all of them, preventing prying eyes from seeing in. A length of iron railings ran in front of the building, some of them rusted, the paint having peeled away. Stone steps led down to a basement.

'What do we do? Just ring the doorbell?' Julie asked cryptically.

'There has to be a back way in,' Donna mused, studying the other structures nearby. She saw what appeared to be a narrow passageway leading alongside a building about twenty yards down the street. 'Come on,' she said and swung herself out of the car, leaving Julie to follow.

They hurried across the street towards the passage, Donna pausing briefly before stepping into the dark walkway. It smelt of stale urine. Donna wrinkled her nose as she made her way along, with Julie close behind her.

The passageway opened out into a large, square

yard. Surrounded on all sides by buildings, it had a claustrophobic atmosphere. Donna shivered involuntarily as she moved over the damp concrete towards the rear of the house.

Another heavy wooden door confronted them, and two ground floor windows. The building appeared to be in darkness. No sounds came from inside, either.

'It's not this house,' Julie said flatly.

Donna moved closer to the window and slid her fingers carefully beneath the sash frame.

To her surprise it moved slightly.

She tried again and a gap about two feet wide opened.

Wide enough for them to slip through.

Donna hesitated.

This was a little too easy, wasn't it?

Perhaps they were expected.

And yet, as she'd said to Julie before, as far as Dashwood and the others were concerned both women had died in the waxworks.

And yet . . .

Could it be a trick?

'Do we go in?' Julie wanted to know, her heart thumping that little bit faster.

A trick?

They had to take that chance.

Donna eased the window up a fraction more, then swung herself over the sill and into the room beyond.

Julie followed.

*   *   *

The woman lay on a rug in the centre of the floor.

She was naked.

So was the man who lay beside her.

The room was silent apart from their low breathing.

The watchers made no sound.

The man finally looked up, as if seeking permission to begin.

Francis Dashwood, seated at a long oak table at one end of the room, nodded slowly, a crooked smile on his face.

As the man in the centre of the room moved onto the woman, his erection bobbing before him, a great cheer arose.

As he thrust hard into her a chorus of hand-clapping and cat-calls accompanied his actions.

The noise began to build to a crescendo. In the brightly lit room sweat glistened on the couple in the centre of the floor.

Donna stood in the darkened room, listening for any sounds of movement. Apart from Julie scrambling through the window, there were none.

Donna closed it behind her.

'No alarms?' Donna mused quietly.

Julie didn't answer. She was squinting around the room, trying to pick out details in the gloom.

The walls were oak-panelled, hung with large paintings in ornate frames. Shelf after shelf of books loomed from the blackness on two sides of them. There was a fusty smell inside the

367

room; it reminded Donna of the odour from the Grimoire. Ancient paper, now yellowing, expelled its stench like decaying flesh. There were four or five high-backed leather chairs in the room, too; the arms were worn, the furniture very old.

On the other side of the room was another door.

Donna moved towards it. Julie followed, glancing up at the stuffed birds that lowered down from the corners of the room like silent sentinels. She recognized the birds as hawks.

There was a strip of light beneath the door and Donna paused, wondering what lay beyond the wooden partition. She could hear no sound from beyond. Even the noise of traffic passing down Conduit Street outside was barely audible, so thick were the walls of the dwelling.

She knelt, trying to see through the keyhole, desperate to know what lay beyond.

She could see nothing.

Just that strip of light beneath it.

Again, almost unconsciously, she allowed one hand to stray inside her jacket and brush against the butt of the .357.

If there was anyone beyond this door she would be ready for them.

She placed her hand on the doorknob and turned it.

Eighty-Seven

It looked like a hallway.

As Donna eased the door open and peered through she saw a large area of black-and-white tiled floor with three doors leading off it. To the right was a staircase. The hallway was twenty feet across, perhaps a little more. It was brightly lit by two enormous crystal chandeliers hanging from the ornate ceiling. Donna could see the clusters of lights reflected in the tiles.

There were no shadows in which to hide.

She eased the door open a fraction more and looked round at the staircase. It looked like bare mahogany. No carpet covered the highly polished wood. The walls were a dark colour completely devoid of decoration of any kind. Not one single painting hung either in the hallway or on the stairs.

Donna eased the .357 from her shoulder holster and steadied it in her hands.

'What are you doing?' Julie wanted to know.

'We've got to get across that hall,' Donna told her. 'If anyone comes out of any of those doors, I want to be ready.'

She took a step out into the brightly lit hall.

Her eyes darted back and forth over the three doors, then up the stairs. She inclined her head, a signal for Julie to follow her towards the stairs.

Donna's eyes never left the top of the flight as they climbed; Julie kept her attention riveted to the doors.

They climbed slowly, step by step, their progress agonizingly slow. Donna was aware how hopelessly exposed they would be, should anyone either enter the hall or approach from the head of the stairs. She could see a large landing at the top with more rooms leading off it.

A step creaked protestingly beneath Donna and she froze. The sound seemed to echo around the hall.

She gripped the revolver tightly, looking quickly around her.

'Come on,' whispered Julie, her own heart beating faster. 'Move it.'

Donna remained motionless. After what seemed like an eternity, she began to climb once more.

Julie followed gratefully.

'Listen,' said Donna.

Julie heard nothing at first then . . .

Breathing.

It sounded as if there was someone close to them, breathing. A low, almost inaudible but laboured breathing.

'Where the hell is that coming from?' Julie said frantically, trying to keep her voice low.

Donna had no answer. All she could do was look around, trying to find the source of it.

Was someone watching them?

The breathing sounded close, as if someone were standing right next to them. Yet they were the only ones on the staircase.

Donna felt cold fingers of fear plucking at the hairs on the back of her neck. She moved further up the stairs until she reached the landing.

The breathing continued, a little more faint now, though. The two women looked round at the doors on the landing. They were all tightly closed. The breathing didn't seem to be coming from any of them.

It still seemed as if it was from an invisible source right beside them.

Imagination?

Julie looked back and forth anxiously. Their assailant could be behind any one of the doors. Just waiting.

'Donna . . .'

Her words trailed off as she heard a sound below.

One of the doors leading into the hall had opened.

The two women ducked down against the landing rail and watched as a smartly dressed man emerged from a room beyond the hall, his shoes beating out a tattoo on the polished floor. He vanished beneath them, then returned a moment later carrying a bottle of brandy. He disappeared back into the door through which he'd emerged.

For what seemed like an eternity Donna and Julie crouched where they were, watching the closed door. Then Donna raised herself up slowly, moving to the head of the stairs.

'Come on,' she said quietly. 'We'll see where he's gone.'

They began to descend, Donna holding the pistol at the ready should the man or any like him appear again.

As they reached the bottom of the stairs Donna heard the low breathing again. She tried to ignore it but she couldn't. Her heart thumped hard in her chest as she looked around.

'I can still hear it,' Julie said, as if to affirm what her older sister already knew.

Donna nodded slowly, and moved across the hall towards the door through which the smartly dressed man had disappeared only moments earlier.

The chandeliers above them pinned them in bright light; Julie could see their reflections in the fine crystal.

There was still no sound except for that infernal low breathing. The entire house seemed to be deserted, but after the appearance of the smartly dressed man, they knew that to be untrue. Could Julie be right? Could this be the wrong house? What if The Sons of Midnight didn't frequent this building? What if they only gathered at certain times?

What if?

There was only one way to find out.

Donna grabbed the door handle, swallowed hard and pushed.

Eighty-Eight

The corridor beyond the door was less than six feet wide and it stretched about twenty feet ahead of them. The walls on either side were bare. Unlike the hallway, it was lit only by two wall lights, one at either end of the corridor. The far end boasted another closed door. The man they'd seen must have come and gone via the door ahead. There was nowhere else for him to go.

Donna wondered how big the place was. It didn't seem this big from the outside.

Where the hell was everybody?

Apart from the smartly dressed man, they'd not seen nor heard a living soul.

Heard nothing apart from that low breathing.

Julie looked into the dark corridor with trepidation.

How much longer was this going to go on? She feared that the end would be signalled by *their* deaths.

Donna moved into the darkened corridor, stepping cautiously, as if she were walking on squeaking floorboards, not carpet-covered concrete.

The wall lights didn't seem to be powered by anything more substantial than forty-watt bulbs. The glow they cast was a sickly yellow light that barely illuminated the narrow walkway from one door to the other.

The two women moved cautiously along, Donna keeping her eyes ahead, Julie occasionally glancing at the door behind.

Donna put out one hand as if to steady herself against the wall.

Something moved beneath her fingertips.

'Jesus,' she hissed, moving away from the wall and looking down.

'What is it?' Julie wanted to know, her eyes wide with fear.

Donna didn't answer. Instead she carefully replaced her hand on the wall where it had been seconds earlier.

She felt it again. Once more the sensation caused her to pull her hand away, as if she'd received an electric shock.

Was she going insane?

She touched the wall again, but left her hand there until she was sure beyond any doubt.

The stonework, the very plaster, was throbbing gently, as if the bricks and mortar contained some kind of pulse.

Donna could see no movement but she could feel the slow, even thudding against her hand.

Dashwood's words came flooding back to her:

'Organic life can exist, can be made to exist, anywhere and within anything. Within the bricks and mortar of a house.'

Donna raised the barrel of the .357. Using the

blade foresight as a tool, she drew the sharp fin across the wall.

'Oh God,' whispered Julie.

Blood oozed from the mark on the wall.

It welled thickly in the narrow mark Donna had made, then dribbled down the paintwork.

She repeated the action on the other wall.

The same thing happened.

She closed her eyes for long seconds, praying that when she opened them the blood would be gone.

It wasn't. The thick crimson fluid ran down the wall in rivulets.

Donna swallowed hard and moved forward, towards the door at the end of the dimly lit corridor.

One of the lights flickered.

They froze momentarily as the bulbs went into a kind of stroboscopic dance before flaring full on for a few more seconds.

Then they went out completely.

The two women were plunged into total darkness.

Julie backed up and touched the wall, feeling the pulse in it, scarcely able to stifle her scream of terror. She bit her fist to muffle the sound.

Donna gripped the .357 tightly and moved towards the door at the far end of the corridor.

'Let's get out now,' hissed Julie.

Donna's answer was to shoot out a hand and grab her sister by the arm, pulling her along with her.

The end of the corridor couldn't be more than about six or seven feet away, she reasoned.

The lights stayed off. Darkness wrapped itself round them like an impenetrable shroud.

They moved forward in the gloom, nearer and nearer to the door.

The light at the far end of the corridor flickered briefly and Donna saw they were a couple of feet away.

'Come on,' she whispered, trying to reassure herself as well as Julie. Her own breathing was heavy now.

She touched something cold and realized that it was the door handle. No light showed beneath. She could only guess at what lay beyond it. *More darkness?*

The lights flickered again and went out. Flashed on.

They enjoyed a few seconds of light, then blackness returned. But at the far end of the corridor there was illumination.

The two women were relieved to see light, until they realized that the door through which they'd entered was slightly open.

Had someone slipped into the corridor behind them while the lights were out?

Donna pushed Julie aside and raised the pistol, sighting it at the far end.

She could see nothing. No dark shape moving furtively in the shadows.

Nothing.

It appeared that they were alone in the corridor.

She turned back to face the next door.

Gripping the gun tightly, Donna took the handle and twisted it, pushing the door open. She stepped through.

Eighty-Nine

The flight of stone steps seemed to stretch away into the subterranean shadows. The bottom of the staircase was barely visible. Only the merest hint of sickly yellow light seeped upwards, barely penetrating the umbra.

Donna moved cautiously down the first few steps, glancing back to make sure Julie was following. She was, her face pale and drawn, ghost-like in the darkness.

She heard breathing, as she'd heard before.

This time it seemed louder, more pronounced, as if some invisible phantom were treading the steps with her. Donna swallowed hard, gripped the .357 more tightly and continued to descend.

The staircase was narrow. More than once she was forced to brush against the wall.

She shuddered with revulsion as she felt the cold stone pulsing. Like a gigantic brick heart it pumped against her. Even beneath her feet she felt a rhythmic movement.

She closed her eyes for a second, still not convinced it wasn't her mind playing tricks.

If only it had been.

Behind her Julie was looking down at her feet, being careful not to slip on the narrow steps. She too felt the thudding. Sweat beaded on her forehead despite the chill in the basement.

They were halfway down the stairs now, within sight of the bottom. Donna saw that it was a hallway similar to the one upstairs. Instead of being lit by chandeliers, however, this one was illuminated by the dull glow of three candles. Halos of subdued light flared from the small flames that flickered and threatened to blow out.

The breathing continued, but Donna was aware her own laboured exhalations were now adding to the sound that filled her ears.

In the silent blackness it seemed deafening.

They reached the bottom of the stairs. Julie looked round to check that no one had slipped through the door behind them, but it was so dark on the steps it was difficult to see anything at all. She stared at the sea of shadow, trying to spot any deviation in a wall of gloom, as if part of that false night might at any second detach itself.

She saw nothing.

Donna stood motionless, surveying the basement area.

The two women stood in an area roughly twelve feet square. Behind them was the staircase. To the right and left were solid walls; straight ahead, they faced three doors. Beside each stood a candle, helping to light the underground chamber.

Which door first?

She listened, trying to hear over the insistent breathing.

Christ, it was getting louder.

If Dashwood had been right about inanimate objects being given life, then they must be at the very centre of the house. It was, she imagined, like walking around inside a huge chest cavity. The infernal pulsing continued, too. Donna thought she could see undulations in the very umbra itself.

She felt perspiration on her palms, the metal and wood of the gun against her flesh. She shifted it to the other hand and wiped her palm on her jeans. She repeated the action with the other hand.

Which door?

She could hear no sound behind any of them. Could the basement also deserted, she wondered? But they had seen the smartly dressed man come down here. There was no other way out but through these three doors.

But which one?

She took a tentative step towards the one on the left, her eyes fixed on it.

The flame of the candle closest wavered, as if disturbed by a breeze. For a second it sputtered but then it flared again. A plume of black smoke rose into the darkness and was absorbed by it.

Donna took a step closer.

Behind her Julie watched, then advanced cautiously, her eyes darting back and forth between the three doors.

Donna was within two feet of the left-hand door.

It was then that the middle door opened.

Light and sound suddenly flooded into the darkened hallway. The figure silhouetted against the sudden explosion of brightness stood motionless, looking first at Julie, then at Donna.

His surprise lasted only seconds.

Peter Farrell reached for his gun.

Ninety

The movement was smooth and efficient.

Donna raised the .357, steadied herself and fired off two rounds.

The roar as the weapon spat out the high-calibre shells was intolerable in the confined space; both she and Julie were deafened by the thunderous retort. The muzzle-flashes seared white light onto their retinas and the stink of cordite filled the air.

The impact lifted Farrell off his feet. The first bullet struck him in the chest, the second hit him just below the chin.

He was slammed back against the wall, blood spouting from the wound in his throat. For long seconds he stood there, eyes gaping wide, his body twitching.

Donna fired again.

The third shot caught him in the face slightly to the left of his nose. The bullet drilled the eye socket empty, powered through the brain and exploded from the back of his skull, carrying a confetti of pulverized bone and sticky pinkish-red matter with it. Farrell pitched forward, what was left of his head smacking hard against the floor, blood pouring from the remnants of his blasted cranium.

Donna stepped over the body and into the room from which he'd emerged, her ears still ringing.

Julie followed, glancing down at the body as she passed.

The room beyond was large and well lit, particularly the area in the centre. It was there that Donna saw a naked man scramble to his feet, a look of horror on his face as he saw the gun. The woman beneath him, also naked, rolled over and tried to get up but she slipped, screaming in terror.

Donna saw perhaps a dozen men in the room, most dressed in suits. And instead of attacking her and Julie, they were fleeing.

A door at the far end of the room seemed to be their only means of escape. They rushed at it *en masse*, struggling with each other in their haste to get out.

Donna spun round, the gun levelled.

Dashwood and Parsons stood immobile at the head of a long table.

The Grimoire was on the table in front of them.

There was another thunderous roar of gunfire. Donna hurled herself to the ground as the bullet sang past her, slicing empty air before blasting a hole in the wall.

David Ryker got off two more rounds before Donna managed to return fire.

The room was filled with the massive sounds, thundercracks of noise that threatened to burst the eardrums.

The naked man ran towards Ryker.

He shot him.

Donna looked on in bewilderment as Ryker put two shots into the man's chest. She saw him hurled backwards by the impact, one shell erupting from his back close to the right scapula. Gobbets of lung tissue sprayed across the room as he fell.

The woman who had been with him went on screaming until Ryker shot her, too, one .45 slug in the head. It smashed in her temple as surely as if she'd been hit with a sledgehammer.

Donna fired and hit Ryker in the shoulder. He dropped his gun and clapped a hand to the wound, feeling jagged bone against his fingertip as his index finger slipped inside the hole.

'Get the book,' Donna shouted to Julie, who sprinted across the rapidly emptying room.

The other people who had been in the room had mostly scrambled through the door at the far end.

Julie picked up a chair and hurled it at Dashwood, who raised his arms to shield himself, falling back.

Parsons snatched at the Grimoire, catching Julie across the face with a swipe of his hand. She shouted in pain, feeling her bottom lip split under the impact.

Parsons gripped the book in his gnarled hands.

Donna stood up and fired at him.

The shot caught him in the left arm, tearing through the bicep.

Blood exploded from the wound, thick, dark blood that spattered the wall behind him.

He dropped the book and Julie made a grab for it, knocking it away, sending it skidding across the floor.

Parsons shouted something and leapt after it.

Donna drew a bead on him and fired.

The hammer slammed down on an empty chamber.

She threw the .357 away, pulling at the other shoulder holster, freeing the Beretta.

Parsons shouted in triumph as he reached the book but Donna swung the 92S into position and pumped the trigger.

One, two, three times she fired.

Parsons was hit in the chest and thigh. The third bullet missed and buried itself in the far wall.

Four, five, six.

The room had become like the inside of a cannon barrel, the noise incessant and deafening. Julie screamed but could not hear her own cry.

Parsons had fallen face down on the floor across the naked woman, his body torn and bleeding from the impact of the 9mm bullets. He reached out towards Donna, his fingers gradually twitching less and less.

He lay still.

Smoke hung like a gauze net across the room.

Julie, on her hands and knees, looked around for the Grimoire. Donna could see that the only living people left now were herself, her sister, Ryker, who was slumped against an overturned table holding his smashed shoulder, and Dashwood, who stood defiantly facing her.

Donna's breath came in gasps as she looked from one man to the other.

The floor was awash with blood from the dead man and woman and from Parsons.

The Grimoire lay in the centre of the floor.

A prize.

The trophy in a game of death.

No one moved.

The retorts of the guns still filled their ears, the muzzle-flashes still flamed in their eyes. But the room was all but silent.

Donna could see that Ryker's .45 was lying within two or three feet of him. She saw his eyes dart to one side.

He moved very slightly towards the weapon, still holding his shoulder. Blood was pumping through his fingers; every movement clearly brought him fresh agony, as the two pieces of his shattered clavicle grated together.

Nevertheless, if he could just reach the gun . . .

Donna shot him three times.

His body jerked as each bullet thudded into him, then he slid to one side and lay still, his chest and face covered in blood. It looked as if someone had upended him and dipped him in the crimson fluid.

Donna aimed the pistol at Dashwood.

Julie was crying softly now. Her hearing all but gone, her eyes stinging from the smoke, she could only watch helplessly as Donna and Dashwood faced each other.

He was smiling.

Ninety-One

'You should have been dead by now,' Dashwood told her. 'Both of you.'

Donna kept her eyes fixed on him and the automatic aimed at his head.

'What did you hope to gain by this little show?' The words were heavy with scorn. 'You think what's happened here tonight will make any difference? Do you think you can stop us? Your husband thought the same thing, and he ended up joining us.'

'No,' said Donna, shaking her head.

'Why do you find it so hard to believe?'

Dashwood asked. 'Did you know so little about him? Or were you too stupid?' He glared at her. 'He knew *this* place well enough. And our other meeting houses. He wanted our knowledge and he found it. He paid the price to be one of us. He abandoned *all* he believed in, all his morals, all his ethics. He had nothing left but us.'

'It's not true,' Donna said tearfully.

'He knew a woman called Suzanne Regan,' Dashwood said flatly, as if he were telling her something she didn't already know.

The surprise registered on her face and Dashwood saw it.

'True?' he continued.

She nodded.

'Do you know what she was? She was what this woman was to have been.' He nodded towards the corpse of the naked female at Donna's feet. 'She was a carrier. She had been for a number of our other members. And she was for your husband.' Dashwood held Donna's gaze. 'You said you had read the initiation rites. You knew of the fornication, the offering of a child, the need to keep that child's skull. Suzanne Regan carried a child for your husband. A child he then killed.'

Donna's body stiffened. She felt an icy coldness envelope her, as if she'd been wrapped in a freezing blanket.

'He knew he had to sacrifice a child as an offering to us,' Dashwood told her. 'He made Suzanne Regan pregnant. She knew what would happen to the baby, but it didn't bother her. She

386

handed it over willingly, so your husband could kill it. He killed it in front of us, just as he had copulated with Suzanne Regan as we watched. He cut the child's head from its shoulders as we watched.' Dashwood shrugged. 'We welcomed him into our ranks and then he betrayed us. He stole the Grimoire and threatened to expose us, as I told you. He knew too much about us.'

'You're lying,' Donna said, wishing she could inject more conviction into her voice. She had lowered the gun slightly.

'You traced us, you learned about us. You know that every member of The Sons of Midnight entered his name in the Grimoire. Your husband's name is there. Look at it.'

He motioned towards the book.

Kill him.

'Go on, look,' he urged.

Kill him and destroy the book.

She had to know.

Donna moved towards the Grimoire and flipped it open. There were hundreds of names there, some faded from the passing of time.

'The last name,' Dashwood told her.

She turned a couple of pages and looked at the list.

'Oh God,' she whispered. She felt the freezing blanket being drawn tighter.

On the parchment-like paper she saw her husband's name, recognized his handwriting.

Donna took hold of the page and tore it out.

Dashwood shouted in pain, his teeth gritted, as he looked at the ripped-out page.

Donna folded it and pushed it into the back pocket of her jeans.

She tore out another page.

'No,' shouted Dashwood. A deep gash appeared above his left eyebrow, as if slashed by an invisible blade.

He lunged at Donna, trying to get hold of the book.

'Leave it, you bitch,' he roared.

She hurled the book away and fired at it, putting two bullets into the ancient tome.

To her surprise and horror, blood exploded from the book.

Dashwood screamed and clapped hands to his chest.

Blood was jetting from two wounds there.

Donna fired more shots into the book.

Pieces of it flew into the air, propelled by the dark blood pumping from it.

Dashwood dropped to his knees, holes appearing in his leg and stomach.

More of the crimson fluid spilled over his lips. He turned to face Donna.

'You know the truth now,' he grimaced, teeth clenched, bloodied. 'Search your house. The cellar.' His eyes blazed. 'He was one of us,' he roared.

Donna shot him in the face as he knelt in front of her.

He raised his hands towards her and she saw

the skin beginning to yellow, to peel away from his fingertips. A nail came free, pus and blood spewing from the digit. Huge pieces of flesh began to curl away from his cheeks, leaving the network of muscles beneath exposed. One eye burst in its socket. Dark fluid began to run from both his nostrils and suddenly the room was filled with an overpowering stench of decay, a nauseating odour that made the two women feel sick.

Dashwood clapped his hands to his face and pulled them away dripping. Flesh was liquefying on his bones, the bones themselves crumbling.

In a corner of the room the Grimoire was dissolving into a seething puddle of reeking muck, a gelatinous mess that looked like the contents of a huge, freshly milked boil.

Dashwood fell forward and his body seemed to fold in on itself, his chest collapsing, lungs transformed into reeking sacks which burst, spilling more black fluid into the cavity of the torso. His legs seemed to shrivel, shrinking up inside his trousers, already stained with blood.

Donna finally managed to stagger away from the sight. Julie followed.

They headed for the door through which they'd entered, hurdling the body of Farrell, aware now that the breathing that had been ever-present since they entered the house had stopped.

Blood oozed from the walls.

All the way up the flight of stone steps and along that corridor the dark fluid coursed down the plaster and stone.

389

They burst free into the hallway, then through into the room beyond, and struggled out of the window by which they'd first entered.

The cool night air washed over them but could not drive the stench of decay from their nostrils.

Julie was already running for the alleyway that ran alongside the house. Donna took one look back at the building, then ran after her.

The wailing of sirens already filled the air.

It would be a matter of minutes before the first police car arrived.

Ninety-Two

From where they sat they could see the uniformed men approaching the house in Conduit Street. Donna watched them scrambling out of their cars, running towards the front door. Others headed off up the alley at the side of the building.

She watched impassively, her mind blank, her eyes devoid of emotion. She felt as if every last ounce of feeling had been sucked from her. She was drained, incapable of movement let alone rational thought.

And yet still Dashwood's words echoed in her mind:

'*He was one of us.*'

She lowered her head momentarily and closed her eyes.

'The police will be looking.'

Julie's voice seemed a million miles away.

Donna raised her head and looked at her sister.

'The police will be looking for whoever killed those men,' the younger woman continued.

'They won't be looking for *us*,' Donna said.

Julie gazed at her for long moments.

'Are you satisfied now?' she said finally.

Donna didn't speak.

'They're dead. You've got what you wanted. How does it feel?'

'We have to go back to the cottage,' Donna said quietly. 'Dashwood said I'd find the truth in the cellar. Only the cottage has a cellar. We have to go back and look there.'

'Not *we*, Donna. *You*. I'm finished. I'm leaving now. If you want to stop me, you'll have to kill me.' There were tears in Julie's eyes.

Donna looked wearily at the younger woman.

'I wanted to hate you for this,' she said softly. 'For what you did. For taking Chris from me.'

'I didn't take him,' Julie protested.

'I know he didn't leave me, but like I said to you before, you shared part of his life. A life that should have been just mine and his. And I *do* hate you.' She felt her own tears beginning to run warmly down her cheeks. A bitter smile creased her face.

'You'll never see me again, Donna, I promise you,' Julie said, wiping her eyes. She opened the car door.

'You think I'd just let you walk away?'

'What else are you going to do? I'm sorry. Believe that, at least. I *am* sorry for what I did.'

Julie held her sister's gaze for a moment, then moved to pull herself out of the car.

'I can't let you walk away, Julie,' Donna said almost apologetically.

'You can't stop me,' the younger woman said, and swung herself out of the car.

Donna slid her hand inside her jacket and pulled out the Beretta, keeping the pistol low, aimed at Julie's stomach.

She shook her head, tears streaming down her face.

A look of fear flickered behind Julie's eyes.

'You're right,' Donna said, her voice cracking. 'It *is* all over.'

Donna turned the gun round quickly, bent her head forward and opened her mouth.

She pushed the barrel into her mouth and squeezed the trigger.

Ninety-Three

Julie wanted to scream but the sight of her sister with the pistol jammed in her mouth seemed to freeze her vocal cords.

Instead she made a frantic grab for the Beretta as Donna fired.

The hammer slammed down on an empty chamber.

The metallic click reverberated inside the car as Julie tore the pistol from her grip and stood panting beside her.

Donna merely looked at the younger woman, then leaned across and pulled the passenger door shut.

Julie looked down helplessly at the gun she now held in her hand.

'Donna, I . . .'

The sentence trailed off, lost in the sound of the Fiesta's engine as Donna started it up.

She guided the car away from the kerb, away from Julie. As she pulled away she glanced one final time in the rear-view mirror.

Julie was standing on the street corner, the empty gun clutched in her hand.

Donna drove on.

The journey became a blur of passing traffic and dark roads.

She didn't look at the clock when she left London; she had no idea how long it would take her to reach the cottage. Donna merely drove, her mind spinning. Two or three times she had to brake sharply to avoid hitting vehicles in front of her. She considered stopping at a service station for a coffee, but then decided against it. If she stopped she'd never start again. It was as if she was being forced on by instinct alone. All she felt was a crushing weariness, a similar feeling to the one she'd felt in the days after her husband's death. A feeling that she had become an empty shell, sucked dry of feeling, unable to think straight.

She stopped for petrol, standing on a deserted forecourt, the cold wind whistling around her. She shivered but the chill she felt came from within.

She had achieved her goal. Parsons and Dashwood were dead. Farrell was dead.

Why then did she not feel a sense of triumph?

Perhaps because she felt that she *too* should be dead.

All she felt was a growing feeling of desolation. Death and loss had become engrained in her life.

She had no one now.

She thought how easy it would have been to drive the car into a tree. She gripped the wheel more tightly and drove through the night.

Ninety-Four

It seemed like years, not days, since she'd been to the cottage.

The assault on the property, which could have cost her and Julie their lives, seemed to have faded into the mists of time. Supposedly the mind pushes unpleasant things to one side in an effort to forget them. Donna had tried to do that with the events at the cottage, but as soon as she saw the building the memories came flooding back in an unwelcome tide.

She sat in the Fiesta gazing at the structure. Even in the darkness she could see bullet holes in the stonework. The wood she'd used to board up the windows was still in place, although a couple of the sheets had come loose. One was slapping against the frame each time the wind blew.

Donna slid out from behind the wheel and approached the cottage, fumbling in her pocket for her key-ring. She selected the front door key, pausing for a moment before turning it, images of her last visit running through her mind like a video recorder on fast-forward. She could see Farrell and his men trying to break in. She could see the blood. She could see Julie.

Julie.

Donna closed her eyes tightly, then took a deep breath. The image faded slightly. She entered.

There was broken glass in the hallway, still. It crunched beneath her feet as she walked, moving through into the sitting-room, not bothering to turn on the lights. She moved quickly and assuredly in the gloom, heading for the kitchen.

There was a torch in one of the kitchen drawers. She retrieved it, flicking it on, allowing the powerful beam to cut through the blackness.

She trained it on the cellar trap door.

'Search your house. The cellar.'

Donna hooked a finger into the ring on the trap and pulled, opening it. She shone the torch down into the underground chamber, ignoring the smell of damp that wafted up from below. She tucked the torch into the waistband of her jeans as she eased herself onto the ladder, climbing down slowly, afraid, as she'd always been, that the wooden rungs would give way. A spider's web brushed against her face as she neared the bottom. Donna snatched at it, anxious to brush it away. The floor of the cellar was partly earth; it was the damp soil that she could smell so strongly.

Donna took the torch from her jeans and shone it around.

The cellar was less than fifteen feet square but it was crammed with tea chests and boxes, some of which were damp and mildewed. Spiders' webs seemed to link the boxes like membranous skin. She shuddered as she looked around. It was the first time she'd had a proper look inside the underground room; already she felt a sense of claustrophobia. Nevertheless she moved towards the first pile of packing cases, rummaging through them, not really sure what she was looking for but fearing what she might find.

The boxes were mostly full of old newspaper, which had been used as padding around items of value. There didn't seem to be much else lurking in there.

She heard a noise from above her and froze.

Instinctively she switched off the torch, standing completely still in the cloying darkness, her heart thudding against her ribs.

Whatever it was appeared to be coming from the sitting-room, above her to the left.

She heard it again.

Donna suddenly realized the source of the disturbance.

It was a piece of wood banging against a window-frame, blown by the wind.

Flicking the torch back on she continued her search, checking more boxes, feeling her feet sinking into the earthen floor. The dirt stuck to her trainers. She muttered to herself, scraping the sticky mud off against a wooden box.

Her efforts to remove the earth caused the box to topple over and Donna saw, beneath where it had stood, a piece of metal; a sheet of rusted iron about a foot square, only part of it showing through the dark earth. She aimed the torch at it, then dropped to her knees and began pulling at the clods. The odour of damp was thick and noxious but she continued with her task, finally exposing the metal sheet.

It was covering a small hole.

Donna laid the torch beside the hole, slipped her fingers under the sheet of iron and lifted, flipping it over.

She snatched the torch up again and shone it down into the hole.

The object inside was small, perhaps twice the size of a man's fist, and wrapped in plastic.

Her heart beat faster as she reached for it.

Leave it. Go now. Walk away forever.

She hesitated a moment.

Get out now and never return.

Donna had to know. She snatched up the

object, pulling the plastic from it like a child would unwrap a Christmas present.

The skull was unmistakably that of a baby.

Parts of it were not even completely formed. The fontanelles had not yet joined.

The child must have been very young indeed. Days old when . . .

When it was killed?

She dropped the skull and closed her eyes, tears beginning to form behind her lids. When she looked down again the skull had fallen back into the hole, the eye sockets gazing sightlessly up at her.

'*He was one of us.*'

She sat down on the wet earth, the torch still gripped in one hand, tears coursing down her cheeks.

Donna felt something digging into her backside and realized that she still had the folded pages of the Grimoire stuffed in there.

Including the page which bore her husband's name.

She pulled it out slowly and unfolded it, shining the light over the other names on the list.

Other members of The Sons of Midnight.

'*They have infiltrated everywhere.*'

Donna read the first of the names.

'Oh, Christ,' she murmured.

She heard the creaking above her, spun round and looked up.

There was a torch beam shining in *her* face

now, held by the figure on the edge of the cellar opening.

It was Detective Constable David Mackenzie.

Ninety-Five

'Come up here, Mrs Ward, and bring the pages from the book with you.'

Mackenzie's words seemed to echo inside the small cellar.

As Donna looked more closely, she saw that he was holding a gun; too. The .38 glinted in the torchlight.

Without a second thought she began to climb the steps, the pages of the Grimoire held in her hand. There was no point in trying to run. Where the hell was she going to go?

She pulled herself out of the cellar and stood facing him, noticing that he'd taken a step back, that the pistol was levelled at her.

'You're part of it,' she said flatly.

'Drop the pages on the floor in front of you and step back,' Mackenzie told her.

She did as instructed, tossing the parchment away as if it was infected with some vile disease.

Mackenzie picked the discarded paper up without taking his eyes off her. He stuffed the pages into the pocket of his coat. He moved away from her again.

'You knew right from the beginning,' she said. 'You knew that first night at the hospital when I came to identify Chris. You were a part of it then. *You're* one of them, aren't you?'

The policeman smiled thinly.

'One of who, Mrs Ward?' he said.

'The Sons of Midnight, or whatever the hell they call themselves.'

'You saw some of the other names on the list,' he said. 'You can't even begin to imagine how far this goes. Who *is* involved. How high up it goes. You've only scratched the surface. I'm a *very* small part of it but there are others who must be protected until the time is right. Your husband knew that, too. He knew who was involved, how important some of the higher ranking members were.'

'That's why you killed him?'

'I told you, his death was an accident.' The policeman smiled. 'Perhaps he was lucky. He died before we got to him.'

'And now it's my turn?'

'Why should I kill you?'

'I've seen the names on the list. I know what's going on.'

'You've seen some of the names, but you have no idea of what's going on. You can't begin to imagine what is going on and who else is involved. Like I said, you couldn't begin to imagine how high this thing goes.'

'No one can be trusted.'

'Who would you go to with your revelations? The press? Television?' There was a mocking tone in his voice. 'Who'd believe you?'

He backed towards the kitchen door, the gun still levelled at her.

'Everything you've done has been for nothing,' he told her. 'You wasted your time.'

Donna watched as he opened the door, then stepped outside into the night. She heard his footsteps in the mud beyond, heard a car engine start up, the vehicle pull away.

She walked through to the sitting-room and peered through a crack in the boarded-up window, watching the car's rear lights disappearing into the gloom.

The package was standing on the table.

Donna saw it. Saw the small red lights winking on it.

She smelled something.

A sickly sweet smell that reminded her of marzipan.

Her husband had once told her that plastic explosive smelled like marzipan.

She guessed that the bomb was about fifty pounds.

There were two red lights on it, and one of them had begun to flicker madly.

Donna took a step towards it.

In the back of the Orion, Mackenzie pressed the red button on the small control panel.

The explosion was thunderous.

Even seventy yards from the cottage the car was showered with debris.

Mackenzie didn't bother to look back; he merely slid the control panel back inside his jacket and nodded to his driver.

The car moved off, swallowed by the night.

'Whom God wishes to destroy, he first makes mad . . .'

Euripides.

<u>SLUGS</u>

Shaun Hutson

They slime, they ooze, they kill . . .

One female slug can lay one and a half million eggs a
year – a fact which holds terrifying consequences for the
people of Merton. As the town basks in the summer heat,
a new breed of slug is growing and multiplying. In the
waist-high grass, in the dank, dark cellars they are
acquiring new tastes, new cravings. For blood. For flesh.
Human flesh . . .

HORROR

CAPTIVES

Shaun Hutson

The murders had been savage and apparently motiveless. Carbon copies of killings committed years earlier and by men currently incarcerated in one of Britain's top maximum security prisons. How could this be? Detective Inspector Frank Gregson must find the answers. Answers that will bring him into conflict with one of those prisoners, a man framed for a murder he didn't commit and determined to discover who framed him and why. These two obsessive men, on their private quests, will clash as they seek the truth that links Whitely Prison with London's seedy underworld of sex-shows and drug barons. One wants vengeance, the other wants the truth. What they discover threatens not only their lives but their sanity . . .

'The man who writes what others are afraid even to imagine'
Sunday Times

HORROR

Time Warner Paperback titles available by mail:

☐	Assassin	Shaun Hutson	£5.99
☐	Breeding Ground	Shaun Hutson	£5.99
☐	Captives	Shaun Hutson	£5.99
☐	Death Day	Shaun Hutson	£5.99
☐	Erebus	Shaun Hutson	£5.99
☐	Nemesis	Shaun Hutson	£5.99
☐	Relics	Shaun Hutson	£5.99
☐	Renegades	Shaun Hutson	£5.99
☐	Shadows	Shaun Hutson	£6.99
☐	Slugs	Shaun Hutson	£5.99
☐	Spawn	Shaun Hutson	£5.99
☐	Victims	Shaun Hutson	£6.99

The prices shown above are correct at time of going to press. However, the publishers reserve the right to increase prices on covers from those previously advertised without prior notice.

TIME WARNER PAPERBACKS
P.O. Box 121, Kettering, Northants NN14 4ZQ
Tel: 01832 737525, Fax: 01832 733076
Email: aspenhouse@FSBDial.co.uk

POST AND PACKING:
Payments can be made as follows: cheque, postal order (payable to Time Warner Paperbacks) or by credit cards. Do not send cash or currency.

All U.K. Orders	**FREE OF CHARGE**
E.E.C. & Overseas	25% of order value

Name (Block Letters) _____

Address_____

_____

Post/zip code:_____

☐ Please keep me in touch with future Time Warner publications

☐ I enclose my remittance £_____

☐ I wish to pay by Visa/Access/Mastercard/Eurocard

Card Expiry Date

_____